For Marjorie and/or Gary Smith,
King of the Côte d'Azur

CHAPTER ONE

I wasn't crazy about the food.

"Is that salmon to your taste, Crang?" Swotty Whetherhill asked me.

"Hold on till I dig it out from under this yellow stuff," I said.

We were eating at one of Swotty's clubs. And not the best of them. I knew he belonged to the Toronto Club, the York, and the Concord. In terms of cuisine, they ranked in that order. We were in the main dining room at the Concord. The chef's specialty was sauces that failed to disguise the sins of his kitchen.

"I imagine you were surprised to hear from me," Swotty said. He was making inroads on a small steak that swam in brown gunk.

"Well, I didn't think it was to cut up touches about the old days," I said. "And I knew it wasn't for legal advice, not unless you've done a major about-face in business ethics."

"Pamela liked that in you," Swotty said, "the cheekiness."

"You didn't."

"Oh, I admire irony as much as the next man."

"As long as we're trading confidences," I said, "I was scared stiff of you."

"That seems appropriate."

Fifteen years earlier, I had asked Swotty for his daughter's hand in marriage. He said he'd keep Pamela's hand and all the rest of her.

Pamela and I got married anyway, and Swotty walked her down the centre aisle at Timothy Eaton Memorial Church. That's a hike of about thirty privileged yards. Pamela was stubborn, an only child, the apple of Swotty's eye. He gave in to her, not me. I was just a criminal lawyer with no prospects beyond a developing facility for defending persons charged with fraud. About five years after the wedding, Pamela and I broke up. I was still representing the con men.

"The fact of the matter, Crang," Swotty said, "is that I have an assignment for you."

"Assignment? In criminal law, we might say a guy has a case for us, or he needs a defence, or he's in the glue with the cops. Assignment isn't up our alley."

"In this instance," Swotty said, frost in his voice, "no one has committed a crime."

The frost was in more than Swotty's tone. He had snowy white hair, and his face was set in long vertical lines, like cracks in a glacier. I used to make up my own names for the guy. Wintry Whetherhill. Swott of the Antarctic. I never said the names out loud. Not even to Pamela.

"The no one who hasn't committed a crime," I said, "anybody I know?"

"Jamie Haddon. He would have been a youngster when you were in the family."

"Sure. The blond kid with the long eyelashes. If Marilyn Monroe had had a younger brother, it could have been Jamie Haddon."

"I would not use your description," Swotty said, icy again, "but, yes, you seem to remember Jamie."

"Your cousin's son, right? Gerald Haddon, the branch of the family that stayed down in Strathroy? The country cousins?"

"Gerald did not stay in Strathroy," Swotty said. "We left him there. Gerald has never measured up."

"Might have something to do with whoever sets the standards."

Swotty ignored this. "There was to be no mollycoddling simply because Gerald is family."

"A man who does household work. I read that somewhere."

"What?"

"Mollycoddle."

A chill wind blew from Swotty's side of the table. "In any event," he continued, "Jamie is the first male Haddon to show real promise. That, of course, is why I brought him to Toronto. To the trust company."

When a Whetherhill spoke of "the trust company," it sounded as if the words came in uppercase letters: The Trust Company. The Trust Company had been one of the two sacred subjects that dominated conversation around the Sunday night dinner table at Swotty's house. The other subject was The Family. Every Sunday night was a command performance for the Whetherhill clan. Always roast beef, always talk about The Family and The Trust Company. The family was Whetherhill, and the trust company was Cayuga & Granark. Swotty's grandfather, a tight-lipped, parsimonious guy, had founded it in Strathroy. His portrait hung in Swotty's front hall. The Whetherhills — grandfather, father, Swotty — were born with a sharp eye for a dollar, and Cayuga & Granark had provided the family fortune. It ranked somewhere in the top ten family fortunes in Toronto. Swotty's father moved Cayuga & Granark's head office out of Strathroy to a steel and glass tower on Bay Street. Among the company's employees, it was known informally as C&G. Among its customers, it was known even more informally as Callous & Grasping.

"What is it about Jamie Haddon that needs me brought into the picture?" I asked Swotty.

"He is on vacation in Monaco."

I stopped scraping yellow stuff off my carrots, and took a slow sip of white wine. It was on the sweet side.

"How is it you know I'm taking a holiday in the south of France? I don't recall releasing the news to the press."

"Pamela told me." Swotty seemed to be getting a kick out of his one-upmanship. "She mentioned that you and, your, um, 'friend' were off in a week or so."

"She has a name," I said. "My friend. Annie B. Cooke."

"A movie critic, I understand."

"Annie prefers reviewer, movie reviewer," I said. "How did Pamela find out about the trip? I haven't run across her more than two or three times in ten years, and none of them has been recent."

"I do not question Pamela on her sources of information."

I let the waitress take away my plate. She had to be nimble not to spill the puddle of leftover sauce. Swotty and I ordered the same dessert, raspberry sorbet.

"Between rambles on the Côte d'Azur," I said, "you want me to look up Jamie in Monaco?"

"Naturally I regard this as a business arrangement. I will pay accordingly."

"As far as I know," I said, "there's nothing criminal about a young guy taking a vacation in Monaco."

"I have already made the point I am not retaining you in your capacity as a lawyer," Swotty said. "Why do you insist on raising the issue of crime?"

"Something weird in the air," I said. "You summoning me from out of the blue. My suspicious nature. All of the foregoing."

Swotty made like an icicle for a few moments.

"It is simply this," he said finally. "I received a disturbing post-card from Jamie two days ago."

"What, a naughty snap of Princess Caroline on the beach?"

"It was the wording of the message that was disturbing," Swotty said. He looked uncomfortable. "Jamie wrote, 'Having a wonderful time. Glad you aren't here.'"

"Cousin Gerald must have been out of the house the day Jamie learned manners."

"Moreover," Swotty added, "the salutation on the card read 'Hi, Cuz.' I have been 'Cousin John' to him from the time he was a small boy, except at the trust company in front of other employees. There, he quite properly calls me 'Mr. Whetherhill.'"

"Let's get off the names," I said. "What's the deal in Monaco? Strictly holiday, or does trust company business come into it?"

"Jamie asked for a leave of absence. Three months. He told me he had never had the opportunity to look about the world. That was quite true. I took Jamie straight into the trust company after he obtained his commerce degree. By all means, I said to him, enjoy the leave of absence. Broaden yourself."

"You didn't have impudent postcards in mind."

"I cannot help thinking something is wrong with the boy."

"How old is Jamie now?"

"He'll be thirty on his next birthday," Swotty said. "This postcard has deeply disturbed me, Crang."

I polished off the watery sorbet and ate the desiccated wafer cookie that came with it.

"On the map, Monaco looks little," I said. "But, I don't know, standing on the local street corners watching out for Jamie Haddon isn't what I had in mind as a holiday. That probably goes double for Annie."

"Perhaps it is far-fetched asking you as I am," Swotty said, "but for all your curious ways, Crang, I regard you as a resourceful man." He almost gagged on the compliment.

"Annie and I are renting an apartment that's in hailing distance of Monaco," I said. "I don't suppose it'd hurt to hop over for lunch. Do our bit for Monacan tourism. Is that the right word? Or Monesque?"

"Excellent," Swotty said. He rubbed his hands together. "I am most grateful, Crang."

The waitress brought coffee. Swotty dumped cream and sugar in his. I took mine black and, courtesy of the Concord's brewmaster, bitter.

"One large point," I said. "How do you know Jamie'll still be around Monaco when Annie and I arrive? Make that two large points. Assuming Jamie is in the country, can you pin down details, like a hotel?"

"Jamie has been gone only twelve days," Swotty said. "I understand his intention is to make Monaco his base for at least the first month of the trip."

"He told you that?"

"No, Pamela told me."

"Pamela again," I said. "She seems to be the fount of all wisdom in the Jamie Haddon case."

"It is not a case, Crang," Swotty said. "Must I keep repeating myself?"

"A situation."

"A concern."

"I'll have to settle for that," I said. "What's Pamela call it?"

"She and Archie have always been very generous with Jamie."

Archie was Pamela's husband. Second husband. He was in a family business too. Cartwright Products. The products were cellophane wrappers, the kind processed food comes in. There was apparently a lot of money in cellophane. Archie Cartwright was a wealthy man. But not as wealthy as Swotty. Or as Pamela.

"What about a hotel?" I asked Swotty.

"I have no information on that, I regret."

"Not even from Pamela?"

"No," Swotty said, "but I have a place where you might inquire."

Swotty permitted himself a small self-satisfied smile around the corners of his mouth. A thaw in the great glacier.

"The postcard Jamie sent me," he said, "is the kind that restaurants give out as advertisements."

"Overlit photograph of the dining room? Name of the place, address, phone number? That type of card?"

"Exactly. The restaurant seems to be close to the Monaco harbour. It stands to reason Jamie had a meal at this establishment. Perhaps he frequents it. The people there might know him by sight."

"I'm not sure where reason stands in this," I said. I was trying not to sound as if I was humouring Swotty. "But, yeah, I'll stop by the restaurant. Might go there for lunch. What does Jamie like in the way of food? I mean, would he eat here? The Concord?"

"The restaurant," Swotty said, skipping past my question, "is called Le Restaurant du Port."

"Just a sec."

I reached for a pen and notebook from the inside jacket pocket of my best blue suit. I'd worn the suit especially for the occasion. Nine hundred dollars' worth of Holt Renfrew fabric.

"Crang, please." Swotty's voice had a note of reprimand. "Remember where you are."

I remembered. The Concord forbade the transaction of business in the dining room. No papers could be examined, documents exchanged, facts recorded. I took my hand out of the inside pocket minus the notebook and pen.

"Close call," I said.

The waitress gave me a big wink. Must have caught my faux pas. She refilled our coffee cups.

"Suppose I do stumble across our Jamie," I said. "Then what?"

"I have a given a great deal of thought to that." Swotty was using the tone he probably adopted for turning down businessmen who hit up C&G for big loans on inadequate collateral. "When you locate Jamie, you are to phone me immediately."

"That's all? I'm just the bird dog?"

"I am placing confidence in you to make an assessment of Jamie. His appearance, his conversation, his demeanor. Your task is to give me information on which I may base a judgment about the boy."

My enthusiasm for the Jamie Haddon project was wavering. I could do Swotty the modest favour for old times' sake, even if those times hadn't much to recommend them except their age. But could he be holding out on me? Was he as shaken up over one snotty postcard as he made out? Or were there bigger issues here?

Swotty's evasiveness put one damper on my zeal. Annie might represent another. The trip was our first excursion abroad in the three years we had been a romantic item. Annie would have one morning's work conducting a seminar on film reviewing at the Canadian university on the Riviera, but the rest of the days were to be our time together, and the thought of scouting after young Haddon paled when I compared it to a vision of Annie and me sauntering hand in hand in the streets of Saint-Jean-Cap-Ferrat.

Lingering over a bottle of *vin rouge*. Driving to Saint-Paul de Vence to lunch at whatever the place was where Yves Montand played boule with the friendly peasants.

"I hope you appreciate the responsibility I am entrusting you with, Crang," Swotty Whetherhill said.

"Oh, yeah, sure."

We finished our coffee. Swotty lead the way to the Concord's smoking room, where two middle-aged fogeys were puffing on cigars the size of Cuba. My ex-father-in-law and I sat in a pair of facing leather chairs while he repeated the name of the restaurant in Monaco and recited the address from memory. I jotted the name and address in my notebook.

Swotty didn't offer me a glass of port or a chance to look over the Concord's bound volumes of Punch. Out on the street, he shook my hand solemnly and turned west, toward The Trust Company. His pace as he walked away from me was stately and remote and inevitable. Kind of like an iceberg.

CHAPTER TWO

I asked Annie what colour my eyes were.

She gave me an intent look from five feet away. "Swamp green," she said.

I was filling out a passport application. Date of birth. Height. Weight. Colour of eyes stumped me.

"Too long," I said. "The form doesn't have room for descriptives."

"Write smaller, big guy."

"Please," I said. "One simple colour."

"Swamp."

"Listen, kiddo, will green do the trick?"

"Actually," Annie said, "your eyes are green with a soupçon of grey."

"I'll put green and hope I don't get picked up for travelling on somebody else's passport."

"I thought all you swift criminal lawyers kept passports at the ready. You know, in case a client needs instant services in Bogota or some sleazy place like that."

Annie was curled on the sofa in the living room of my apartment, leafing through Premiere magazine. I live on Beverley Street, across from the park behind the Art Gallery of Ontario. I own the house the apartment is in, and rent the first floor to a gay couple and their dog. Annie had on a black wool dress with big black buttons all the way up the front. Annie is small and dark and beautiful in a gloriously old-fashioned way. Myrna Loy beautiful.

"I let my passport lapse," I said. I was sitting in an armchair kitty-corner to the sofa. I had the passport application propped on a record jacket. The record was playing low on the stereo, Billie Holiday from the 1950s. I said, "The last trip I took out of the country was a week in Baja."

"You must have left me at home."

"Before your time."

"Oh." Annie put down the Premiere. Behind the "oh" there was a curiosity that might set the room ablaze. "Okay, fella, so who did you go to Mexico with?"

"Myself. I was mending a broken heart. Or that's what I was supposed to be doing."

"Oh." Flat and anticlimactic this time. "When you split from old what's-her-name," Anne said. She picked up the Premiere. "Your ex-wife."

Under "in case of accident or death, notify:" I wrote Annie's name and address. She lives in a third-floor flat over in Cabbagetown. Her movie reviewing is freelance and not conducive to a paycheque every Friday. She discusses movies twice a week on *Metro Morning*, the local CBC radio wake-up program, and writes features for whatever newspapers and magazines she can wangle commissions from.

"Speaking of whom," I said, trying for a casual delivery, "her father bought me lunch today."

"Old what's-her-name's father?"

"Pamela's."

Annie swung her legs out from under her and set her feet on the floor.

"What did her dad want all of a sudden?" Annie asked. "Anything about patching up the family dynasty?"

I shook my head. "He wanted a favour." I told Annie about Swotty Whetherhill and Jamie Haddon and Monaco. I used sentences that I hoped came across as off-hand.

"Gee, rich guys don't mind presuming," Annie said. "You're gone years from his life, and he thinks he can crook his finger in your direction and you'll snap to attention."

"Maybe I felt a little sorry for him. Maybe I felt a little intimidated by him. Maybe a little of both."

Annie smoothed the skirt of her dress over her thighs. "It wouldn't do any harm," she said.

"What?"

"Looking up this Jamie Haddon."

"You noticed the circumspection of my approach to the subject?" I said. "I thought you might be pissed off."

Annie shrugged. "Monaco could fit nicely into our program." Annie's shrug looked Gallic. Insouciant, yet assured.

"You're in charge of the itinerary, sweetie," I said.

"Monaco's vulgarity quotient is awfully high. But there's the Oceanographic Museum. Very Jacques Cousteau. And you'd get a kick out of the decor in the Casino. I'd estimate a half day's worth of sights."

"Built around a lunch at Le Restaurant du Port?"

"Well, you have to ask after the rude cousin somewhere."

I balanced the passport and the record jacket on the arm of my chair. "I'm not questioning your innate good nature, my love," I said, "but why are you being so accommodating all of a sudden?"

Annie curled back on the sofa. She gave me a smile. It may have had a trace of the sheepish in it.

"Well, you've got this case to take care of," she said. "And as a matter of fact, a potential job … more than potential … a sure thing … came my way this morning."

"In France?"

"In Cannes."

"He doesn't call it a case, by the way. Swotty doesn't. Very adamant on that point."

"I love that part, the man's name."

"You should have met his father," I said. "The late Bubs Whetherhill."

"I always wondered about upper-class nicknames," Annie said. "Do the parents dish them out at birth?"

"Swotty got his at prep school. He's really a John."

"What did you call him when you were his son-in-law?"

"Sir."

"Oh, so that's the way it was."

"Uh huh," I said. "Tell me the other half of your news."

"The job is for the *Sun*," Annie said. Eagerness was building in her voice. "And it is definitely big time. They're accrediting me to the film festival."

Behind us Billie Holiday was singing "Easy to Love," medium tempo and heartbreaking. Annie and I were trivializing Lady Day's music, half-listening to it the way we were, treating it as a backdrop to conversation. I got up, and turned off the stereo.

I said, "Doesn't the *Sun* have a regular guy they send to Cannes?"

"Bruce Kirkland, yes," Annie said. "Bruce phoned me himself. This year they've decided they want somebody over there doing capsule reviews. Not for every day's paper. I'm just to pick out movies I think are relevant to your average *Sun* reader and write short takes on them."

"Your average *Sun* reader?"

"I shouldn't have said that," Annie said.

"Would he or she, this average *Sun* reader, be the person you see on the subway, lips moving, little bit of drool maybe?"

"Such an obvious straight line." Annie shook her head. "Why did I hand it to you?"

I slid onto the sofa beside her.

"So it isn't the *New York Times*," she said, "the *Sun*'s still a better paper than you think it is. Some sections are."

"Where does that leave Kirkland?" I was unwilling to debate the *Sun*'s journalistic merits.

"Free to do the newsy stuff."

I put my arm around Annie's shoulders. "How long were you intending to hold out on me about the job?" I said. Annie wasn't ready to melt into my arms.

"I was monkeying around for the right approach," she said.

"While I was tiptoeing into the Swotty Whetherhill errand."

I squeezed Annie's shoulder. She turned her head toward me. Our faces were six inches apart.

"You're not upset?" she said.

"It's a great career chance."

"Or disappointed? This will mean me seeing a couple of films a day. Hanging out some with the movie people."

I shrugged. "Exposure in a daily," I said. "Who knows where it'll lead." My shrug was pure Canadian. The French would spot me for a tourist every time.

"I know this is putting a crimp in our original plans," Annie said, "but we've got the first week clear for ourselves. And the hotel room in Cannes is for the two of us, the same with the movie passes. I told Bruce you had to be part of the package or forget it."

"I'll supply the common man's touch. Very useful at the *Sun*."

Annie closed the gap between our faces. We kissed lightly on the lips. The kiss lingered until I had to detach my hand from around Annie's shoulder. The hand had gone to sleep. I stood up and shook it.

"You think the sun's over the yardarm?" I asked her.

"Probably over Hawaii by now."

Outside the window, the street lights had come on. I looked at my watch. Not quite seven. For late April, it had been a murky day and close to the freezing mark.

"White wine, please," Annie said. She had Premiere open again. "It says here Marcello Mastroianni's in a film that's set for competition at Cannes. Lucky you, your very favourite actor."

I went into the kitchen. I poured Annie a glass from an open bottle of Orvieto. The Wyborowa was in the freezer. I put three ice cubes in a glass that I'd got for buying two tanks of gas at a Texaco station. I filled the rest of it with vodka. The glass was imitation crystal and spectacularly ugly. I bet a Pole wouldn't sully his Wyborowa with ice cubes. Probably wouldn't drink it out of a

Texaco glass either. There was a tin of unsalted nuts on the counter. I managed to open the tin without cutting myself and dumped the nuts into a cereal bowl. I got the wine, the vodka, and the nuts in delicate balance in two hands. The telephone rang.

"You mind getting that?" I called to Annie.

I have two phones, one in the kitchen, the other in the bedroom. Annie came into the kitchen. I passed her at the door and put down the glasses and the bowl on the pine table behind the sofa. I could hear Annie talking on the phone, not words, just tones. She wasn't long.

"Is old what's-her-name's mother still living?" Annie asked me.

"Pamela's?" I said. "As far as I know."

"In that case, she'll probably be the next member of the family wanting to bend your ear."

"Pamela's on the phone? Right now?"

Annie pointed a thumb over her shoulder in the direction of the kitchen phone. "It's a woman, and she wants to speak to you, and when I asked 'Who may I say is calling?', she said 'old what's-her-name.'"

"She did not."

"You're right," Annie said. "She said 'Pamela Cartwright.'" I lifted my glass from the table, and swallowed an inch of vodka.

"Well, now," I said. "I wonder what she wants."

CHAPTER THREE

Pamela wanted me to come to tea at four o'clock the next afternoon, Thursday.

"Well, sure, that'd be just fine, you bet," I said on the phone. I sounded like Jimmy Stewart in *Mr. Smith Goes to Washington*.

"Until tomorrow then," Pamela said, crisp and categorical.

"I clocked that at a forty-second call," Annie said in the living room. "You and Pamela aren't much for trips down memory lane."

I swallowed another inch of vodka. My hand shook slightly.

"She invited me to tea tomorrow."

"That's wild."

"The tea?"

"No, that's quaint," Annie said. "Her asking to see you, that's wild."

"Tea might be a euphemism for scotch whisky."

"What's she after, any hints?" Annie was sitting up on her knees on the sofa. "More about this Haddon bounder? Or deeper matters? I put my money on deeper."

"The only reason Pamela would call me is if she wants something very special," I said. "Special to her."

"Not your body, I trust."

"The implication when we got divorced was she'd had her fill of it."

I made myself another vodka on the rocks. I finished it while Annie drank half her wine. Annie was an absent-minded drinker. Then we walked down to Queen Street and ate chicken and shrimp at the Rivoli while Annie pumped me about Pamela.

I told her that, in a marriage that had lasted five years and change, Pamela had been bright, sexy, caustic, profane when angry, and no more self-absorbed than any other young woman who'd inherited several millions of dollars from her grandfather. Marrying middle-class me represented Pamela's one departure from the normal course of moneyed life. I was never sure whether it was true love or an act of rebellion.

This was territory Annie and I had covered a dozen times before. Annie brought it up every few months, like a kid asking for a favourite bedtime story. Never got bored with it, even if she kept up the running joke of calling Pamela old what's-her-name. And now that Annie had spoken to the woman herself, her fascination had increased.

"She's got one of those great throaty voices," Annie said. "Or was that just the phone?"

I said it wasn't the phone.

We had two espressos each and went back to my place. I played Billie Holiday again. Annie and I sat on the sofa and listened. The lights were out. Lady Day sang "I've Got You Under My Skin." I held Annie in my arms. We didn't talk.

In the morning, after Annie had left the apartment on movie duties, I got busy on the passport drill. Went downtown and had photos taken. Buttonholed a lawyer I'd known for more than two years to sign in the spaces where a doctor or lawyer or minister guarantees I am who I say I am. Crang. Criminal lawyer. Green eyes and all. And took everything to the passport office in the government building near the corner of Dundas and Yonge.

The lineup lasted an hour. I read a copy of the *Sun* somebody had left behind. It had a fat sports section. Too bad Annie's specialty wasn't baseball. Or violent homicides that involved motorcycle gangs or distraught spouses.

When I got my turn at the front of the line, a sunny East Asian woman said I could pick up my passport in four days, any time after nine a.m. Monday. A near thing, I told her. Annie and I were to leave on an Air Canada flight Monday night.

At home, I made a meatloaf sandwich. The meatloaf was from Ian downstairs. He's a wizard cook, and offloads on me whatever he and Alex and their dog don't consume. The dog's name is Genet.

I considered a visit to my office. And rejected it. I run a one-man practice out of a second-floor space on the north side of Queen near Spadina. I've been a tenant there for twenty years. In recent weeks, I had let things wind down in anticipation of my sojourn in France.

Two o'clock. Two more hours until tea with Pamela. I puttered. Smoothed out the duvet and patted the pillows on the bed. Took out the clothes I would pack for the trip. Tied up all the magazines that were a month old in a bundle for the recycle pickup. *The New Yorker. Downbeat. Saturday Night.*

"Damn," I said.

The puttering wasn't doing what it was supposed to do: take my mind off the Pamela appointment. I felt apprehensive. I felt damp in the armpits. I went into the bathroom and stood under the shower for five minutes. That took care of the armpits. The apprehension remained intact.

Pamela had occupied a significant chunk of my life; she was a woman I'd fallen in love with, a woman who had ditched me. And the ditching, in my opinion, was for a lousy reason. Because I wouldn't go out and play. When Pamela flew to Gstaad for the skiing, Manhattan for the shows, Lyford Cay for the sun, I stayed home. I had clients and trials. Pamela decided the arrangement wasn't working and asked for a divorce. Not so much asked as ordered one up, the same way she used to have catered lunches for eight whipped over from Paul's Fine Foods in the Village.

She sent down to the Supreme Court of Ontario for one divorce, and had it delivered for a Friday before she jetted to London for the shopping. I felt bitter for a couple of months. I phoned Pamela's new condo in Granite Place and told her that skiing, shows, and the sun were no substitute for me. More accurately, I told it to her answering service. Pamela wasn't home. She never returned my call.

And now, ten years later, I said I'd have tea at her house. Was I nuts? Possibly. Curious? Slightly. Apprehensive? Definitely.

CHAPTER FOUR

Pamela lived on Ardwold Gate. I drove over in my white Volks Beetle convertible with the dent in the passenger side. Ardwold Gate is a cul-de-sac that curls behind Casa Loma at the top of the steep hill on Spadina Road. The houses on the street are a jumble of architectural styles, most of them ersatz. Georgian. Spanish. Edwardian. They have nothing in common except price, a couple of million per house. It takes big money to get ersatz just right.

The Cartwright place was built of heavy grey stone and filled a double lot. I gave the polished brass knocker on the front door a solid thump. A hefty woman in her fifties opened the door almost immediately. She had on a severe black dress and spoke with a Hungarian accent. She verified that I was Mr. Crang and ushered me into the living room.

It was a room that had chic stamped all over it. Walls painted terra cotta. Furniture covered in pale grey fabric. Oils and water-colours by Canadians who worked in contemporary realism. I looked out through the French doors. There was a tennis court at the back. It had a red clay surface. Not many of them left in the city.

"How have you been?"

Pamela spoke from the living-room entrance behind me.

I turned around. "Since when?" I asked. "The whole last ten years?"

"You're looking well."

"That makes two of us."

Pamela had blond hair cut short and flipped to the right. She had eyes that looked out through a brown mist, a slightly stuck-out upper lip, and a figure that was slender all the way down. She was wearing a white silk blouse and cream-coloured trousers with many pleats in front. There were three or four thin gold bracelets on her left wrist and a thick gold wedding band on the appropriate finger. I would wager the blond hair still didn't need much help from a bottle.

"Please have a seat." A small wave of Pamela's hand told me I was to sit in one of the wing chairs. She sat on a sofa opposite me. In between us, there was a marble-topped coffee table with a bowl coloured a deep inky blue on it.

"Thank you for coming," Pamela said.

"Glad to oblige."

"I hope it didn't interfere with your work schedule." Pamela was perched on the edge of the sofa, her legs crossed at the ankles. "I know how important your practice is to you."

"You going to keep on like we're diplomats exchanging bows or are you going to get down to why I've been summoned?"

"Shut up, Crang," Pamela said. "This isn't particularly easy, and I want to get through it my own way."

There was a cigarette box on the coffee table near the inky-blue bowl. Pamela reached over and lifted off the top. The box was light green. It looked like wood to me, studded with pieces of white glass. Pamela put the lid on the table. It made a sharp clink against the marble. The box wasn't wood. It was some kind of metal, and I was probably wrong about the white pieces too. They were probably antique ivory.

"Do you mind?" Pamela asked. She was lighting her cigarette from a lighter that matched the box.

"I didn't before," I said. For sensuous smoking, Pamela was in a class with Simone Signoret in *Room at the Top*.

"I want to talk to you about Jamie Haddon."

"I already got my marching orders on him from the top guy."

"There are some facts about this mysterious trip of Jamie's to Monaco that Daddy doesn't know. And will never know, as far as that goes."

"You're going to tell me, and it doesn't leave this room."

"Goodness," Pamela said, "aren't we a very clever criminal lawyer."

When Pamela and I were married, I used to let her sarcasm fly by. No call to change old habits.

"What's the mystery about Jamie's trip to Monaco?" I asked.

"To start with," Pamela said, "I'm not paying for it."

I gave Pamela my uncomprehending look. "Did I miss a step?"

"For the past year, I've paid for practically everything Jamie has. Everything that's any good. His suits, the apartment, rental on the Jag he's so fond of ..."

"Why did you —?" I started to ask. And stopped. I recognized the step I'd missed.

"I was having an affair with Jamie," Pamela said. "Am having an affair with Jamie. At least I think I still am."

"You're cheating? Oh, my. On Archie?"

"Why the shock?" Pamela blew smoke out both nostrils in matching streams. "I cheated on you, for heaven's sake."

"This conversation isn't turning out to be a ton of fun."

"If it makes you any less scandalized, Jamie has been the only time I've betrayed Archie."

"It wasn't Archie I was thinking of."

"Betrayed. God, I sound like Mata Hari or someone."

"There was the Swedish guy in Sardinia."

"What Swedish guy in Sardinia?"

"How soon they forget."

"Oh, him."

Pamela pushed out her cigarette dead centre in the deep inky-blue thing. It wasn't a bowl. It was an ashtray. Nothing in the damn room was what I thought it was.

"You amaze me, Crang," Pamela said. "That was a million years ago, the Swede. Not much on talk, now that I think about it, but he had an absolutely heavenly body."

"Nice to hear you didn't betray me with just any old chap."

"Stop saying betrayed."

"That was only my first time."

"I must have been terribly naive when we were married. To have told you about the Swedish man, I mean."

"You said you hadn't committed adultery before. You wanted me to forgive you."

"Remind me what you answered."

"I said I forgave you. But I had my fingers crossed when I said it. Didn't count."

"That was wise of you, because I'm sorry to say there were one or two 'any old chaps,' as you put it."

"That you had affairs with when you were my wife?"

"Only towards the end," Pamela said. "And none of them was a friend of yours."

"That doesn't narrow the field much. I hardly had any friends in those days."

"And now you have one very close friend." Pamela did little arching numbers with her eyebrows, like a bad imitation of Groucho Marx.

"Annie," I said. "Annie B. Cooke. Why can't anybody in your family come right out and say her name?"

"I know her name, and I'm grateful to her."

"That has an ominous ring," I said, "coming from you."

"Nothing ominous. I heard the people on the radio in the morning say they envied your friend's trip to the Riviera. Pardon, Annie's trip. And I guessed she wouldn't be going alone. That's why I'm grateful to her. I phoned a friend with a rather good job at Air Canada and got the rest, about the two of you leaving Monday."

The hefty woman in the black dress was halfway across the pale grey broadloom before I realized she had entered the room. She

must have mastered the servant's art of stealth. She set a large lac-
quered wood tray on the marble in front of Pamela. The tray held
a teapot, matching cups and saucers in a pretty tangerine shade,
milk, sugar, lemon slices, and a plate of cookies.

"How do you take your tea, Crang?" Pamela asked.

"Clear."

That was a mistake. At home, I drink gentle herbal teas. Pamela's
was straight-ahead English power tea. Taken untempered by milk,
sugar, or lemon, it tasted like shellac. I tried an oatmeal cookie to
take the taste away.

"Well, okay," I said, "you had an affair with Jamie Haddon, maybe
still are having one, which is something you'd better clear up, the
maybe part, and you spoiled him rotten. Car, clothes, other treats."

"Yes."

"It's a cliffhanger so far," I said. "What next?"

Pamela put down her cup and saucer. She'd polished off the tea.
The woman had a cast-iron stomach.

"Five weeks ago," she said, "Jamie sprang this silly three-month
leave of absence on us all. I hadn't an inkling until he announced
it one night when we were all at Daddy's for dinner. There I was,
I'd invested so much of myself in him, affection, time, gifts, God
knows I even risked my marriage for him, and he decides to traipse
off to Europe."

"I see," I said. "A woman scorned."

"That's just it, scorn didn't come into it as far as I could make
out, not the way Jamie behaved. He continued to act as passionate
and attentive as he'd been all through our relationship. Nothing
seemed to change in his attitude to me except that he picked up
and left for three months."

"Ah well, the spontaneity of youth."

"Don't give me that crap," Pamela said. The harsh shift in her
voice brought back memories of the tiffs we'd had during our married days. "This kind of spontaneity needs a few thousand dollars."

"Which you didn't give him."

"For once."

My tea was a quarter of the way down the cup, where it was leaving a dark ring. What was it doing to the lining of my stomach? I ate another cookie and left the tea alone.

"Jamie has a job, right?" I said. "He must be earning good bucks of his own at C&G."

"Loan officer," Pamela said. "That's his title, not bad for someone of Jamie's age and experience. But you know Daddy, he really does pay his junior people dreadfully."

"Explains how the rich stay rich," I said.

"To be fair to Daddy," Pamela said, "there's another side to the story. Jamie knows he'll be brought up through the ranks, as far as he wants to go. He's family, even if he does come from those addled Haddons." She interrupted herself. "You do remember the Haddons?" she asked me.

"Gerald's the one who didn't come in for mollycoddling."

"Honestly, the man practically cornered the market on hopelessness. He's been very lucky Granddaddy gave him that little job at the C&G branch in Strathroy."

"Gerald's still there?"

"Who else would hire him?" Pamela said. "Anyway, where was I? Oh yes, Jamie. He's very much the Haddon exception, bright and charming. Daddy's very supportive of him, he's the son Daddy never had, I sometimes think. Daddy put him through school, you must remember that, Ridley College and then Queen's. And he'll bring Jamie along at the trust company. At Daddy's own speed, that goes without saying."

"I feel like I'm on the inside of the Forsyte Saga."

"In the meantime," Pamela said, "Jamie has no money to speak of."

"Well, maybe not for you to speak of."

"Crang," Pamela said, edgy, "keep your eye on the main question. All right, of course, I wanted Jamie to live well, dress well, be fabulous, while we had the affair. Are having the affair. So I paid for things."

"What's the main question I should be keeping my eye on?"

"Where did Jamie get the money to finance three months in Europe?"

"Ask him."

"I asked."

"And?"

"Basically evasive." Pamela reached for another cigarette. "He let on the trip was going to be on the cheap. A big adventure, camping out, drinking the inexpensive local wines."

"Nothing wrong with inexpensive local European wines."

"There is when somebody's been stocking your cellar with Châteauneuf-du-Pape for a year."

The lighter in Pamela's hand went snick. She took a drag on the cigarette and blew a wispy cloud of smoke.

"So, the chores you want done," I said. "One, I track down Jamie in Monaco and two, I ask after the source of his travellers' cheques."

"Ever heard of finesse, Crang?"

"Put my mind to it, I do excellent finesse."

"Please. And let me know what you've found out when you get back."

I shifted in my chair as a prelude to standing up and saying goodbye.

"Not yet," Pamela said. Her hand was waving me back into the chair.

"There's more?" I said.

"Dante."

"I take it we're not talking Italian poets."

"Dante Renzi," Pamela said. "He's a young man Jamie met through business at the trust company. That's what Jamie said at any rate. He said Dante had lost the place where he was living and did I mind if he stayed at the apartment till he found something new."

"You gave Jamie an okay?"

Pamela nodded. "But Jamie knew I was annoyed." She had a retrospective look of annoyance on her face.

"Not your type?" I asked. "This Dante?"

"Nice-looking. I didn't mind that, nice-looking in a dark, soft sort of way. But, Lord, he blew it whenever he opened his mouth." Pamela shook her head back and forth. "Completely inarticulate. No breeding."

"Listen, I don't want to sound like I'm in a rush to wrap up our little chat, but is this dark, dumb chap relevant to what we've been hashing over?"

"Wait for it, Crang," Pamela said. "Dante put in his appearance five weeks ago."

"Aha. Do I detect an uncanny coincidence?"

"I didn't put two and two together until after Jamie left, but the announcement of the bloody trip to Europe and the arrival of bloody Dante happened at about the same time."

"Suspicious," I said, "but not necessarily an authentic four. If we're speculating that Dante might have some bearing on the leave of absence, wouldn't it depend on whether Jamie and Dante left for Europe together?"

"They didn't."

"You phoned your man at Air Canada?"

"Air France. No record of a D. Renzi on Jamie's flight. I don't know where the little shit has got to."

"The apartment?"

"Not him or his clothes." Pamela lifted her cigarette from the blue ashtray. "Thank God."

"Want me to check out Jamie's companions in Monaco for some-one along the Dante Renzi lines?"

"Do that."

I started shifting in my chair again, but something in Pamela's attitude kept me in place. She was hunching forward, gener-ating an atmosphere I interpreted as a windup to even more intimate revelations.

Pamela tapped her cigarette lightly on the edge of the blue ash-tray. She had a way of rolling the cigarette that left the ash looking like a miniature log.

She started again. "Thinking back now, I get the feeling … or it could be I always had it and wouldn't admit it to myself … that Jamie rushed me."

Pamela stopped. I said nothing. It required a mighty effort.

"If you want it phrased vulgarly," Pamela said, "he might have put the make on me."

Another pause.

"Started the whole damned affair on purpose. In a funny way, inveigled me into it, lured me, you know what I mean? I hope to God I'm just acting crazy. The older woman-younger man relationship doesn't matter to me one way or the other. It's almost trendy these days. I could spin endless stories about middle-aged friends of mine and their twenty-five-year-old beaus. But I had no particular yearning to have an affair. Archie's a perfect husband. I wasn't thinking of straying. I certainly wasn't thinking of straying with Jamie. Not that he isn't divinely attractive and the rest of it. He definitely is. But he'd always sort of been around since I was a teenager, this little blond cousin stuck with the dim Haddons in Strathroy. Then he came to Toronto, and he was even more around. And then, somehow or other, I'm forty-two, he's twenty-nine, and we're in bed, and I'm uneasy, rightly or wrongly, about how we got there."

Pamela came to another stop. I judged this one signalled the end of true confessions. I tried for something to say that fit the occasion. The trouble was I hadn't experienced an occasion before when Pamela had seemed vulnerable.

"So," I said, "you think Jamie might be lacking in the chivalry department?"

"Just keep my unease in mind when you talk to him."

Pamela gave me the smile I used to call her hired-help smile. It accompanied tips to headwaiters, compliments to chefs, congratulations to jockeys.

She said, "You're being a pet about this."

Pamela's hired-help smile also went with pats on dogs' heads.

"I haven't much to do the next couple of days," I said. "Why don't I nose around? Ask about Jamie at the trust company? I know a lawyer who works there. And maybe I could rummage through Jamie's apartment."

"I already rummaged."

"Find anything?"

"I didn't know what I was rummaging for."

"Takes a pro."

Pamela looked doubtful. "Well, you could be right," she conceded. She stood up. "I'll get the keys."

"And something else, if you don't mind."

"A drink? You hardly touched your tea."

"A recent photograph of Jamie. I'll take a rain check on the drink."

Pamela was gone from the living room for five minutes. When she came back, she handed me two keys on a Gucci key ring and a photograph with an address written on the back.

"That's where the apartment is," she said. "The ground floor in a house on Rowanwood just over from Chestnut Park."

"Nobody'd accuse you of skimping on Jamie," I said. Addresses didn't come much more old-Toronto posh than Rowanwood Avenue in Rosedale.

"It's a sweet little flat," Pamela said.

The keys were to Abloy locks, real toughies even for break-and-enter specialists. I'd learned that from a client who pursued the B&E trade. In the photograph, Pamela was standing between two men. I recognized Jamie from the times I'd seen him years earlier, still California blond, all grin and eyelashes, slim, holding himself in a pose that said nonchalant. The other gent was older, straight as an arrow, tall, fit, good smile. The two men looked formal in dark suits. Pamela was wearing a red dress with frou-frou trimmings at the neckline and hemline. Her arms were around both guys' waists.

"The other one's Archie?" I asked.

Pamela nodded. "It was taken last Christmas."

I looked again at Archie's face. He had a great set of choppers.

"He is handsome," Pamela said.

"Jamie?"

"Archie."

Pamela's eyes were fixed on the photograph in my hand. She had a wistful expression. First, vulnerable. Then, wistful. It was more than an ex-husband should be expected to fathom.

"Jamie's the immediate problem."

"Of course," Pamela said. Her attention was back on business. "Call me the moment you return."

"You bet," I said. "Three weeks."

Pamela saw me to the front door, stretched up on her toes, and gave my cheek a glancing kiss.

Outside, sitting in the Volks, I took stock. No sweat in the armpits. No apprehension in the gut.

I wheeled the car in a U-turn and drove over to Rosedale.

CHAPTER FIVE

Somebody, somewhere in Jamie Haddon's apartment, was whistling "Memories."

I was standing inside the apartment door. The first Abloy had got me into the house, the second into Jamie's part of the house. The small outside lobby, which must have been the foyer before the old mansion was divided into flats, had dark wood panelling and shiny hardwood floors which continued into the part of Jamie's apartment I could see from the doorway. The door opened directly into the living room. The whistler was deeper inside the apartment. As far as I could tell, he or she was whistling in tune.

I slammed the door hard. The whistling stopped in mid-bar. Silence took over the apartment. I didn't move. Neither did the whistler. The standoff kept up for about fifteen seconds. Maybe my tactic of the slammed door had been too impetuous.

The whistler moved first. Firm footsteps, growing louder, echoed from a hall across the living room and opposite the door. Two lamps were on in the living room. The whistler walked into the light.

He was a guy about five-seven, four or five inches shorter than I am, but he didn't look like anyone's pushover. He was solid and muscular and barrel-chested. His black hair was clipped to within a quarter inch of his scalp. The cut gave his head the aspect of a missile.

"Hi there," I said. I left my hand on the knob of the shut door behind me.

"Hello, my friend," he boomed back. Even his voice had muscles.

"That's kind of a record for me," I said. "Only been here thirty seconds and already we've made friends."

The little guy shot across the room and pumped my hand.

"You are a friend of Jamie, why else you come here?" he said. "And this makes you a friend of mine because Jamie, I am best friends with him."

He had an accent. Nothing impenetrable, but he pronounced "him" as "heem." And he didn't use contractions, not "you're" or "I'm," but a precise "you are" and a definite "I am." Italian maybe?

I played along with the instant friendship game. "My name's Crang."

"Michel Rolland," the little guy said. "Call me Mike. All my good friends call me Mike."

Not an Italian name. French?

"Jamie's away," I said.

"Of course." The two words came out like an explosion. "That is how we are friends, Jamie and me. I meet him where I live. He comes to my condo."

"This is where?"

Another explosion. "Monaco."

"Ah."

He could be French or Italian. Or French and Italian.

"Come in, my friend Crang," Mike said. "Why not we sit down?"

Mike acted the host, ushering me to a pair of easy chairs. The chairs were covered in chintz, large red flowers against a fawn background. Pamela's decorating hand. Across from me, short, forceful Mike was hard on the eyes in a head-to-toe silvery getup. Silver grey shoes, pants, shirt. A solid silver windbreaker was draped over the chair he sat in. None of the silver items had little pink polo players on them or miniature green crocodiles, but they looked to be in the high-priced bracket.

"What brings you to Canada, Mike?" I asked.

"Cats bring me."

"Really? What, some special breed? You a vet?"

"No, no, on the stage. I watch it. I know all the songs by heart."

"Oh, that *Cats*. Andrew Lloyd Webber and the other guy."

"Beautiful music."

"Listen, it's too bad you came all this way, Mike. *Cats* closed in Toronto, I'm not sure, a year back."

"No problem. *Cats* is opening in the city of Winnipeg, Canada, on Friday … where is Winnipeg, my friend Crang?"

"Keep going west, Mike. Can't miss it."

"I fly there tomorrow. This will make twelve times I have seen *Cats*. I love the songs. I love all musical shows. Everywhere there is a new show, I go. Or if I have not seen a show for a long time, I just go. *Les Miserables* is my best. I have been five times in three cities each time. Paris, London, and New York City. Incredible, you agree?"

"Took the adjective right out of my mouth."

I had Mike tagged for a fanatic.

"What else do you do, Mike?" I asked.

"I shoot."

Was he also a hit man?

"Pheasant is my favourite."

A sportsman.

"Very big birds, but fast. Zip, zip, they go by. You need the good eye, my friend Crang."

"I guess."

"Last month I was in Scotland for the pheasant. Eight guns was on the shoot. In two days, we kill ninety-eight pheasant. Thirty-six were mine."

"The good eye."

"For sure," Mike said. His voice came close to rattling the windows in the apartment.

"When I asked just now what you did, what I meant was, this is a very Canadian question, Mike, what's your business?"

"Oh, I see. Lot of businesses. I have business in Antibes that sells cars. I have business in Nice sells houses and apartments. Real estate, yes? And in Monaco, my business is boats. That was how Jamie became my good friend."

"Enlighten me."

"Pardon?" he said with a French inflection.

"What's the connection between selling boats and Jamie?"

"He bought one from me."

"Little sailboat you're talking about? Something to catch the light breezes?"

"That is funny. No, no, Jamie bought from me a Hatteras. Sixty feet."

I drew a blank on the Hatteras, but the sixty feet caught my attention. That made it sound more like an aircraft carrier than a punt.

I said, "This is Jamie Haddon we're discussing, young blond guy?"

"For sure."

"He bought a sixty-foot boat?"

"Hatteras."

"Cash money Jamie paid?"

"What else? Two guys go with the boat, crew. One guy is the captain. Other guy we call the mate, but he serves the drinks, you know, different things you ask him."

"Big cash money, I'm getting the impression."

"Very big. For sure."

Mike stretched the "very" into two long syllables.

"Well, this is gratifying to us here in Toronto to hear how splendidly Jamie's doing overseas."

"Jamie be big man in Monaco, you wait, and Monaco, honest to God, this is a place where we got a lot of big men."

"He's only been there twelve days."

"Spend the money, you get to be big man fast."

"Really spreading it around, is he?"

"You know the American bar at the Hôtel de Paris?"

"Can't say I do."

"This is where I meet Jamie. Most beautiful bar in entire world. Jamie, the night I meet him, he buys drinks for everyone. For me, for this Spanish guy who is a count, for an American guy with his wife who is in the music business. Own a record company, I think. Jamie says to all these rich guys, your money no good here. They love him, new young guy in Monaco, handsome, lot of charm. Everybody think Jamie the greatest."

"A vodka on the rocks, how much would that set me back at the American bar of the Hôtel de Paris?"

Mike shook his head.

"You have to ask," he said, "you never go there."

"I'm curious. Polish vodka."

"Thirty dollars, probably."

"You're right. I don't qualify."

"Can I ask you, my friend Crang," Mike said, "why you drop in? In this apartment?"

"Request of the landlady," I said. "She wants me to keep an eye on the place."

While Mike digested my improvised answer, I grabbed the initiative.

"What about you?" I asked.

"Me?"

"Why are you here?"

Mike didn't miss a beat.

"Shirts," he said, broadcasting the word with so much power I thought I felt the wind of his voice ruffle my hair.

"You looking for something in silver, Mike?" I said.

"Shirts for Jamie," Mike said. "He tell me, long as you be in Canada, why not you please stop at my apartment and get me some more shirts."

"The sort of chips Jamie seems to be in," I said, "he could probably buy out every Hugo Boss outlet along the Mediterranean."

Mike shifted his shoulders in what I took to be a shrug native to Monaco. It was less Gallic than Annie's, less Anglo than mine.

"Jamie's favourites," Mike said. His eyes were steady on my face. "He wants his favourite shirts he left behind. Funny guy, Jamie."

As a liar, Mike had a flawless delivery. But the shirt story didn't hold water. Didn't wash either.

"Well, Mike," I said, "Why don't I give you a hand?"

"Huh?"

"Round up the favourites."

"Oh, for sure."

We went down the darkened hall off the living room, Mike in front. The hall branched to the right at the far end. There were two rooms opening off the stretch we were in, one room on either side. I poked my head into the room on the right.

"No, no, my friend Crang." Mike spoke quickly as well as loudly. "That is not the room for the shirts."

Mike was right. A lamp was on in the room, and in the seconds I had for a fast glance, I'd say the room was Jamie's den.

Mike ran his hand up and down the wall inside the room on the left side of the hall. He found the overhead light switch and turned it on. The room was a bedroom. A hell of a bedroom.

The bed was king-sized, set high off the floor. It had a frilly white canopy. The carpeting was white too. Mike and I stood in it up to our ankles. The walls were painted off-white, but what counted were the pictures that hung on the walls. Two Robert Markle drawings that concentrated on female crotches. A Dennis Burton painting from his garter-belt series. And a big Graham Coughtry canvas of a pair of entwined lovers.

"A fella could get horny just standing here," I said.

"Merde," Mike said.

I cleared my throat. "The shirts, Mike," I said.

"For sure," Mike said. He seemed to be having trouble taking his eyes off the Graham Coughtry.

There were doors on either side of the canopied bed. Mike mushed through the white carpet and opened the first door. A bathroom. He tried the second door and got lucky. It was a clothes closet. Shirts hung in it on hangers. So did a couple of sports jackets, a charcoal grey suit, and three or four pairs of slacks. The shirts, half a dozen of them, looked top quality, in silks and broadcloth and in elegant colour combinations.

"Just look, my friend Crang," Mike said. He had a wide grin on his face.

"I'm looking."

What I read on Mike's face was the expression of a guy who was flabbergasted to find shirts that supported his cockamamie story about the favour for Jamie Haddon.

"I think Jamie will like for me to take all of these beautiful shirts," Mike said.

He arranged the shirts neatly over his arm, and the two of us left the bedroom. I turned the light out on all that female flesh.

"Mission accomplished, Mike," I said in the living room. I didn't sit down. It might have encouraged Mike to remain on the premises.

"You too, my friend Crang?" Mike asked. "You have done the job for the landlady?"

Mike and I appeared to be operating from the same motive. I wanted him out of the apartment. He wanted me to leave first. I dug in.

"Plenty more to do, Mike," I said. "Read the meter. Check the pipes. Speak to Jamie's upstairs neighbour."

Would Mike swallow that line? I didn't think he had a choice, unless he was inclined to make a fuss.

"Well, my friend Crang," he said, "we meet again maybe."

"Wouldn't be surprised. I'll be in your corner of the world myself next week."

"For sure?"

The hesitant sound in Mike's voice said he hadn't decided whether this was good news or bad news.

"A holiday," I said. "Near Villefranche for a few days, and after that, Cannes. Me and a swell lady."

"Oh, a holiday, my friend Crang." Mike had decided. A holiday was okay. "You look me up for sure."

"Any place except the American bar of the Hôtel de Paris," I said.

I picked up Mike's silver windbreaker from the armchair and folded it on top of the armload of shirts. I put my hand on Mike's back. I may have been pushing him lightly as he went through the apartment door.

CHAPTER SIX

Whatever Mike Rolland came to fetch in Jamie Haddon's apartment, it wasn't shirts. Hell, the guy hadn't been in the bedroom. Didn't know where the light switch was. Hadn't even taken in the erotic glories of the crotch collection.

Whatever Mike came to fetch was probably in the den. Where the whistling had issued from. Where the desk lamp was switched on. Where Mike had apparently been poking around when I put in my unexpected appearance.

I walked back down the hall to the den. Its decor was in a masculine motif, crimson and military wallpaper, soldiers marching, horses rearing. The rug was Indian, and the desk was black and sleek. Along one wall, there was a large-screened TV set, a VCR, a CD player, and a stack of CDs. One short shelf held eight or nine books. All dealt with the esoterica of computers. A computer sat beside the shiny black desk. The computer was called a NeXT in jaunty colours. Tidy-looking machine, as black as the desk.

I went over to examine it at a closer range. On my way, behind the desk, I stepped on something that went crunch under my foot. It was a rectangular metal disk, a couple of inches wide, about three inches long, and not much thicker than a wafer. I picked it up. My foot hadn't cracked it. An elephant's foot wouldn't have cracked it. The thing felt indestructible in my hand.

I hefted it. Very light. It was black all over except for a silver band down the middle. I knew vaguely what it was, a disk that went into the computer. And a dozen more like it were scattered at my feet.

I sat in the chair behind the black desk. Comfy. The chair was upholstered in soft red leather. Jamie kept a clean desk top, nothing on it except the lamp, a red touch-tone telephone, and a pair of pens mounted in a clear glass holder. The pens looked like they were used for ceremonial purposes only.

I leaned out of the desk chair and scooped up the disks strewn on the floor. There were twelve of them, thirteen counting the one I'd stepped on. I turned over the first disk. It had a strip of paper taped across the bottom. On the paper someone had printed four words in neat block letters: "INVESTMENTS – STOCKS AND BONDS."

The printing was probably Jamie's, and he probably kept a record of his dabblings on the stock market on it. With Pamela's backing and his own salary he ought to have enough cash to take a modest flyer on the market.

Each of the other disks had the same sort of neatly printed label. "Correspondence and letters," I read on one. "Dictionary, thesaurus, quotations" on another. Well, okay, Jamie was hooked on self-improvement. Build up his word power. Stagger Pamela with his erudition.

I riffled through the rest of the disks. Nothing set off alarm bells. All struck me as straightforward and aboveboard, the kind of stuff a computer guy, which Jamie apparently was, might store on his computer disks.

So why were the disks scattered on the floor and not filed in the tray next to the NeXT where they clearly belonged? Jamie wouldn't have left his disks in disarray.

Pamela had been in the apartment after Jamie's departure. If she had seen the disks on the floor, and she would have if she'd been thorough in her rummaging, she would have put them back in their proper place. Pamela's motto had always been "tidying as you go is half the fun."

That left my new best friend, Mike Rolland of Monaco.

Mike had been in Jamie's library when I arrived, and he went out of the apartment wearing the face of a man unhappy with what he was leaving behind. Why was he unhappy? Because he'd been in the apartment on a search and hadn't found the object of his search.

That was a surmise on my part, but not a bad surmise. Another pretty fair surmise: he was looking for a computer disk, one that fit into the NeXT.

I pulled open the drawers to Jamie's desk. Time to launch my own search. The desk drawers didn't hold much. Stacks of computer paper. The Toronto telephone directory. A guide book to Monaco. I flipped through it. The proper adjective wasn't Monacan or Monesque. The book said it was Monégasque.

I got down on my hands and knees and rubbed my hands across the bottoms of the drawers. No disk was taped to the undersides.

I shook out the books in Jamie's single-minded little library, removed the CDs from their plastic containers, lifted the pillows off the maroon leather sofa against the opposite wall and jammed my hand into its lining. No disk.

I rolled up the Indian rug and rolled it down again. I unscrewed the base of the lamp and re-screwed it. I spent thirty minutes in the den. The room, I would've sworn, was clean of concealed disks.

I gave the same treatment to the living room, the dining room, the undersized kitchen, and the bedroom that Dante Renzi must have once occupied. It was empty of Dante and his effects and of a disk. I had narrowed the search to Jamie's bedroom. I made my way methodically through its closets, the two bedside tables, and a high bureau that held a few stray socks, some briefs in shocking shades, and nothing else. I pulled the drawers out of the bureau and turned them over. I patted the thick white carpeting for unnatural lumps. Nothing. I stuck my hand under the mattress. Nothing.

Had I exhausted all possibilities? All potential places of secrecy? Was there an ingenious hidey-hole somewhere in the apartment? Inspiration failed me.

I sat on the bed. It had a white satin spread. The pillows had satin covers. Seven pillows, one in mauve, two in silver, one in apple green ... seven pillows? What practices did Pamela and Jamie get up to in bed?

I stretched out on the satin spread and dropped my head on a white satin pillow. From where my head was positioned, I was staring at the Dennis Burton garter-belt painting. The woman in the garter belt was bending to one side. She showed a lot of haunch.

I stared some more. And noted a flaw. Either the woman was bending at a very tricky angle or the painting was hanging crooked on the wall.

I skidded off the satin and walked over to the painting. The garter belt was black, the haunch was pink, and the painting was tilting an inch too much to the right.

I straightened it and stepped back.

Nah. I'd made it worse, a couple of inches too far left.

I put my fingers under the bottom of the frame and started to ease the picture back into line.

On the back of the painting, at the bottom, the fingers of my right hand were touching something that definitely wasn't frame.

I unhooked the painting and turned it over.

Paydirt.

Layers of Scotch tape held something that looked remarkably like a disk to the back of the frame. I peeled off the Scotch tape. It was a disk under there, and it had a label with the familiar neat printing.

"Operation Freeload."

I rehung the lady in the garter belt and backed off two steps. She looked straight to me.

In the den, a small liquor cabinet nestled into the panelled wall beside the desk. Bottles, glasses, an ice-making machine. Jamie kept

Russian vodka on hand. Or Pamela kept it for him. Stolichnaya. I built a drink on the rocks, raised the glass in a toast to my own perspicacity, and sat in the chair behind the NeXT.

As a rule, I'll take the quill pen over the computer any day. That isn't a smart attitude in my profession and getting less smart awfully fast. Somewhere around fifty percent of my clients are charged with crimes of fraud, and lately too many of the people who beat a path to my door are accused of perpetrating their frauds with the accursed computer. I have to refer them to computer-friendly lawyers. It's embarrassing, especially when the computer-friendly lawyers don't send any quill-pen felons my way.

I had a stiff swallow of Stolichnaya and thought, what the hell. Take a flyer. Fire up the NeXT. Stick "Operation Freeload" into the thing. Maybe divine its contents. Solve the mystery right out of the box. Why not? What was the worst that could happen? I considered the question, but I didn't know what the worst could be.

A button on the NeXT's keyboard was labelled "Power." A logical starting place. I pressed it, and the machine went into a mild convulsion of drones and quavers. When the dust cleared and silence reigned again, a box in the computer's screen, black letters on an off-white background, seemed to require the answers to two questions. Name and Password.

Name.

Well, not mine.

Jamie's.

I typed "Jamie" into the indicated space.

Password?

I typed in "Freeload." It was worth a try.

Did the NeXT like what I'd fed it? I couldn't tell. Maybe it needed to chew on a disk. I looked around for an appropriate slot and found one on another black box that seemed to be a partner to the main computer. I slid in "Operation Freeload." The disk disappeared into the slot, making a polite slurping sound in the process, and right away, the screen blipped up a bunch of lines.

First, "Loading from disk."

Then, "Checking disk."

"Checking network."

"Starting system services."

Was this fun or what, a NeXT in high gear?

Something titled "Directory Browser" settled onto the screen. Under it, there was a long list of one-word titles. Browser? Jeez, computerspeak was turning mundane. Whatever happened to "interface" and "IBM-compatible"?

I gathered I was supposed to select something from the "Directory Browser," and move on to the next step.

Uh huh. I tried tapping keys on the keyboard, but nothing happened.

Hovering in the corner of the screen was a tiny arrow. Intuition told me the arrow was the little devil that handled the selecting chore. But how did I make the damn thing move?

To the right of the computer, resting on the table, there was a small rectangular gizmo. It was in the usual black, and it fed into the computer through a cable arrangement. Something about the little gizmo ... what was it? The rodent? The rat? The bug? Wait a minute, it was the mouse. I'd picked up that piece of dope somewhere along the line from one of the computer-friendly lawyers. The mouse acted as a sort of remote-control guide to the arrow on the screen.

Right.

I began to move the mouse around, and, presto, magic, computer science at work, the arrow moved around the screen.

Oh-kay.

The mouse had a button on top. I moved the arrow on the screen to a title under "Directory browser," and pushed the button on the mouse. Did I know what I was doing? Hell, no, but at least things were happening on the screen.

One by one, positioning the arrow and clicking the mouse, I got a series of lines of type popping up on the screen. I rattled through "NeXT Developer" and "Demos" and "Score Player."

Fascinating. I hadn't a clue what it all meant.

Could I penetrate into "Operation Freeload"?

Well, anything was possible.

On the screen, I had somehow summoned up a curious list of titles. The list was stacked vertically, and it read, "clouds, eagle, fish, gravity, holey, hotspin, mosaic …"

"Holey?"

I moved the arrow to "holey" and clicked the mouse.

All of a sudden it was like Chicago and the St. Valentine's Day massacre on the screen. Bullet holes, authentic-looking bullet holes, shreds around the edges and everything, studded across the screen, and the sounds of gunfire erupted into the room.

I jumped in the chair and spilled vodka on my pants.

"Holey?" Bullet holes! Was this a computer joke? Swell sense of humour, guys.

The screen went quiet. I mopped my pants and poured a new drink.

The weird list was back on the screen. "Clouds, eagle, fish, gravity …"

Was any of this going to lead me to Operation Freeload? Or had I stumbled into some kind of computer backwater? I couldn't fathom what was happening, but there didn't appear to be any turning back. Where could I turn back to? I pointed the arrow at another entry on the list, "Bach fugue." Well, why not? And I pushed the mouse's button. I got sound again, music this time. Or something approximating music. A Bach fugue came out of the computer, but the guy at the piano wasn't Glenn Gould. In fact, the closer I listened, the more I realized it wasn't a person at the piano and it wasn't a piano. The computer was playing a synthesized brand of Bach. Disillusionment was beginning to replace the euphoria I'd had when I embarked on this journey into the computer universe. The answer to Operation Freeload lurked somewhere inside the computer, but did I want to have a relationship with an instrument that sullied the works of a revered eighteenth-century German composer? Gimme a break. I went back to the oddball list and pointed the arrow at "fish." No surprises there. A fish swam across the screen. Actually a drawing of a fish. Lot of detail in the drawing too. Same thing with "eagle." The eagle swooped and dived and generally behaved like a patriotic American bird. I drank some more vodka and pondered the wisdom of pushing ahead. I could be sitting at the damn machine all night and never come within hailing distance of Operation Freeload. Or I could go home and think about rounding up someone who would handle the computer detail for me.

I positioned the arrow opposite "gravity" and clicked the mouse.

Everything on the screen bounced and vibrated. Words and symbols and boxes trembled as if an earthquake had struck.

Then — zip — nothing. The screen went blank, nothing except a sea of off-white.

Was this a silent metaphor? Was there a hidden message in the damn blank screen? Was the computer telling me to sign up for a course at George Brown College? Study up your Disk Drive 101 and come back in a year, fella.

"Well, thank you very much," I said to the NeXT.

Talking out loud to an inanimate object. Bad omen. Maybe a sign I should bid adieu to the NeXT. But not to the disk. I pushed the Power button, and the machine went into another round of hums and drones. As they dwindled toward silence, the light on the screen faded to black and the slot on the annex box beside the main computer burped out the disk. Good old Operation Freeload, whatever it was.

I stuck the disk in my pocket, made one more small vodka, and organized myself to head home. The hell with technology.

CHAPTER SEVEN

At home, I phoned Pamela.

"This is the Cartwright residence."

It wasn't the housekeeper who answered, not unless her voice had dropped an octave since the afternoon. It was a man on the line, sounding as pear-toned and snooty as Arthur Treacher used to in the movies. I gambled it wasn't Archie being funny, or even being serious, and asked for Mrs. Cartwright.

"May I say who is calling, sir?"

"The credit manager at Creed's."

"One moment, please."

Pamela took less than one moment to get to the phone.

"Is this a joke?" she said into the receiver.

"It's Crang."

"Close enough."

"Was that a real butler who answered?"

"Real part-time butler. He comes in when we have a dinner party. Which is what's going on right now. Why are you calling? And speak fast."

"Jamie's got a NeXT in his den."

"A birthday present from me."

"What's he do with it?"

"Plugs into the Pentagon for all I know," Pamela said. Behind her, I could hear the subdued buzz of the party.

"There are little square disks that go with it. With the NeXT."

"Optical disks. Get the terminology right, Crang. Those, if you want to know, hold words and pictures and sound. A person could store a whole novel on one disk, a James Michener, though God knows why anyone would want to."

"Gee," I said, "you're practically an expert."

"I couldn't help picking up something, the way Jamie rabbits on about that bloody NeXT."

"Did he ever rabbit on about an optical disk labelled Operation Freeload?"

"Should he have?"

"I was hoping."

"He didn't, and, listen, couldn't this wait? The dinner party's really for Archie's sake, business friends of his. It isn't polite for the hostess to ignore them. Or good for Archie's business either."

"Michel Rolland, heard of him?"

"Who's he, the director of Operation Freeload?"

"He was in Jamie's apartment when I went over. He's from Monaco. A guy in his late thirties, looks prosperous, obviously tough, a cagey sort of cookie."

"Hold on."

She must have put a hand over the receiver. At my end, I got muffled half-words. One of the half-words was "hole." I had an inkling the other half was "ass."

Pamela came back on the line, unmuffled.

"Archie's getting antsy," she said.

"Did I half-hear you describe me as an asshole?"

"You half-heard me describe the credit manager at Creed's as an asshole who's bothering the wrong Mrs. Cartwright at an hour when sensible credit managers should be in the bosom of their families."

"I got more on Jamie," I said. "We should meet again. Not for tea."

"Whatever you've been doing in the last few hours, Crang, you'd better not have blown my problem into major proportions. This isn't a criminal case, you know."

"Those are just about the same words Swotty used at lunch."

"Well, Daddy is usually right."

"A meeting?"

Pamela didn't hesitate. "Saturday at five-thirty," she said. "The Courtyard."

She hung up.

I spent another five minutes on the phone talking to a young criminal lawyer I know, one of the new computer-friendly breed. He said he'd be free to look at the optical disk and its contents Sunday morning. I thanked him, and thought about hiding the disk until Sunday.

If the disk was important enough to conceal in Jamie's apartment, it merited the same treatment in mine. I moseyed around the living room and out to the kitchen checking for a hiding place that qualified as cunning. In the end, after fifteen minutes of moseying, I settled on the white globe around the overhead light in my bedroom. I stood on a chair from the kitchen, unscrewed the globe, took out the light bulb, dropped in the disk, and re-screwed the globe. Maybe not out-and-out cunning, but fairly crafty.

I phoned Annie and got her answering machine. Annie was busy with movies. She had to see six or seven before we left for France and put reviews of them on tape for Metro Morning to use in her absence. I made a sandwich out of three-grain bread and some turkey slices that were just beginning to harden at the edges. A rerun of *L.A. Law* was on TV. I watched it, ate the sandwich, and helped it along with a Wyborowa and soda. When *L.A. Law* ended, I tried to decide whether I identified more with Jimmy Smits or Corbin Bernsen. Tough call. I was still working on the decision when I fell asleep.

CHAPTER EIGHT

On Friday morning, I called Trumball Fraser. He said sure, he was free for lunch. Did I know Coaster's? Little place over by the St. Lawrence Market? Trum said he was a regular there. I didn't know Coaster's, but I knew Trum. When he said he was a regular, it meant Coaster's must be an out-of-the-way spot where Trum could have long lunches and longer drinks without other Cayuga & Granark employees crowding his noon hour. I said I'd meet him at twelve-thirty.

Trum Fraser was a lawyer about my age. Professionally, he had two strikes against him, his father and his older brother. They were both civil litigation lawyers whose names looked incomplete unless the adjective "distinguished" was inserted up front. Distinguished counsel Justin and Roger Fraser. They argued before the Supreme Court of Canada about every other week and had their cases written up in the Dominion Law Reports. Trum got the short end of the stick in the family when it came to the law. He had most of the brains but not much of the ambition. He took the path of least resistance: a job as an in-house lawyer at Cayuga & Granark. He read contracts, wrote memos on changes in laws that affected trust companies, nothing terrifically demanding in the legal line. If litigation loomed, a lawsuit against C&G, Trum briefed counsel outside the trust company, someone like his distinguished father or his distinguished older brother. They ran with the case in court while Trum stayed snug in his office at C&G and had lengthy lunches at Coaster's.

The weather had turned close to balmy. I left the Volks at home. Nice day for a walk. Tulips were starting to bloom red and yellow in the boulevards that divide University Avenue. Secretaries and guys in shirt sleeves ate lunches out of paper bags on the benches around the plaza behind the Toronto-Dominion Centre. And in the little park next to the Flatiron Building, people reclined in the grass with their faces up to the sun, getting a head start on their summer tans. If I were Gene Kelly, I'd have broken out the taps for a chorus of "It Might as Well Be Spring."

Coaster's was down a short sloping street that ran alongside the market. Delivery trucks jammed up the traffic, dropping off crates of lettuce and sides of beef to the vendors in the market building. The restaurant was on the opposite side of the street and up two flights of stairs. I climbed the two flights. The room was agreeably ramshackle and felt like it'd be easy on the noon-time nerves. The only flaw was the place's sound system and the owner's lousy taste in tapes. Willie Nelson was whining about another cheatin' woman.

Trum Fraser had a table for two beside one of the windows. The table and chairs were like the rest of the restaurant, somewhere between unpretentious and rickety.

"Know what I like about this joint?" Trum said.

"Everything except the music."

Trum listened as if he were taking in Willie's droning for the first time.

"Not that shit," he said. "What I like, the bartender here understands the connection between the words bathtub and martini."

"Makes them ample, does he?"

"The guy must be American," Trum said. "Ever notice how unsatisfied you feel after a Canadian martini?"

Trum's face was that of a man on a lifelong search for the sat-
isfying martini. Flushed cheeks, veins beginning to break, nose
headed in the direction of W.C. Fields'. He was about thirty pounds
too heavy, stuffed into his brown suit, the collar of his white shirt
digging a crease in his neck. But as lushes went, Trum was a thinking man's lush. I'd never seen him drunk. Never seen him when his
brain wasn't taking care of business.

"You could've had it made, Crang," Trum said to me. He must
have arrived five or ten minutes earlier. The level of the martini in
his hand was two-thirds of the way down the bathtub.

"If you're talking about life in general, I'm not doing too badly," I
said. "If it's the law, I never counted on getting it made. Just getting
a light grip on it is sufficient."

"I mean business, the trust company, good old C&G," Trum
said. "After you got off the phone this morning, I was thinking,
when you were married to Pamela, Jesus, if you'd played your
cards right, you'd be up there on the thirty-second floor today,
right down the hall from Whetherhill."

"You know how much fun that'd be, Trum?"

"Fun, hell. Think of the power."

"About as much fun as you in partnership with the other two Frasers."

"Oh, low blow. I'd be honoured to serve alongside my papa
and sibling."

"Bull."

"Fortunately they never asked me."

A waitress showed up at our table.

"Connie, my little petunia," Trum said to her, holding out his
empty martini glass, "I trust you're keeping count."

"When I come back," Connie said, "it'll be with the third."

"What time'd you get here, Trum?" I asked.

"Noon," Connie answered for him. "Stroke of. As usual."

I asked for a glass of white wine. The menu was printed in small
type on the place mats. Trum said he'd have the Friday special. I
went for a dish billed as half an appetizer plate.

"Speaking of your shop," I said to Trum, "how's business?"

"Be specific."

"Jamie Haddon."

"There you go, old buddy, another case of nepotism. But he's smarter than you, Crang, young Jamie is. He has tied himself to old Whetherhill's coattails, and he's not about to let go."

"I think you got your metaphors mixed up there, Trum."

"Jamie also knows which side his bread is buttered on."

Connie made the round trip with my white wine and Trum's third martini.

"Leaving aside family advantages," I asked Trum, "how is Jamie on his own merits, in your humble opinion?"

"Well, one talent of his, he's hot stuff in the boardroom. Very organized with the reports when his turn comes around. Doesn't say a whole lot, but he drops the odd harmless witticism. Knows how to butter up the guy in the chair without brown-nosing. He's a political guy, Jamie."

"Young man going places is what you're telling me?"

"Listen, I'll lay it out for you from the top. C&G isn't a bad place to work, not for Jamie, not for me, not for anybody. You think of it, we're talking about the last of the old-school trust companies in this country that hasn't been gobbled up by a bank or some marauding American. The company is solid as a rock, and it's Whetherhill, him and his family, who built it. Swotty's idea of a lavish salary doesn't happen to coincide with mine, but there are other benefits. Stock options, smart people to work with, and God knows the place is going to be there forever. That's all Whetherhill's accomplishment, and you're asking about Jamie Haddon, well, Swotty treats the kid like he's seen the future and Jamie Haddon's in it."

Connie plunked down two plates. The Friday special was chili. My half appetizer plate held a full complement of fish, crustaceans, and molluscs. Shrimp, lobster, herring, two oysters.

"Computers," I said to Trum, moving along my list of topics. "I assume C&G is chock-a-block with them."

"I love those suckers."

"You personally? You use a computer?"

"I got a little honey right beside my desk. Every day I ask myself, how did I ever work, how did I live, before whoever invented computers invented them."

"You should understand this is coming as a cruel disappointment to me, Trum. I had you down for a fellow Luddite."

Trum pointed his fork at me.

"I got something I want to give to my secretary ... follow me on this, Crang, it's a good example of what my computer does for me ... and the secretary isn't at her desk. Do I chase after her, wait around, look for another girl? Hell, no, I bang the message, the memo, whatever, into my computer and press a button and, zip, it's in her computer. Or, get this, I'm setting up a short meeting with a couple of other people, say some guys two floors down from me. Am I gonna take the elevator, and it ends up these guys are out of the office, in a conference, something like that? You kidding me? I do the whole arrangement on the computer. Never leave my desk. Those examples, I save myself, easy, thirty minutes out of every day at the office."

Trum was serious.

"That's great," I said. "What do you do with the extra half-hour?"

"Get out to the golf course a half-hour earlier."

Trum was still serious.

"What about Jamie?"

"Never played golf with him. He looks more of a squash type to me."

"Come on, Trum, you know what I mean. Jamie and computers."

"Now you mention it, he's pretty sharp. He talks all the time about ways we can use computers I never thought of. The truth is I don't frankly understand it when Jamie gets on one of his kicks. 'Your programming's out of date, Trum.' Shit, gimme a break, I'm only sending memos to my secretary. But, you know, to each his own. Jamie knows computers. I know law."

"Don't undersell yourself, Trum. You're sitting next to one of them all day, you must have a notion about the machines, how computers work."

"A thing I learned, lemme tell you, Crang, they're resilient little suckers. There was a hell of a flap two, three weeks back. I'm punching away at my computer, putting in this big deal report to the head guy over in the securities department. My screen all of a sudden goes berserk. Jumping around like a bitch, like a movie out of focus, except sometimes the screen would be absolutely blank for long stretches. This wasn't just my computer. Same thing all over the entire trust company."

"What'd happened?"

"Some kind of massive short circuit, I don't know. But never mind that. It isn't the point of the story."

"I'm still listening."

"All right, you know the old brick warehouse, looks deserted, right at Spadina and Wellington, far side?"

"No, but if you say so."

"That building, it isn't empty at all. In there, they got a computer backup system for the C&G computer. It takes over in case the computer at the main office blows. Which it did. Okay, within minutes, the backup over at Spadina and Wellington kicks in."

"Trum, I'm astounded, really am. Totally awestruck."

"You don't give a rat's ass, Crang, I can tell. But to me, it was amazing. One minute, I was running around the hall. The computer's out, I was saying, my report's lost, the sky is falling. And next thing, a couple of minutes later, I was back in my office, and everything was normal. Not a syllable got lost. My report to the head securities guy was right there, right in the middle of the sentence I was typing. Fucking-A amazing."

Connie reappeared.

"You going for four, Trum?" she asked.

Trum wiped chili from the side of his mouth.

"Not till I've called my friend here's bluff," he answered.

Connie went away. I waited for Trum to call my bluff. What bluff? I was guarding a secret about Pamela and Jamie, but I wasn't trying to blow anything past Trum.

"I guessed soon as you started in with the Jamie Haddon questions." Trum looked satisfied with himself. "You're acting for a client, correct me if I'm wrong, but I'm not, and the name of the client, the reason you're having lunch with me, is Archie Cartwright."

"You're wrong."

"Okay, confidentiality, I understand. You're not gonna level with me."

Trum's eyes, I hadn't realized before, were surprisingly clear and sharp, a minimum of red for a man as dedicated to martinis as he was.

"But if you expect me to go further," Trum said, "I want it between us, officially, you heard nothing from me."

"About what?"

"The affair, for chrissake."

"The affair?"

I knew what affair Trum meant. But how did he know about it? And wasn't Pamela going to blow her stack when I told her Trum knew?

"Yeah," Trum said. "The affair."

"Pamela and Jamie?"

"See? I knew you were acting for Archie."

"Trum, not that it matters, but I don't take matrimonial cases."

"Sure, you're criminal. But I'm thinking to myself, maybe Archie found out Pamela's screwing around, and he wanted someone to do a little preliminary digging before the divorce lawyers come in and the fees hit six figures, and he arrives at you because for reasons of your own, Pamela giving you the brush years ago, you might be willing to throw yourself into the job."

"I'm wounded, Trum, hurt to the quick. You'd think that of me?"

"Must be my lawyer's training," Trum said. "Anyhow, I'm with Pamela if the time comes for choosing up who you have to be with."

"Archie Cartwright — listen to my every word, Trum — Archie Cartwright has never communicated with me by letter, by telephone, by an intermediary, by telex or fax, or by semaphore."

Trum eased his stomach away from the edge of the table. He looked at me from over his swelling nose.

"Pamela and me," Trum said, "we go back. I remember, years before you ever came along, I was at UCC, she was at Branksome. We went to the formals, the battalion balls, her father's house, my father's house. Same gang of us did all that teenage crap together. That's why I still got a lot of time for Pamela."

"Very touching, Trum," I said. "Now, how did you find out about the affair?"

"Jamie told me."

"Holy shit."

"That's what I thought too. An affair, you only tell your best buddy about, and I'm not Jamie's. He's just a guy I work with on projects at the office. But a while ago, he says, let's have lunch. First time that happened, believe me. Anyhow, I'm into my second silver bullet, he starts in about him and Pamela. Wouldn't shut up."

"How much did he tell you?"

"That it's been going on a year, that Pamela set him up in an apartment, and that, in so many words, she's a great lay."

"Charming."

"I would've punched him, except I wanted to hear more."

Connie took away our empty plates and brought coffee.

"You holding at three?" she asked Trum.

"I'm saving number four for my confreres at the bar," Trum answered, nodding toward the centre of the room.

"Just another couple of questions," I said. "Anybody else privy to all this?"

"Two, maybe three other people at C&G. They found out the same way as me, same general time too. From Jamie, last month. The guy that runs the investment department, he knows, and Jamie's immediate boss, him as well."

"What about Swotty? Any chance of these guys passing it to him?"

"Are you nuts?" Trum jerked his hand and spilled coffee on his placemat. "Can you see one of us dropping in at Whetherhill's office. 'Oh, by the way, Chief, your married daughter's banging a guy from the trust department. And, hey, you'll never guess, Chief, the guy's a relative of yours.'"

"Yeah," I said. "Dumb question."

Trum lifted his cup and mopped the spilled coffee with a paper napkin.

"Sure sign," he said. "When I start dumping coffee all over the place, I need another drink."

"This has been a large help, Trum," I said. "I'll let you know how it develops."

"You won't need to. If anything hits the fan, it'll be all over the office." Trum put his hands on the table and levered himself out of his chair. The table rocked on its legs. "I did all the talking," he said. "So you get to do the paying. Fair? Not at the bar though. I'll pick up for what I drink there."

"Number four?"

"All this shit we been talking about, I might feel a fifth coming on."

When Trum reached the bar, the guys sitting there opened up a space for him. A martini was waiting on the Formica top.

CHAPTER NINE

I got home just after seven, laden with purchases. I had Miles Davis's autobiography, thick and in paperback. That was for overseas reading. I had two new shirts, a French-English dictionary, and, best of all, a beret in a raffish black model. I tried it on in front of the bathroom mirror. Someone resembling the young Maurice Chevalier stared back at me. Ah, France. Ah, Gigi. Ah, thank heaven for leetle girls.

"Yo, Crang." Alex of the downstairs duo of Alex and Ian called up the stairs. "You all alone up there?"

I went out to the landing. "Annie's working tonight."

"Poor you. Had dinner yet?"

"I was planning on something from the kitchens of Campbell's."

"Well, Ian's cooked pots of *ragoût d'agneau*. We'd adore it if you came down and made us green about your big trip."

"What did you call the meal?"

"Lamb stew, numb nuts."

I got two bottles of Côtes du Rhône out of the cupboard over the refrigerator. Alex and Ian and I ate, drank, talked, and laughed until almost midnight, and when I arrived back upstairs, I was feeling no particular pain.

In the bedroom, I turned on the lamp beside the bed. A little breeze was floating through the open window. I walked over to the window and got closer to the breeze. It felt soft and sweet. I stood there and wondered, idly, vaguely, why a soft, sweet breeze was coming into the room. As far as I remembered, before I joined the guys downstairs, the bedroom window had been shut tight.

"Be cool, my man."

The voice was a relaxed tenor, and it seemed to be emanating from somewhere over by the closet.

"Stay steady, man," the voice said. "Three things I don't need you be doin.'"

I turned around.

"Ah, now, man, that there's one of the things I didn't need you be doin.'"

The guy might have been Patrick Ewing, except I knew Patrick Ewing was playing for the Knicks at Madison Square Garden that night. The guy looked about as big as Patrick Ewing though, close to seven feet and two hundred and fifty pounds, and he was just as black. He had a ski mask pulled over his face, but his hands were the hands of a black man. There wasn't a weapon in either hand. A guy built like Patrick Ewing doesn't need a weapon.

"Other two things," the giant said, "don't go talkin' loud and don't go doin' any brave shit."

"No problem." My voice hadn't progressed past the croak level.

"Long's we got an understanding."

"Urn, would you perhaps care for a drink? Vodka?"

"Not on the job, man."

"Yeah, I didn't think this was a social call."

"Workin.'"

"You want me to raise my hands or anything?"

"Want you be tellin' me where the disk's at."

"You too?" The surprise in my voice lifted it a notch in volume.

"Man, what'd I tell you 'bout no loud talkin'?"

"You said there was an interdiction against it. Sorry."

"Don't give me no interdiction shit. Just don't be shoutin' or nothin' along those lines."

My heart felt like it was pounding someplace close to my throat, but the terror was receding, and I was beginning to feel a trifle silly standing in my own bedroom chatting with a large visitor who was apparently bent on burglary.

"What do you think?" I said. "Could we adjourn to the kitchen? You know, pull up a chair. Talk over issues."

"Ah, man, you one of those discussers!"

The guy sounded disgusted, but he didn't object when I stepped past him and led the way out to the kitchen. My kitchen is a roomy space, large enough to accommodate a wooden table and four chairs in the centre. The giant and I sat across from one another at the table. His size had the effect of cutting down the room's dimensions.

"Well, look, um, friend," I said, attempting a hearty line, "my name's Crang."

"Already know that, man. How you think I got here?"

"Right, yeah. And your name would be?"

"It would be none of your business, man, but it might be Curtis."

"Okay, Curtis, feel free to take off the mask. Must be kind of warmish, and, you want the truth, it has the effect of restricting conversation. Like a barrier between the two of us."

"You 'bout finished, man?"

"I take it you're going to leave the mask on."

"Part of the costume, man. You see the way I got myself duded up?"

Curtis had on black-topped Nikes, black jeans, a navy blue turtleneck, and the forbidding ski mask, which was dark blue wool with large holes for the eyes, nostrils, and mouth.

"Very authentic, Curtis," I said.

"This here disk, it ain't in the living room and it ain't in the kitchen, 'less you got a real smart place you concealin' it. And the bedroom, I just started, you come in."

"You were as quiet as a mouse in your searchings, Curtis. Congratulations."

"All that gigglin' and laugh'n downstairs, nobody's gonna hear nothin' no way anyway, man."

"Good point."

"You gonna save both us wastin' whole lotta more time and tell me where the disk's at?"

"Am I right, you don't want it for personal reasons of your own?"

"Come on, man."

"You're present in my home on a contract basis?"

"Man, you are a trial."

"Had any second thoughts about that drink?"

"I can see this gonna be a long night."

"In that case, mind if I help myself?"

I didn't wait for Curtis's approval. There was a full bottle of Wyborowa in the freezer. I reached in and brought it out by the neck. It felt cold and heavy. In one motion, gripping the neck of the bottle, I whirled around and slammed the bottle at Curtis.

Before the bottle got within two feet of my target, Curtis's head, he stuck up his left hand, which looked like it had a span big enough to palm a basketball, and plucked the bottle out of the air. The gesture struck me as remarkably casual, as if Curtis was used to intercepting hard objects that were aimed at his skull. He remained in his chair holding the vodka bottle. I stood in front of him experiencing a new spasm of terror.

"Urn, Curtis," I said, "I hope you're going to accept that in the nature of a necessary gesture."

"Sit back down, man."

"Under the present circumstances, you know, a guy's expected to make a stand. The manly thing and all that."

"Sit the fuck down."

I sat.

Curtis got up and went straight to the cupboard that held the glasses. He chose an old fashioned glass and poured two inches from the Wyborowa bottle into it. He handed the drink to me.

"Thanks, Curtis," I said, "but I generally have my vodka on the rocks."

"Man, you really tryin' my patience."

I drank some of the Wyborowa. "Very smooth this way. Sure you won't change your mind?"

Curtis shook his head.

I took another swig. It seemed to be soothing the most recent onslaught of fear.

"The kind of dude you are, man," Curtis said, "it probably be a long time before you tell me where you got the disk hid."

"A French or Italian guy named Michel Rolland hired you, correct?"

"That's exactly what I'm talkin' about, man. You shoot the shit, ask questions, drag ass, you never get round to tellin' me the facts."

"Curtis, perhaps I could propose a meeting of minds here."

"Man, keep this shit up, I meet your mind with my fist."

Curtis took two long and limber strides across the kitchen to the big drawer beside the stove. He moved like he was loose all over, loose in the limbs, loose in the joints. His hand went into the drawer and came out with a roll of thick twine. He seemed to approve of it, and reached back in the drawer for some tape.

"Really know your way around the old homestead, Curtis," I said.

"Been familiarizin' myself, man."

"About the twine, I use it for tying the newspapers into bundles. You know, for recycling?"

"Wanna finish your juicin', man?"

"Curtis, I have an inkling you're not intending to bundle up my *Stars* and *Globes*."

"Drink, man."

The rest of the vodka burned its pleasant way to my stomach. I set the empty glass on the table.

"Your nose, man," Curtis said.

"Huh?"

"Breathe through it." Curtis ripped off a piece of tape and slapped it over my mouth.

I said, "Argghh."

"Man, don't you ever shut up?"

"Grrrrr," I said, and tried to rip the tape off with my hands.

Curtis swatted my hands and gave me a glare I interpreted as menacing. I left both hands in my lap.

"Round behind you, man," Curtis said.

I swung my hands to the back of the chair, and felt Curtis go to work with the twine. He looped it around my wrists three or four times and did something intricate with a knot that tied the wrists to the rungs of the chair. He gave my ankles and the chair's legs the same treatment. If I'd been able to make myself understood, I would have complimented Curtis on his efficiency.

"Don't go 'way, man," Curtis said.

"Sssssrrrrr."

Curtis left the kitchen in the direction of the bedroom. I took a couple of exploratory tugs at the twine around my wrists. Nothing yielded. Ditto with my ankles. I pushed my tongue against the tape. It stayed in place. I decided I wouldn't be going anywhere soon. Maybe it was better that way. Going some place with Curtis could be dangerous, especially if he rethought the episode of the vodka bottle and elected to take it personally. I waited. The second hand on the kitchen clock dragged around three times. Nothing except silence came from the bedroom. The second hand completed another sweep, and Curtis reappeared in the kitchen.

"Cuuuuurrrr," I said.

Curtis bent over the drawer that had held the twine and tape.

"Bedroom's awful dark, man," he said.

Oh, damn.

Curtis produced a package of sixty-watt bulbs. He unwrapped one bulb and went away with it.

The second hand didn't make it half way around the clock before Curtis was back in the kitchen.

"Put in a new bulb for you, man." he said.

In his large palm, Curtis held the disk, good old Operation Freeload, and for the first time, Curtis was showing a lot of teeth in the dark blue mask. His teeth were exceptionally white.

"Yarggg," I said.

"Dig it, man," Curtis said, "the Billie Holiday album in the livin' room?"

I nodded from my place of confinement.

"Lester Young, Duke's band, Ahmad Jamal? Those all your phonograph records on the shelf, man?"

I nodded again.

"Man plays Billie Holiday, Lester Young on his phonograph, he likely got a soul."

My nodding grew more vigorous.

"Don't merit I should slap him upside the head. Little payback for wingin' that there bottle from the icebox."

I was bobbing my head like a frantic fool.

"Stay cool, man."

Curtis took a step back, turned, and flowed out of the kitchen. From the bedroom, I heard faintly the sound of the window coming down. Curtis was no doubt lowering it from the outside. Immediately below the window, there was the roof over the downstairs patio. From there, it was a short drop to the ground, particularly short for a guy of Curtis's proportions.

I sat in the bright light of the kitchen and reviewed my position. Physically, my position was humiliating. In strategic terms, it was just as bad. Curtis the Hip Giant almost certainly burgled my apartment on a consignment basis. He was sent in to steal one object, the disk, and the employer who had sent him must have been Mike Rolland. Mike had probably gone back into Jamie Haddon's place, failed to find the disk, reasoned that I had taken it, and called on Curtis's services. The only other person who knew the disk was in my possession was Pamela, but she had no reason to retain Curtis to repossess the thing. Hell, Pamela wouldn't even know how to contact a guy in Curtis's line of work. But I wouldn't put it past Mike Rolland to know and employ a Curtis or two in every country he dropped in on. Given the events of the evening, Mike would soon be on his way with the disk to *Cats* in Winnipeg. And I was in Toronto with egg on my face. Egg and tape.

I took a few more tugs at the twine around my wrists and ankles. All I accomplished was to remove a few layers of skin. Curtis knew more tricks with twine than an Eagle Scout. The tape wouldn't budge either.

Maybe a different mode of escape might work. If I couldn't get out of the chair, I'd have to take it with me. I gave the chair a preliminary rock. It wasn't heavy, just a collection of wooden slats and a fatter piece of wood for the seat. I gathered my strength and lifted upwards and outwards. The chair came with me, hippety hop. I kept up the motion, and the chair went hop, hop, hop across the kitchen floor.

My forehead started to break out in beads of sweat, and breathing through the nose wasn't entirely comfortable. But I made steady progress across the kitchen and into the hall.

Hop, hop, hop, I went, and then crash.

The legs of the chair had caught in the folds of the hall rug, and I tipped over sideways. I landed on my elbow and lay on the floor, right side down. The elbow ached, the twine was digging into my wrists and ankles, and I felt like a helpless idiot.

"What is the racket up there?" Alex's voice came from the bottom of the stairs.

"Yoo hoo, Crang." It was Ian. "People down here are trying to watch Letterman."

"Ruffff," I said.

"Crang?" Alex called.

"He didn't have that much to drink," Ian said in a lower voice.

"And he does hold his liquor well," Alex said.

"Gets so much practice with that Slavic stuff."

"Polish."

"Whatever."

"Arghhh," I said.

Footsteps sounded on the stairs, and in a few seconds, Ian and Alex came into view. Ian had on a long nightshirt in red and white vertical stripes. Alex was wearing a silk dressing gown. Both were barefoot, and when they saw me lying on the floor, tied to the chair, both developed expressions somewhere between shocked and amused.

"Really, Crang," Alex said, "have you been up to something kinky?"

Ian set the chair upright, and Alex peeled back the tape, trying to do a slow and painless job. He almost succeeded.

"My Lord, what happened?" Alex asked in a solicitous voice.

I ran my tongue over my lips. "A tall dark stranger came calling."

"Ooooo," Ian said, "lucky you."

CHAPTER TEN

A strapping young guy inside the door of the Courtyard cafe asked me if I wanted smoking or non-smoking.

"I'm meeting Mrs. Cartwright," I said.

"Say no more."

The young guy had on a sweater that probably cost a dozen yaks their lives, and his hair came in two shades, gold and fuchsia. He didn't resemble many maitres d' of my acquaintance, but he was carrying two menus.

"Pamela prefers to sit back here," he said.

Back here was a booth against the wall farthest from the restaurant's entrance. Secluded, but with a clear view of most of the room. The hour was early for the dinner crowd, but the place was two thirds full. Everybody looked glittery. It helped that the ceiling was one huge skylight letting in plenty of late afternoon sun. But even without the dramatic lighting, the Courtyard was a fashionable joint. Very jet set. A home away from Hollywood for movie types. Deals got cut at the Courtyard. The people who did lunch there had names that turned up in the Sunday *Sun*'s Panache column.

Pamela arrived right after me, escorted to the booth by Gold and Fuschia Hair. He was gabbing up a storm.

"This woman, a countess she claimed," he was saying a half inch from Pamela's ear, "when she found out Norman was a writer, she said he had to do her biography. Well, Norman heard her out, and then he said ... Norman was sitting right over there at his usual afternoon table ... he said to her she was no countess because he knew all the Romanian nobles left in the world, and, lady, you ain't one of them."

"Too much," Pamela said. She laughed more than politely.

"Thought you'd appreciate it."

The maitre d' hovered over Pamela as she sat down across the table from me. "So," he said to her, "what can we bring you and your guest?"

"Crang?" Pamela said to me.

"Vodka on the rocks."

The maitre d's eyes didn't leave Pamela's face.

"I'll have Campari and soda," Pamela said.

The maitre d' tore himself away from the booth.

I said, "I suspect that lad's vaulting ambition is to be your personal lap dog."

"Pip's a sweetie."

"Pip?"

"He picked it himself. He was born Elmer in Owen Sound or somewhere awful."

Pamela opened a black leather handbag and took out a gold cigarette case and a gold lighter. Both were uncluttered by initials or any other design. She set them on the table within easy reach.

"Isn't this a shade public for an intimate tete-a-tete?" I said. "The Courtyard?"

"I don't see why."

"Well, you know, I can just imagine a line in Panache. 'Caught bending in one another's direction at the Courtyard, Pamela Cartwright and the former Mr. Pamela.'"

"They wouldn't dare."

"Never had my name in a real gossip column."

"And you're not starting today," Pamela said. She tapped her cigarette case on the table, but didn't open it. "'Operation Freeload' you said on the phone. Translate it into something that makes sense to me."

"As a matter of fact, I got some late-breaking news that supersedes the disk."

"Let's do it my way. I have an agenda in my head, and it begins with Operation Freeload."

"Well, listen, this just in, a report from a lawyer at Cayuga & Granark."

"Indulge me, Crang. Operation Freeload."

"I lost it."

A waiter brought the drinks. He made a beautiful ceremony out of placing them before us. Pamela and I sat without talking. I was watching the ceremony of the drinks. Pamela was watching me.

"You what?" she said when the waiter went away.

"'Operation Freeload' were the words printed on one of Jamie's computer disks, presumably by Jamie himself. At least it was in the same hand as the printing on the labels for the other disks beside his computer. But it had to be special, this disk, because it was hidden. Scotch-taped to the back of the Dennis Burton painting."

"Scotch-taped?"

"The one of the lady with the splendid thighs in the garter belt."

"I know the damn painting, Crang. It belongs to me."

"That's a vivid collection you've got in the bedroom."

If I expected Pamela to blush or otherwise show embarrassment, I expected wrongly.

"Jamie's idea," she said matter-of-fact. "I had all the paintings in storage. He wanted to see them grouped in one room."

"With the seven pillows."

"That's enough inventory, Crang. Now get on with it about the disk."

"Okay, Jamie is probably the guy responsible for hiding it. Who else had access to the apartment? Just him, you, and lately, Dante Renzi."

"I never heard of Operation Freeload until you mentioned it," Pamela said, "and that moron Renzi hasn't got the brains to realize paintings have backs to them."

"So we go with Jamie as the hider of the disk."

"Which you found."

"And lost."

"To whom?"

"Michel Rolland."

"What was he doing in the apartment?"

"Trying to find the disk."

Pamela looked down at her Campari and soda, studied it, took a taste, and raised her eyes back to me.

"How's your law practice going, Crang? Doing all right?" she said. "What I'm getting at, do you make your instructions to clients as confusing for them as you're making your explanation of the goddamned disk for me?"

"Michel Rolland lives in Monaco. He met Jamie there. He came to Canada to see *Cats* … No, scratch *Cats*. It's a red herring … Jamie asked Rolland to stop by the apartment to pick up some shirts … Ahhh, scratch the shirts too …"

"Another red herring perhaps?" Pamela had acid in her voice.

"More like an outright lie. The real goods is that Rolland knew the disk existed. Knew it was in the apartment. But he didn't know where. I walked in in the middle of his search. And after he left, I completed the search. Successfully."

"So how did he end up with the disk?"

"Went shopping for the world's largest second-storey man and pointed him in the direction of my place."

"Crang, don't exaggerate."

"Hey, this was a potentially life-threatening situation. I could've been maimed."

"You're telling me your apartment was burgled?"

"More than burgled. My safety was at risk."

"If you were diddled out of this elusive bloody disk, just admit it and never mind the dramatizing."

"I carry wounds." I started to roll up the cuff of my shirt. "Scars of battle."

"Please, Crang."

I left the cuff alone. "But I'll level with you, I'm beginning to get my back up about this whole deal, about your pal Jamie and his pal Rolland and Rolland's pal Curtis the burglar."

"It isn't your back I'm counting on." Pamela looked slightly exasperated. "It's your head, but I may be overestimating its usefulness."

"You should've been in my kitchen last night."

"Crang, I'm not interested in the details of how the disk got away from you."

"Yeah, well, here's a detail that ought to grab you. It seems that Mike Rolland ..."

"Mike?"

"Actually, morality aside, he's an entertaining guy. Says to call him Mike."

"Keep in mind you're supposed to be on my side in this."

"No fear," I said. "Anyway, Mike is a big shooter along the Côte d'Azur. Sells cars, real estate, goods in the conspicuous consumption line. It seems, according to Mike, he made a large sale to Jamie. A boat."

"What kind of boat?"

"You ever heard of a Hatteras?"

"Of course I have," Pamela said with a bit of a snap. "What length?"

"Sixty feet."

"Eight hundred thousand dollars more or less, depending on how it's equipped."

"Mike gave me the impression Jamie's spending like a drunken sailor."

Pamela raised her hand for the waiter.

I said, "In Jamie's case, that might be closer to spending like a drunken commodore."

Pamela said to the waiter, "A double Johnny Walker Black, please, water on the side."

If Pamela ordered a big scotch when I told her about Jamie Haddon tossing around money, what would she order when I told her about Jamie bandying about her name? A twenty-sixer?

I said, "There's a disk in his collection with a label on it about investments and stocks and bonds."

"That's pocket money," Pamela said. Her lips seemed to have gotten tight and thin. "The entire portfolio, cashed out, wouldn't come to more than fifteen thousand."

"I wouldn't mind pockets like that."

Pamela's double arrived at the table. She took a long tug at the scotch.

"That's better," she said. She opened the gold cigarette case and lit a cigarette with the gold lighter. She blew smoke into the air over the table, inhaled more scotch, ignored the water, composed herself.

She said, "I suppose you're going to tell me Jamie took the money from the trust company."

"Crossed my mind."

"Get one thing straight in all of this," Pamela said. "Jamie wouldn't embezzle. Not from the trust company. Not from Daddy."

The way Pamela made her statement, I knew she didn't think of it as a debatable point.

"Urn," I said, "I suppose if he stole to the tune of eight hundred thousand dollars somebody down there might have noticed."

Pamela nodded as if I'd come up with something sage.

"Now," she said, "you mentioned a Cayuga & Granark lawyer a few minutes ago. Who?"

"Trum Fraser."

"I know Trum. Where does he come into this? Don't tell me he knows about the money?"

"What Trum knows is probably worse."

"I can't imagine anything worse."

"Trum knows about you and Jamie."

It was what Pamela didn't do that surprised me. She didn't signal for more reinforcements of scotch. Didn't scream for Pip to come hold her hand. All she did was sit very still and soak up more information.

"Tell me what Trum knows."

"About the apartment," I answered, "and about how long the affair has been going on. I don't think he knows intimate details, the white rug practically to a person's shins, that sort of intimate detail."

"And how did Trum find out?"

"This is the freaky part. Jamie told Trum. Told a couple of other people too, guys around the office."

"Jesus." Pamela got a slitty-eyed look that told me her calm was about to come unravelled. "As if I'm the prize among the bimbos, he can treat his friends to stories about how he got into my drawers."

Pamela's voice was close to a whisper and hoarse. She was also paying more attention to the scotch supply. She polished off the drink on the table and whistled up another from the waiter. I slipped in an order for a second vodka.

Pamela said to me, "You know, don't you, that the Côte d'Azur is six hours ahead of us?"

"The way I hear it, they're in front in a bunch of ways. Wine. Painting."

"I'm not in the mood."

"I was going to add sunshine and pizza. But, okay, I'm aware of the time difference."

"Keep it in mind," Pamela said, "when you phone me."

"I'm going to phone you?"

"That's what I'm asking you to do."

"Swotty wants a call, remember, after I've scrutinized Jamie."

"Phone me first," Pamela said, "and don't bother with the scrutiny."

"Swotty got his dibs in first."

"We'll discuss Daddy when you call," Pamela said. "All I'd like from you is the name of the hotel where that graceless swine is staying."

The fresh shipment of scotch and vodka arrived.

"Let's get the hours in sync," Pamela said to me. "Phone the house, Toronto time, after ten in the morning and before six-thirty at night."

"When Archie's at the office."

"How perceptive of you, Crang."

"What if you're off being fitted for jodhpurs or something?" I said.

"Leave the message with Hilda, the hotel's name and address."

"Hilda? She's the housekeeper?"

"And totally trustworthy."

"The hotel's name," I repeated. "What are you planning? Ring Jamie and give him a rocket?"

"Uh, uh." Pamela's voice dropped close to bass-baritone territory. "I'm going to handle Mr. Haddon face to face. And his'll be the face covered in shit."

"Fly over? You?"

"How else do you think I can get at his face?"

Damn, the Riviera was going to be overcrowded by one too many Canadians.

"Is that advisable?" I said. "Won't Archie get his antennae up?"

"That isn't your worry. I'll think of ways to keep Archie out of harm's way."

"Yeah, well, practice makes perfect."

Pamela must have been putting so much energy into fuming over Jamie that she let my little jab bounce right off.

"I know what's bothering you," she said. "Me in the vicinity. You're afraid I'll spoil the fun for you and Annie."

"You read my mind."

"But don't you see, the minute you phone me, you can toddle off to the beach or wherever you please. To the movies. You won't have to bother any longer with me or Jamie. Your obligation will be over."

"Except to Swotty."

"Oh, just tell Daddy Jamie was in culture shock when he wrote the postcard. Daddy's so anxious to be understanding and forgiving he'll believe anything about Jamie."

"Swotty might not be so understanding and forgiving when he hears Jamie is on board a sixty-foot yacht he's the proud new owner of. Especially, as you yourself may be rethinking at this very instant, if the cash that bought the boat isn't Jamie's and it is Swotty's."

"Crang, please."

"Not Swotty's own, but possibly C&G's."

"Will you lighten up a minute."

"Or a C&G client's."

Pamela paused for a beat of silence.

"Two things, Crang," she started up again. "Number one, are you familiar with the term 'alleged'?"

"Very popular in circles I work in."

"For heaven's sake, the only indication we have on Jamie and the alleged money comes from a complete stranger named Rolland with whom you spent, maximum, a total of forty-five minutes."

"Granted."

"Number two, who was it that raised the issue of Jamie and money in the first place? Who said to you, how is Jamie financing his leave of absence in Europe? Who?"

"You did. You, Pamela."

"Now I'm saying to you, me, Pamela, I'm saying I withdraw the money issue from your list of assignments."

She had a point. Tenuous, but a point. Pamela could be likened to a client who was taking back a case, dispensing with my services. Still, I felt myself resisting her orders. I owned a small personal stake in events. It was my house that big, scary Curtis, undoubtedly hired by Mike Rolland, broke into to swipe the disk I had swiped from Jamie Haddon's apartment. In my mind, the pair of swipes didn't cancel out one another. The personal element was one reason for not abandoning a search for the source of Jamie's money. Another reason to resist Pamela was that I'd made my commitment to Swotty Whetherhill first. I didn't like the thought of short-changing him.

"Supposing," I said, "we put off all final decisions until I suss out the situation in Monaco?"

"Is this a compromise?"

"Of sorts."

"I loathe compromises."

"How can you be sure?" I said. "As far as I know, you've never entered into one."

Pamela laughed. It wasn't a hearty guffaw, just a small indication that something risible had crossed her horizon.

She said, "You can be a bastard, Crang."

"Better than having a Mr. Nice Guy tend to your interests."

"We shall see."

Pamela absorbed more scotch, and checked the watch on her wrist. It was about the size of a thumbnail.

"I have to be going," she said. "Archie's playing tennis at the club. I'm meeting him there when he's finished."

She started to slide out of the booth. I managed a half rise. Pamela stopped her slide.

"Are you and your Annie doing anything special tonight?" she asked.

"Well, thanks, but I don't think it's such a hot idea us double-dating with you and Archie."

"Don't be gauche. I meant if you'd care to keep the table, I'll speak to Pip. My treat."

"Annie's occupied, real marathon session, seeing movies, writing reviews."

"You stay," Pamela said. "They do wonders with veal here."

"Veal? I accept."

"That's settled." Pamela stood up. "And bon voyage for Monday, Crang."

CHAPTER ELEVEN

If I turned my head to the left, the Mediterranean came into view. It gleamed azure in the afternoon sun. Straight ahead, across the harbour, the houses of Villefranche spilled from the top of the steep cliff to the water's edge. The cliff looked smooth and weathered. The houses were pink and yellow and ochre. On the distant right, I could make out the peaks and crests of the Alps. The tallest had wreaths of snow.

"I believe I've died and gone to the south of France," I said to Annie.

"Half right, big guy."

Annie and I were drinking glasses of *vin rosé*. Annie's French friend who had rented the apartment to us had left the bottle in the refrigerator. Welcome to the Côte d'Azur. The apartment occupied the top floor of a three-storey white stucco house on a hill over a narrow, twisting street called Avenue Denis Semeria. All streets in the south of France seemed to be narrow and twisting. Some were named after guys better known than Denis Semeria. In the taxi over from Nice Airport, I had noticed boulevards for a Roosevelt, a Kennedy, and a de Gaulle. Maybe Denis Semeria had been a resistance fighter or a soccer player. It was mid-afternoon on Tuesday. I was standing on the balcony of the Mediterranean villa, sipping the dry *vin rosé*, absorbing the Riviera view, and feeling one hell of a worldly fellow.

"When can we get the sightseeing underway?" Annie asked me.

"I'm way ahead of you, sweetie. Sightseeing is what I've been up to out here the last fifteen minutes."

"This long-range stuff is okay," Annie said, "but tame. Your veteran tourist gets down to it and slogs."

Annie listed the wonders within walking distance of the apartment. Villa Ephrussi de Rothschild. La Chapelle de Saint-Pierre. Villa Kerylos. She gave the names of the places their correct pronunciation. Annie speaks French like Isabelle Adjani. She speaks Italian like Claudia Cardinale. She has some Portuguese, but I don't know any movie stars from Portugal. Annie picked up the languages and her intimacy with Europe's countries in the three years she drifted around the continent in her mid-twenties. She says she travelled alone most of the time. I never asked about the rest of the time.

Annie said our apartment was in Pont Saint-Jean. Very convenient location, she said. It was at the conjunction of three towns. Saint-Jean-Cap-Ferrat was further south on Avenue Denis Semeria, on a peninsula sticking into the Mediterranean. Beaulieu was behind us and around the corner. It had the nearest train station, Annie said, and an open-air market that sold fish unknown to Canadian cuisine. The third town, Villefranche, lay shining at our feet.

We finished the wine. We unpacked. I shaved. Annie sat in the bathtub for three minutes. At five-thirty, we went down to Avenue Denis Semeria. We found a back road that took us past palm trees and large flashy residences and deep driveways with expensive cars parked in them. The road petered out at a descending cement staircase. The staircase ended at a walkway around the harbour to Villefranche.

"Watch your step," Annie said to me.

"You're talking about this obstacle course of dog shit?" I asked as I stepped over a mutt's recent deposit.

"Dogs are allowed pretty much freedom of place," Annie said.

"Nobody heard of poop and scoop?"

Annie shook her head. "Strictly a North American concept."

"Know what I think?" I said. "A guy could run for mayor on a platform of no more doggie doodoo. Just from the evidence I see around me, the guy would win in a landslide."

"Uh, uh," Annie said. "The French love their dogs more than their grandmothers. Your politician would go zero at the polls."

I zigged and zagged past a lumpy mass.

"Whoever sells door mats," I said, "must clean up, you'll excuse the play on words."

The harbour was in the shape of a new moon. Villefranche, as we circled closer to it, looked postcard pretty. Beige and cream buildings sitting tight to the water, open-air cafes, gaily-coloured tablecloths, people being leisurely over drinks in funny-shaped glasses. A sign read La Vieille Ville. An arrow on the sign pointed up a ramp of stairs. We followed the arrow. We were in a maze of cramped alleys and tiny vaulted passages. Annie said the old town's staunch greystone buildings dated from the Middle Ages. A kid in a space helmet ripped past us on a dirt bike. I told Annie I was having trouble with the collision of centuries. Dirt bikes in medieval alleys. Above us, jeans hung out to dry from the windows of apartments that had been built for guys who had carried longbows into battle.

Annie conducted us back to a gorgeously-proportioned little building on the waterfront. Another dislocation in time. The building was the Chapel of St. Peter, lovingly erected in the fourteenth century. Its decorating scheme was more recent, by Jean Cocteau in 1957. Inside the chapel, Cocteau's paintings flowed around the walls and ceiling in an airy swirl of gypsies and angels, musicians, a Virgin and Child, and fisher folk of both sexes.

"Not profound," Annie said, "but a beaut of a tourist attraction."

We settled at a cafe in the square. It was under a hotel that was five storeys high and painted orange. The hotel had a name that put Holiday and Ramada to shame. It was called the Hotel Welcome. Annie spent a long time in discussion with the waiter.

After a while, he brought six dozen fresh mussels drenched in some kind of divine-smelling juice. There was a green salad and white wine. The wine came in a jug that, back home, shoppes on Avenue Road would label an antique and price at seventy-five dollars. We started on the mussels.

"A schedule," I said to Annie.

"I've thought about that," she said. "Roquebrune should be our first stop. It's got the most sensationally picturesque citadel

"By schedule, I had reference to business."

"Oh, that."

"Duty," I said, "then pleasure."

"Well, the film festival doesn't open until next week, and my seminar at the university, which" — Annie turned sideways in her chair and waved an arm in the general direction of the hills — "is somewhere above us, is on for Thursday morning."

"What's a Canadian university doing in the land of bliss?"

"Prospering, I gather."

"Turning out students with suntans and majors in hedonism."

"Your jealousy's showing, buster," Annie said. "The place is perfectly legitimate, L'Université Canadienne en France. It's administered out of Toronto, Canadian subjects and teachers, lectures in English, all like that. The students that come over, they get the same credits for a degree they'd get at a school back home minus the snow and ice."

"Plus the benefit of beautiful and intelligent guest lecturers."

Annie smiled. "Somebody heard me on the radio, a woman who used to teach here. She recommended to the university I do the seminar. The honorarium's three hundred francs."

"Don't bother translating. I might be shocked."

"I'll buy you a dinner."

I speared a mussel. "My quest for young Haddon isn't as cut-and-dried as your tasks," I reminded her.

"How easy it is for his name to slip my mind."

"Fair's fair. My Jamie Haddon for your film festival."

"Yes," Annie said, "but in movie reviewing, a person doesn't run into dissembling, stealing, and skulduggery.... Well, not on the same scale as you seem to have turned up in the Haddon thingamabob."

"My accumulation to date may not merit the term skulduggery. What have I got? A May-December affair in which May can't keep his mouth shut. A computer disk that's slippery to get a grip on. And some suspicious spending habits." I stopped chewing. "Actually that's not a bad list."

"You left out the burglar."

"Large Curtis. Yeah, I may be trying to suppress the memory."

"If this Mike Rolland is calling in that sort of person and if the burglar was as big as you say, it could mean that your simple little investigation for the Whetherhill family might be more physical than you can handle."

"Curtis was as big as I say."

"I rest my case," Annie said. "Look, suppose Mike Rolland pops up over here, as I've no doubt he will, he could arrange to cuff you around again, and I didn't come all the way to the Riviera to sit with you in a doctor's office."

"I don't know," I said. "As far as Mike goes, guile and wit ought to carry the day. Mine, I'm talking about, my guile and wit."

"Oh, brother."

Annie concentrated on her food and wine for a minute.

"Deep down," she said, "what do you suppose Pamela thinks is the source of Jamie Haddon's eight hundred thousand dollars? Deep down in Pamela, I mean."

"I don't think she wants to know. I think she wants to put herself between me and Swotty."

"Understandable."

"Yeah. If I report to Swotty that Jamie is rolling in francs ... are francs the currency of Monaco?"

Annie nodded.

"... then whatever's going on, if anything, could come undone, not excluding Pamela's dalliance with Jamie. Pamela couldn't bear to have Swotty find out. It would rock him to the foundations."

Annie had a knack of using an empty mussel shell as an implement to scoop a fresh mussel from another shell and convey it to her mouth. I admired the technique, but didn't copy it. I might cause damage to myself. Maybe a lip impaled on a mussel shell.

"Let's visit Monaco tomorrow," I said. "First thing."

"Get it out of the way," Annie agreed. "Right. We'll go over by train. They're fantastic along the coast, just like the subway at home, except the stops are more exotic."

"Jamie may be the fly in the ointment. Finding him, that is, if he doesn't care to be found."

"What's Plan A?"

"No Plan A."

"Ah, then we go directly to Plan B."

"Yeah, the one where I poke and prod and nudge until someone comes from under."

The mussels were gone, and jet lag was beginning to set in. Annie and I walked back to the apartment along the quay just as the sun, showing plenty of vermilion dazzle, dropped behind Villefranche's hills.

CHAPTER TWELVE

From the Monaco train station, the streets sloped at a precipitous angle in the direction of the sea. Annie and I tottered down them for four or five blocks until we arrived at a broad, level section of boulevards and sidewalks. The buildings of Monaco were behind us, running back up the hill and into the lower levels of the Alps. There were rows of low-rise villas, the pink and pale brown stucco and stone buildings I'd seen all along the coast. But shoehorned into every free space, on every block, high-rise apartments and condos, graceless and disruptive, poked fifteen and twenty storeys into the air.

"My God," I said to Annie, "the developers around here could teach the Japanese a few things about stacking people on top of one another."

"These last twenty years," Annie said, "speculation in Monaco land has gone kind of bananas."

From where we were standing down by the harbour, approximately at the centre of everything, the city was enclosed by two high rocky promontories. On top of both, there were clusters of pastel buildings. From a distance, they looked like sets left over from a 1930s MGM musical.

Annie pointed to the promontory on the west. "Up there," she said, "that's the real Monaco, the original. The old town is there, and those walls you can see, light coloured, with all the crenella-tion, they're part of Prince Rainier's palace."

"I thought it might be the Nelson Eddy Retirement Villa."

Annie said, "Where you and I are standing is called La Condamine. More humble, you notice, commercial. And up there" — Annie was pointing to the eastern promontory — "that's your renowned Monte Carlo. The Casino, L'Hôtel de Paris, untold wealth."

We dodged the traffic to cross the street and get closer to the water. The harbour was small and orderly. The jutting promonto-ries formed a natural protection from the Mediterranean. There were wide docks with berths for boats to tie up. Annie and I walked around the harbour, gawking at the boats. For a long time, neither of us spoke.

"I may barf," I said.

"Kind of rich for the stomach."

As a word, "boats" was grossly inadequate to describe what Annie and I were looking at, though "gross" was probably on the mark. These boats, replete with several levels of decks and gang-ways and saloons and aft quarters and fore quarters and quarters amidships and passages in between, were castles that happened to sit on water instead of land. They were painted a white that glared in the sun, and they were equipped with every electronic gizmo except maybe rocket launchers.

We followed the walkway around the harbour and out to a man-made seawall. The boats moored at the inner wall, closest to land, were smaller than the others. Smaller in relative terms: they were larger than a house, my house anyway, but not as large as a mansion.

"Hey." Annie stopped dead. "I think your guy may be in the neighbourhood."

We were in front of one of the smaller boats. A man in nautical workman's gear was putting the finishing touches to a paint job. He'd painted the name "Freeload" on the transom. Underneath were the letters "YCM."

I said to Annie, "Does that look like sixty feet to you?"

"Yep. And the builder's trademark on the side is Hatteras."

"What's YCM in English?"

"Yacht Club of Monaco, you fish."

"It'd be a heck of a coincidence if there was someone besides Jamie Haddon in the good old YCM who would name their brand-new sixty-foot Hatteras by the same name as Jamie Haddon's disk."

The workman was wiping his hands clean of paint.

"Excuse me," I said to him, "any idea where I might find the owner of this man o' war?"

The workman frowned at me. He answered in French. Annie spoke up in the workman's own tongue, and the two of them fell into an animated dialogue. The only words I made out were "*monsieur*" and "Haddon."

"*Merci, m'sieur*," Annie sang out to the workman, "*et au'voir.*"

Annie and I walked away from the Hatteras.

"It's Jamie Haddon's all right," Annie said. She looked pleased as punch. "And the nice man back there says Jamie's staying at the Hôtel de Paris."

"Splendid piece of work, Cooke. Might be persuaded to keep you on as official interpreter."

We went at a leisurely pace back around the curve of the harbour all the way to an elevator built into the side of the rock on the Monte Carlo side. The elevator went in only one direction from the harbour. Up. We got on board. Annie pressed the top button.

I examined the elevator panel. "Somewhere I pay for this ride?"

"Relax," Annie said. "Elevators are the one thing you get free in Monaco. They're how people move around. Move up anyway."

The elevator didn't take us all the way to the heart of Monte Carlo. We climbed one more steep hill on foot, turned two corners, and went past a hotel called L'Hermitage, which looked to be the last word in ornate architecture. We arrived at a small green square. On the south side, a building announced itself in gilt lettering across the front as the Casino. The Hôtel de Paris took up the square's west side. I had been mistaken about L'Hôtel Hermitage. It wasn't the last word in ornate architecture. It was the antepenultimate word, after the Casino and the Hôtel de Paris.

I said to Annie, "I think I saw these buildings on the top of a cake once."

We went into the Hôtel de Paris. Its lobby was massive and marble, and populated mainly by poker-faced men in dark suits and shades. I read the menu outside the main dining room. Its prices were in francs with many zeros at the end. Annie went to the front desk, and spoke at friendly length to a clerk who was decked out in braid and brass buttons. The clerk placed a telephone call for Annie. He bestowed many smiles and bows on her.

"What did the obsequious clerk advise?" I asked when Annie was finished.

"The concierge, Crang. Mr. Haddon is staying at the hotel, *oui*, in a suite, if you please. But he isn't answering his phone at the moment. Perhaps, the concierge thinks, we should try *la piscine*."

"*La piscine*. Ah … the sauna?"

"Good try. The swimming pool."

La piscine, down two flights from the lobby and on the hotel's south side, wasn't the kind of setup that folks who swim at the Y would call a swimming pool. It looked like a large sculpture, scooped into the floor and painted a brilliant aqua. Around the sides there were dozens of tables set for lunch with cutlery and crystal that had been cleaned and polished to a high gleam. The tablecloths and napkins were white and aqua, the same colour as the swimming pool.

The south wall was glass and opened on to an enormous deck with white lounge furniture and a spectacular view over the sea. The deck also had most of the action. Inside, two couples sat over green drinks and one elderly gent was using the sidestroke to plough gamely up and down the pool. But outside, dozens of people sat and lay in groups, talking, gesticulating, drinking, soaking up the rays.

"See anyone who answers the description?" Annie asked.

I saw Mike Rolland before I saw Jamie Haddon. And I saw the young woman who was with Mike and Jamie before I saw them or much else in the vicinity. She was tall, if I could judge the height of someone who was more or less horizontal on a deck chair, and she had legs that went on for days. Her mouth was in the pouty thrust style that Brigitte Bardot introduced to the world thirty years ago. Her hairstyle was from the school of reckless abandon, trails of light brown curls running over shoulders and deck chair. She was wearing a yellow string bikini. Cellulite didn't seem to be a problem.

"Guess who?" I said to Annie.

"Miss All-World Sexpot of 1990."

"I mean the guys flanking her."

"That's the quarry?"

"Jamie Haddon is the blond smiler in the green tank top," I said. "And the guy dressed like Ricardo Montalban in the coffee commercial, the guy doing all the talking, that's Mike Rolland, musical connoisseur and my newest best friend."

"You left out the dark kid just to the right of Haddon. See, the sunglasses in the hair?"

"I don't know Dante Renzi by sight, but the dark kid's particulars are about right."

"Oh yes, the unwelcome lodger."

I put my hand under Annie's elbow.

"Let's get to it, babe," I said. "Do the up-close assessment."

CHAPTER THIRTEEN

Mike Rolland came belting across the deck. I couldn't tell whether it was to greet Annie and me or to head us off. Was he worried about my arrival on the scene? Did I read anxiety in his expression or merely surprise? Was it an earthquake or simply a shock?

"My very good friend Crang," Mike bellowed. Whatever was cooking in his head, he projected the hail-fellow front. "And this must be your very charming companion."

I introduced Annie. Mike reached for her hand, turned it over, and kissed the back. Annie didn't seem to know what to do with the hand after Mike had finished with it.

"This is marvelous, Annie and Crang." Mike's voice was at peak amplification. His shirt, slacks, and shoes were white but with some kind of silvery sheen. "On your holiday, I am right, yes? What a great place to come, for sure. Have you seen the sights? The Casino?"

Annie started to say something about the extravagant nature of Monte Carlo's architecture. Mike galloped over her.

"You must meet other good friends of mine and drink champagne with us," he said. "From Toronto, like you, but you will not know them, I think for sure."

"Well, Annie doesn't, Mike, but you know that I know ..."

Mike trampled on top of my sentence.

"They will like to meet you, my friends Crang and Annie."

If there had been a table between Mike and me, he would have reached his foot under it and kicked my shin. He was giving me every other signal in the book that Jamie Haddon and Dante Renzi, if that was who the dark kid was, were supposed to come as a surprise to me. Or that Mike and I hadn't met at Jamie's. If Mike was playing a game, I didn't see any harm in going along with it. Just let matters unfold, I told myself. Let Mike keep up his deception, if that was what was afoot. Maybe I'd find out about the disk and its whereabouts. At least I'd get a free glass of champagne.

"You will love these friends of mine, for sure," Mike boomed.

He trotted ahead of us, back to the grouping of chairs around Mademoiselle Bombshell.

I spoke to Annie from the side of my mouth. "It's okay if you put the hand down now."

"What's the etiquette?" she whispered. "Do I wipe it on my skirt or just leave it damp like this?"

Mike was standing beside Jamie Haddon and the others looking as if he were Alex Trebek shepherding the players on *Jeopardy!* Big smile, hands outstretched to encompass the bunch of us, making a show of the introductions.

"My very good friends Crang and Miss Annie Cooke," Mike announced. "From Toronto also. Wonderful, I think, all of us, what is the expression, bumping into one another in this marvelous hotel. The sun, you know, the sea, everything so beautiful, good friends together."

The long-stemmed glamourpuss's name was Babette. Her response to Annie and me was no response I could detect. She lay back in the deck chair and practised her languid air. The dark young guy was, as anticipated, Dante Renzi, though if I followed Mike's introduction, Dante preferred Dan. Under either name, he was polite about standing up and saying hi to Annie and me. So was Jamie Haddon.

Jamie had high cheekbones and small hollows under them. His eyes were pale grey. He wore his blond hair gelled in short waves, and his face and shoulders were lightly tanned. He had the grin I'd seen in the photograph Pamela gave me, nonchalant, and he remembered who I was. I could read it in his face. I could hear the wheels turning.

"Two more chairs I need here," Mike said. He had a hand in the air, snapping his fingers. "Which you like?" he asked Annie. "Which kind of chair?"

Annie said, "The one Babette's in looks like it does wonders for a girl."

Someone snickered. It was Dante. Or Dan. Babette continued to concentrate on her sang-froid.

"For sure," Mike said to Annie.

Two guys pulled up in answer to Mike's fingersnaps. They had on sports jackets and ties. One was lanky and had a black beard streaked with grey. The other was built lower to the ground, with the general contours of a large stove. Mike spoke to them in French. They hopped to their assigned tasks.

The bearded one dragged up two chairs, one like Babette's for Annie, a white wooden armchair for me. The Stove brought a waiter from the restaurant section. He had the waiter by the arm. Mike ordered three bottles of Piper-Heidsieck. The two guys in the sports jackets retreated to the edge of the deck and didn't take their eyes off Mike.

"You may not remember me, Crang," Jamie Haddon said. He was displaying a low-key grin. It still managed to put dimples in his cheeks. "It was a long time ago. I'm Pamela's cousin. Pamela Cartwright? Used to be Pamela Whetherhill?"

"And my wife in between," I said. "Nice to see you, Jamie."

"Wonderful." Mike sounded elated. "You two guys, I bring you together, my good friends, and you each know the other one already."

"Fortuitous," I said.

"For sure," Mike said.

"You're still a criminal lawyer?" Jamie asked me.

"Can't break the habit," I said. "And you? See much of Pamela?"

"Constantly," Jamie said. I had to give him credit. He didn't smirk.

"I work for her father, you know," he went on. "At Cayuga & Granark. The old boy invites me to family dinners and so on. And I see Pamela on her own."

"With Archie?" I said.

"Oh, Archie, sure."

"Pamela is a load of laughs," I said.

Dan Renzi piped up. "She's got a tongue on her if that's what you mean," he said. Dan looked to be in his mid-twenties. Dark and attractive, as Pamela had said, but not soft, as she'd also said. Closer to delicate. He was wearing a chocolate-brown jumpsuit.

"On the subject of Pamela's tongue, Dan," I said. "I can show you a few scars."

Dan smiled. It made him look even younger and more delicate.

The waiter returned with two sidekicks, transporting three silver buckets holding bottles of champagne and a silver tray with six champagne flutes. Mike supervised the popping of the corks and the filling of the flutes. Jamie took care of the signing of the waiter's chit.

"To all my very good friends," Mike said. He lifted his glass to the toast.

Babette's glass overflowed, and a splash landed on her stomach just below the navel. Her skin was a tawny colour. The champagne trickled down her stomach, leaving a clean, wet path until it disappeared into the bottom of Babette's yellow string bikini. Babette giggled. It was the first sound that had emerged from between her sullen lips since Annie and I arrived.

"I was wondering," Jamie said to me, "how did you meet, you and Mike?"

"Over a disk," I said.

Mike choked on his champagne.

"What sort of disk?" Dan Renzi asked. He had a light, almost adolescent voice. It may have been registering concern.

Jamie didn't say anything. His head made a swivel from me to Dan to Mike and back to me.

"CD," I said. "Compact disk. You fellas know how Mike is about musicals. Keen as mustard. Well, I was able to put my hands on a boot-leg CD of Evita. Absolute top-drawer quality. This is Meryl Streep's secret audition tape, the one she cut when it looked like she was going to do Evita for Oliver Stone. Very big deal. I made Mike here a copy."

"In Toronto?" Jamie asked.

"You'll like this part, Jamie," I said. "You know Sam the Record Man's main store on Yonge Street at home? Mike and I, two complete strangers, we reached for the same album at the same moment, and that just got us talking. Liza Minnelli Sings Neil Diamond."

Annie made a noise at my side that sounded like grrr.

"In Toronto?" Jamie was talking to Mike. "You said your business was in New York."

"Oh, those guys on Wall Street," Mike said, "they tell me, okay, Mike, we do the deal for sure, but one part of it, you go see broker in Toronto. So I go, and lucky for me, I meet my very good new friend Crang the way he say."

"How'd you like the shirts, by the way, Jamie?" I said.

Mike had some more trouble with his throat and his champagne.

"What shirts?" Jamie asked.

"Something between Crang and me," Mike said. He seemed to be regaining his grip on the story. "I told him I want to take a present back to a very good friend in Monaco ..."

"And I said shirts were always nice," I finished for Mike.

"Jamie's bought drawers of shirts since he got here," Dan said. His voice had an aggrieved tone.

"Nobody's stopping you from buying whatever you want," Jamie said to Dan. Jamie sounded no more than mildly perturbed.

"A man can't have enough shirts," I said.

Mike jumped up and poured more Piper-Heidsieck. I watched to see if Babette would do her party trick again. But the glass didn't co-operate.

I said to Jamie, "Annie and I were admiring your boat."

"How did you know it was mine?" Jamie asked. "I just bought it."

"From my company he buy it," Mike said.

"Too big," Dan said. "The boat's way too big."

"It was the name," I said to Jamie. "Freeload."

"By that, you knew I owned it?"

"The workman down there told us your name," I said. "But it was the boat's name that caught our eye in the first place. Very original. Witty. A hidden meaning perhaps? Free? Load?"

"It's symbolic," Jamie said.

"Of what?" It was Annie who asked the question.

"Annie's a movie reviewer," I said. "Occupational hazard with her, symbols."

"Of a certain style of life," Jamie said.

"Not exactly a style worth emblazoning on a boat, is it?" Annie said. She wasn't inclined to let go.

"Everybody does it in different ways," Jamie said, "and nobody complains."

Before Annie could pursue Jamie's enigmatic remark, Mike charged in.

"For sure," he said. "Jamie is looking at a penthouse around the corner from here. Same building as me, that I live in, also a penthouse."

"Useless place to buy," Dan Renzi said. He seemed to be filling the role of wet blanket.

"As long as I can afford it," Jamie said, "what's the problem?"

I said, "All the signs I read, Jamie, the boat, penthouse, shirts, Babette here, I'd say you got the world by the tail."

"Babette belongs to Mike," Dan piped up.

"Belongs?" Annie said sharply.

"Well, I don't know how else you'd describe it," Dan said. "Talk about beck and call."

Babette held silent and steady with her pout. I gathered her English was a match for my French.

"You might say, Crang," Jamie said, apparently getting back to my remark about him and money, "that a few plans have worked out for me."

"Ships come in, so to speak?"

"Exactly."

Talk lurched on to tourist topics after Jamie's one-word summation. The change in subject came as an obvious relief to Mike. He waxed on about the treasures available in Monaco. Many of them, according to Mike's lights, were the kind of bauble one might pick up at a shop I'd noticed across from the hotel. Van Cleef & Arpels. Babette snapped to attention at the name. Maybe they were her only three English words.

Jamie didn't contribute much. He sat in his chair, affable and smiley, but also close-mouthed and attentive. He might have been pondering my presence in Monaco. Or maybe the transparently phony exchange between Mike and me over the disk had tripped some kind of radar. Or maybe, behind the easygoing facade, he was a guy who instinctively played his cards close to the vest.

In the general scramble of talk, Annie got to discuss Monte Carlo's architecture. That spurred Jamie to open up briefly.

"They give the gambling a nice sense of formality at the Casino," he said. "We wore tuxedos when we went last night."

"Just to play the slots?" I said.

"No, no, my friend Crang," Mike said. He looked disgusted at the thought of vulgar slot machines. "Baccarat. Very superb, my friend. This is in la salle privee. You must pay just to get in."

"Jamie lost fifty thousand francs," Dan said. He sounded like a tattletale.

"Wait till I develop my own system," Jamie answered. "I'll win it back. No sweat."

"Systems are what you're good at?" I asked.

"A hobby of mine." Jamie grinned. "You could say that. Or maybe" — the grin stretched — "you could say an obsession."

"For bringing in ships?"

Jamie didn't bother answering, and I couldn't see much reason for Annie and me to stick around any longer. The champagne bottles were upside down in the buckets. Babette's appeal had worn thin. And the conversation wasn't as bracing as it'd been when Mike and I were exchanging falsehoods.

"Time for Annie and me to push on," I said. "A sightseer's feet never rest."

"For sure you will be busy," Mike said. He didn't seem inclined to prolong our visit. "If you are in Monaco again, I buy you vodka on the rocks. But, you know, you will not have the time probably. Next visit, for sure."

"Until then, Mike," I said. "And don't forget to play the disk for the fellas."

"The disk?"

"Meryl Streep not crying for Argentina. Or is it the other way around?"

"Oh, Evita, for sure." Mike smiled broadly.

Annie and I went out through *la piscine*. The elderly gent was still in the pool. He'd switched to the breast stroke.

CHAPTER FOURTEEN

We retraced the route that had got us up to Monte Carlo. Past L'Hôtel Hermitage, down the almost vertical street.

"Honestly," Annie said, "Liza Minnelli Sings Neil Diamond, two people you can't abide."

"Well, let's see, how about Tony Bennett Sings Johnny Mercer? No, that wouldn't have sparked the same recognition from the gang on the deck."

"I didn't get the reason for all the blarney in the first place."

"It was a way of seeing which way the wind was blowing," I said. "Finding out who was tuned in to what information. The other reason was that I got a kick out of the bullshitting once Mike Rolland set the pace."

"That man. Five minutes in his company, I was expecting him to sell me a piece of the rock."

"Sincerity isn't Mike's strong suit. Or honesty. Some chaps wouldn't fault his taste in female pulchritude, though."

"Oh sure," Annie said, "as long as you don't mind if the beautiful bundle has the sensibility of a mud wrestler."

The elevator carried us to harbour level. We started toward La Condamine.

"I deduce from Mike's dipsy-doodling he's got the disk and

doesn't want Jamie to know it's in his possession."

"That's obvious," Annie said. "Haddon was surprised to hear Rolland had even been to Toronto."

"So Mike wasn't on a mission for Jamie."

"Then how did Rolland know about the disk?"

"And who stuck it behind that piece of garter belt mania?"

Behind us, running feet pounded on the pavement. I glanced back. The runner was Dan Renzi. The beginnings of sweat stains showed in the armpits of his chocolate-brown jumpsuit.

"Mr. Crang, sorry." Dan was puffing hard. "I need to talk to you."

"Go right ahead, Dan," I said, "as soon as your lungs deal out more oxygen."

Dan stood with his hands on his hips, taking deep breaths. He looked at Annie.

"Don't worry about me," Annie said to him. "Whatever you tell Crang, I'll worm out of him anyway."

I put my arm around Annie's shoulders and winked at Dan.

"All right," he said. He had his air intake under control. "You're a lawyer, Mr. Crang, and I think I have a problem."

"Good opening, Dan," Annie said. "Crang's clients always begin that way."

"If you want to discuss something," I said to him, "let's make it over lunch. Except not at the prices you may be growing accustomed to."

"There's a nice place I go to on my own," Dan said. He favoured us with a guileless smile. "Sometimes when we eat at the hotel," he added, "I'm not sure what it is on the plate."

Dan's restaurant was two more blocks along the harbour and another two into the heart of La Condamine. It was called Le Texan. A large primitive painting of the Alamo graced the wall inside the door. The menu on display by the bar advertised burritos and chili dogs.

"We come to the Riviera," Annie said, "and for our first lunch, we might as well be in Laredo."

A waiter who spoke American showed us to a table under a rack of ten-gallon hats. I asked if Tom Mix had ridden by lately.

"No," the waiter said, "but Hopalong Cassidy's in the back room drinking sarsaparilla."

"Everybody does schtick these days," Annie said.

Dan fiddled with the empty wineglass at his place.

I said to him, "Is your problem the kind that could run you afoul of any country's laws?"

"Well, I don't like to think so," he said.

I waited.

"It's about a disk," Dan said. He checked my reaction. I had my noncommittal expression in place. "When you and Mike Rolland were talking about a disk earlier," Dan said, "neither of you meant a CD. Am I right?"

"As rain, Dan. You caught me in a fib. The disk wasn't Evita."

"It was a computer disk?"

"One that has 'Operation Freeload' printed on the outside."

"How in the world do you know about it?"

"Uh, uh, Dan." I waggled a finger at him. "That's my story. At the moment, we're focusing on yours."

Dan took a breath. "I sneaked it away from Jamie," he said. "Then I hid it."

"Scotch-taped it to a painting in the Rowanwood apartment?"

"In Jamie's bedroom, yes."

"This will come as a blow to Pamela Cartwright," I said to Dan. "She's got you pegged as underequipped in the cerebral department."

"I never could stand the woman." Dan's delicate features did their darnedest to look irate. "It was hopeless between us from the start. I just clammed up whenever she was around."

I asked, "What is it about the disk that makes it such a valuable commodity to everybody?"

"I'm not sure."

"Let me try again," I said. "Why did you, in your own description, sneak it away from Jamie?"

"As protection."

"For whom?"

"Me. And really for Jamie's own sake."

"Dan, this is getting to be in the category of pulling teeth."

"Well, the worst is that Mike Rolland has the disk now."

"Nice going, big guy," Annie said to me. "That's one solid fact you already had nailed down."

We ordered. I asked for chicken tacos. Dan wanted a cheeseburger. Annie said she'd try a salad called the Rio Grande. She looked skeptical. We got a big carafe of the house white.

"Autobiography might be in order about here, Dan," I said. "How long have you known Jamie?"

"Oh, it seems like years. We recognized we were kindred spirits the day we met."

"There's a phrase I haven't heard in a while."

"It's true," Dan said. His tone was hurt and earnest. "We want the same things from life. Travel and freedom and, you know, no more suits and ties."

"That's what you wear in your job?"

"I did when I had one. I was an assistant manager at a Bank of Nova Scotia branch. That's how Jamie and I met. About eight or nine months ago, one of the bank's clients needed more financing than we could advance. I phoned Cayuga & Granark on the client's behalf. Jamie was the trust officer assigned to the file. He and I started talking, and really we've never stopped."

"Talking about what?" I swallowed some wine. Dan hadn't touched his. Annie was being forgetful about hers. Fine, left more for the serious drinker in the group.

"We talked about getting away from the rat race," Dan said. "About taking off to countries we had always dreamed of visiting. Stopping at funny little places that appealed to us on the spur of the moment. Working at jobs along the way when we needed money. But keeping on the move, living simply."

"L'Hôtel de Paris isn't exactly a youth hostel, Dan."

Dan's lower lip trembled. "That just shows you how Jamie has changed."

The waiter brought lunch. Annie's salad was inside a thin pastry shell. It had marinated chicken slices, wedges of cucumber and tomato, sprinkled cheese, salsa. She ate some and looked much less skeptical.

"Exquisite," she said.

My tacos fell short of exquisite, but they were damned tasty. Dan took a nibble from his cheeseburger and began to talk again. He exuded youthful candour. I wasn't sure whether it was genuine or adopted for my benefit.

"Right out of the blue, Jamie started making everything more grand," Dan said. "All of a sudden, it was to be the best hotels. We were going to find a ski chalet in Austria. Buy our own cottage on a Greek island. Jamie's attitude got away entirely from our original plan of keeping things simple and going on that way forever."

"From what I've heard," I said, "Jamie's definition of forever stops at three months."

"Oh, you know about the leave of absence?"

I nodded.

"Well, it isn't true at all." Dan sounded miffed. "I thought it was true. Partly true, that is. See, Jamie originally told me we'd go back to Toronto after three months and he'd formally resign from C&G and everything, and then we'd get on with, you know, travelling the world. But I came over here a week after Jamie, and he said, 'Oh, forget the three months thing. I'm never going back,' he said, and 'The trust company can just stuff it.'"

"And Pamela could do roughly the same? Stuff it?"

"She is going to be stunned." A half smile came and went from Dan's face. "I shouldn't sound callous, I guess," he said.

I lifted the carafe and topped up Annie's glass and Dan's. My own required filling from the bottom.

"What about the financing, Dan?" I asked. "How were you two drifters intending to pay for Austrian chalets and Greek cottages?"

"That wasn't a problem. Jamie told me it wasn't."

"You accepted his word?"

"Why shouldn't I?" Dan's voice became firm and virtuous. "I still wanted to stick to the simple approach we had in the first place. In fact, I know we'll go back to it when Jamie gets over his craziness. But the money, well, Jamie said we could afford expensive places. I believed him."

"When did Jamie's switch happen?" I asked. "When did he start talking rich as Rockefeller?"

"A month or so ago."

"Around the time the disk made its appearance?"

"That's right." Dan sounded cautious.

"And you made a connection between the disk and Jamie's glimpsing of golden horizons?"

"I guess I did."

"Which explains why you took possession of it?"

"Of the disk, yes." Dan pushed his cheeseburger about three inches to the right on his plate. He had eaten no more than a couple of mouthfuls. "Getting it wasn't difficult," Dan continued. "Jamie kept the disk in his safety-deposit box. I borrowed the key and went to the box at Jamie's bank. I signed his name, and nobody there noticed I wasn't the box's owner. Banks are like that."

"What did you have in mind? Holding the disk for ransom?"

"You might say so."

"I just did."

"I told you earlier it was for Jamie's own good, Mr. Crang. I knew the disk was important to Jamie. My idea was to tell him I was going to keep it until he came to his senses about the way we were supposed to be organizing our lives."

"I've often found confrontation an effective tactic myself, Dan," I said.

Annie made a rude noise into her salad.

"How did Jamie react?" I asked Dan.

"He didn't," Dan said. "Well, what I mean is I haven't told him about the disk yet. I only got it from the safety-deposit box on the day Jamie left for Monaco. I was saving it as a last resort."

"In the meantime," I said, "you taped the disk behind the woman in the garter belt."

"I thought it would be safe there until Jamie and I went back three months later. If things were settled between us, I'd just return the disk to the safety-deposit box and never say a word. If not, well, I could use it in whatever way I had to."

"Except," I said, "at the time you laid your little plan, you didn't know Jamie had canned the idea of going back in three months to resign and dump Pamela and one thing and another."

Dan blinked at me. His eyes were dark and moist. "That's right. I didn't know about Jamie changing his mind."

"Or maybe," I said, "he never intended to go back. Maybe the leave of absence was part of a bluff, something to keep the Whetherhills at bay while he got out of town, something he didn't bother letting you in on, Dan."

"I hate to think Jamie would have secrets from me, Mr. Crang."

"Either way, the situation over here meant you had to find a way of retrieving the disk from its hiding place back home behind the woman in the garter belt."

"I was desperate," Dan said, sounding desperate.

Annie spoke up. "Know who you two guys remind me of?"

I answered, "Of a crafty lawyer quizzing a potential client?"

"Uh, uh." Annie shook her head. "Of Abbott and Costello."

"Who's on first?"

"You got it, Buster."

"Sweetie, it must be my trained analytical mind, but the sequence of events is clear as crystal."

"Yeah," Annie said, "and what's on second?"

"Come on," I said. "Dan here snaffled the disk from Jamie's safety-deposit box to use as a weapon to get Jamie back on track. He figured to use the disk, if necessary, when the two of them returned to Toronto."

"Three months hence," Annie said.

"Right, except that when there turned out to be no three months, and Jamie really was spending beyond what Dan considered their means, the Hatteras and so forth, Dan had to get the disk over here pronto."

"As leverage," Annie said. "Okay, awfully labyrinthine, but I'm with you."

"And what I see coming up next," I said, speaking to Dan, "was a serious error in judgment. To retrieve the disk from Toronto, you threw yourself on Mike Rolland's mercy."

"Of which," Annie said, "he might not have as much as Mother Teresa."

"Well, don't you see, I had to have the disk actually in my hands before I spoke to Jamie," Dan said defensively. "Otherwise Jamie might not believe I really had taken it from his safety-deposit box."

"Granted, Dan," I said. "So you rung in Mike?"

Dan let out a long quavery sigh. "How can I put this?"

"As straightforwardly as possible," I said.

"Straightforward?" Annie said. "Now there's a novel concept."

Dan went on. "I didn't really know Mike, the kind of person he is, when I brought up the disk to him. I mean, honestly, Mr. Crang, I'd just got here, and I was sick over the whole situation, desperate like I said. So, this one night in the bar at the Casino, I was alone with Mike, and he was being, um, ingratiating. He mentioned his business trip to New York, and I had the thought I might, you know, ask him to stop in Toronto and bring me the disk."

"Must've been more than a thought."

"Well, I started telling him about the disk, and right away, he was all over me with questions. So aggressive and everything. Just too interested. So I backed off."

"But it was too late."

"Oh, God, I know I gave him the idea how important the disk is, but I had enough wits to stop before I gave away where it was hidden. In the apartment, okay, Mike got that part, but not behind the painting."

"The upshot was Mike declared himself in the game."

"Isn't he sickening? He gives everybody that best-friends line, but underneath he's just another hustler."

"Solid thinking, Dan. He hustled you out of the disk."

"It's unbelievable." Dan's eyes were as damp as Bambi's.

"How'd Mike get the Rowanwood address?" I asked.

"From the hotel register, I suppose."

"And the keys?"

"He stole mine from the suite. At least, somebody did." Dan made a snuffling noise. "But I never dreamed in a million years he'd find the disk's hiding place."

I restrained myself. If I revealed that I was the smarty-pants who had ferreted out the disk, it would only confuse the lad.

"What about it, Mr. Crang," Dan said, "can you help me?"

"What do you want me to do?"

"You're a lawyer. You must know a way to get back stolen property."

"It might be too late, Dan. Mike's been babysitting the disk long enough for him to have found out what's on it."

"Oh, no. He only got back to Monaco yesterday. He was seeing some stupid musical."

"You've already discussed the disk with Mike?"

Dan sighed. "You couldn't call it a discussion. He practically ordered me over to his place last night. Threw the disk on the desk. Said if I couldn't tell him what it was all about, he'd get it transcribed. I thought I was going to throw up."

"Mike has what intentions for the disk after he's made the acquaintance of its contents?"

"Using it to get some sort of advantage over Jamie. Financial advantage." Dan looked close to tears. "That's why I'm so worried. Jamie will know I've let him down terribly."

The waiter came by to collect our dishes. Annie and I had left a few scraps. Most of Dan's cheeseburger sat cold and lumpy on its plate. We ordered coffee.

"Where did your interview with Mike take place?" I asked Dan. "At the Monaco penthouse?"

"No. He has a house out on Cap Ferrat. It's called Villa Pomme. Pretty hard to miss the place."

"That's curious," Annie said. "All the orange trees and olive trees in this part of the world, I haven't noticed a single apple tree."

"The name of the house doesn't come from the kind of tree," Dan said. "It's the way they're shaped, cedar trees trimmed so they look like huge green apples."

"Topiary," Annie said.

"No," Dan insisted. "Apples."

"Topiary is what sculpting trees and bushes is called," Annie said patiently. "Revolting custom if you ask me, like the poor little poodles you see on the streets, sheared down to the bone practically."

"Well, anyway," Dan said.

"Who lives in the apple villa besides Mike?" I asked him.

"Babette, and there's a cook I saw when I went out there last night. And those two assistants were around the place. Very much around, if you follow me."

"The guys who jumped to attention when Mike snapped his fingers at the hotel?" I said.

"They're brothers." Dan provided the names. Georges and Emile. The surname sounded like "Klootch." I asked Dan to spell it. It came out C-l-u-t-c-h. "Ah," I said. "*Les frères Clutch.*"

I pronounced it the same way as the word that describes the time in a basketball game when Michael Jordan goes to town.

"You say it like this, Klootch," Dan corrected. "They drive the cars, and get things for Rolland, and give everybody sour looks."

"Muscle," I said.

"Georges is the tall one with the beard," Dan said, "and Emile's the other one."

"Shaped like a stove," I said, "and it isn't topiary."

Dan took one quick hit from his cup of coffee. "I'd better get back to the hotel," he said. "I wish you'd help me get the disk back, Mr. Crang. You're my last hope."

"Where's Mike keeping it?"

"The last I saw of it was in the centre drawer of the desk in his den at the villa."

"Not in a safe or some place more secure?"

"Why bother when the Clutches are right there?"

"You got a point, Dan."

He stood up and showed Annie and me another of his frank and open smiles. "Please, Mr. Crang," he said.

I waited until he was out of the restaurant. "You feel anything coming off Dan in the sexual department?" I asked Annie.

"No gonads, as far as I could tell."

"How about whiffs of Ian and Alex?"

"Do I think Dan's gay?"

"That's my question."

"Well, Dan's not quite as macho as Rock Hudson."

"Is that your roundabout way of saying Dan could be homosexual?"

"It is," Annie said, "and doesn't that just open a can of worms?"

I leaned back in my chair and looked at the painting of the Alamo. The artist's style was primitive bordering on incompetent.

"What's crossing your mind?" Annie asked.

"We should make a pact," I said. "Let's agree to spare Pamela our thoughts on Dan's sexual orientation."

"Really, Crang, she's probably figured that out for herself."

"Well, yeah, she's not Dan's biggest fan. She was more than direct about her dislike when I talked to her, but she didn't let on it might be because Dan was, um, a possible rival for Jamie's affections."

"Hey, a girl isn't going to blab it around she's having an affair with a guy who may be having an affair with another guy."

"I guess not."

"Of course not." Annie patted my hand. "But if you'd like us not to raise the subject, though heaven knows I'll probably never even meet the woman, I'll go along with you."

"Just that it might be unnecessary embarrassment."

"Such a sensitive guy." Annie patted my hand again. "Anyway," she said, "Dan's gayness is only the second most interesting item that came out of his conversation."

"You're referring to the perhaps self-serving nature of the story he told us?"

"Oh, lordy, the big wet eyes, the quivering lower lip, all that effort he put into portraying himself as Mr. Innocent."

"The impression I got," I said, "Dan might be editing out facts to protect his own hide."

"Facts about the disk?"

"Yeah. If the disk has criminal content, which is shaping up as more and more of a possibility by the minute, Dan could be trying to establish distance between him and it in case the crime comes to light."

"Hmmm," Annie said. She read her watch. It was a man's pocket watch that she wore on a chain around her neck.

"Not boring you with the disk conjecture, am I?" I asked.

"No," Annie said, "but according to our agreement, I'm just about due to get my innings in."

"For sightseeing?"

Annie nodded. "But we've got time for a second cup of coffee, fella."

"Before what?"

"Before the next train to Nice. I'm about to earn my spurs as your personal guide to the Riviera."

CHAPTER FIFTEEN

To say that Annie liked to sightsee would be like saying that Marco Polo took a couple of trips. With her, it was an educational route march. We looked at the paintings in the Matisse Museum. We inspected examples of architecture that Annie said were baroque and Italianate and *belle époque*. We cruised the tiny streets of Nice's Old Town and walked a promenade that snaked the length of the waterfront, part patrician, part tourist trap. My legs held up, but by six-thirty, the head was surrendering to a floating sensation. Maybe it was the cars. In Toronto, we'd call what was going on in the streets a demolition derby. In Nice, they said it was light traffic.

"Anybody keep a body count around here?" I asked Annie.

She flagged a taxi. The guy behind the wheel drove like Starsky or Hutch. But he got us all the way back to the apartment on Avenue Denis Semeria.

Inside, I settled beside the phone in the living room. Annie retired to the kitchen with a string bag full of goodies she'd bought in Nice's food shops. My first long-distance call was to Pamela. Hilda answered, the Cartwright housekeeper in the black dress and the veil of silence.

"Madam is not at home," she said.

"Would you inform Madam that Jamie Haddon is at the Hôtel de Paris," I said.

"Yes."

"In Monaco."

"Yes."

"And tell her Mr. Renzi is likewise in residence."

"Yes."

Hilda's monosyllables ruled out any thought I might have had for a freewheeling exchange of views on matters of household protocol. If Pamela was "madam", was Archie "mister"?

"Well, okay," I said, "thanks a ton."

A click came blipping down the line.

At Cayuga & Granark, I was passed through three levels of personnel. Each asked my name. And spell it, please. The third level was Swotty's private secretary. She buzzed me straight through to le grand frontage.

"Extraordinarily prompt, Crang." Swotty was almost buoyant. "I take it you've spoken to Jamie."

"He's in the pink."

"How do you mean, Crang?"

"Mostly physically. Jamie's got some sun on his face. Done wonders for his colouring."

"Yes." Impatience was collecting at the fringes of Swotty's voice. "Naturally I'm pleased to know that Jamie looks healthy. But if you will recall our conversation at the Concord, it is his state of mind that concerns me."

"That's dandy too. Anybody's state mind would be dandy at the place where Jamie's put himself up."

"Oh? Where is he staying?"

I gave it a nasal Anglo pronunciation. "The hotel duh Paris."

For a moment, nothing reached me except the telephone line's random pops and gurgles.

"Perhaps I didn't hear you correctly, Crang," Swotty said. He was speaking slowly and cautiously.

"I could do it in French. L'Hôtel de Paris. It still comes out a pricey spot to hang your hat."

"Has Jamie to your knowledge been at the hotel since his arrival? The entire two weeks?"

"Yes."

"He appears to be paying for the accommodation himself?"

"Yes," I said again.

"Do you see other indications of Jamie's mode of living?"

"Champagne before lunch. And a brand new Hatteras."

"That is a boat, I believe?"

"Like Rolls-Royce is a car."

There was another lull from Swotty's end. I made a bid to fill it. "Listen, Mr. Whetherhill, if you've got ideas about the source of Jamie's ..."

"Crang." Swotty's voice snapped down the line. "I may need you to see Jamie again. Is that possible?"

"Sure, but ..."

"And if I decide to contact Jamie myself, would it be at L'Hôtel de Paris?"

"Saw him there this morning."

"Hold on, Crang." Swotty was gone for fifteen seconds. I heard the sound of a hand wrapping around the receiver. The hand pulled away. Swotty spoke again. "All right, Crang, my secretary is on the other extension. If you would just give her your number over there, I will be back to you in due course."

"Hey ..."

"I'm ready, Mr. Crang," said a neutral, polite female voice.

I read her the digits from the phone I was holding in my hand. The neutral, polite voice thanked me and hung up.

Annie walked past my chair. She was carrying a clear glass salad bowl and two dinner plates from the kitchen in the back of the apartment to the sunroom in the front where we had set up a perch for eating. The sunroom had the view over the water toward Villefranche.

"I only heard your end of the conversation," Annie said, "but I have the impression the flow of information was one way, you to him."

"I wasn't at my most adroit," I admitted.

Annie made another shuttle from kitchen to sunroom with wineglasses and a bottle of Beaujolais I recognized from purchases at home when I felt flush.

"We're going first cabin on the wine," I said.

"In Ontario, sure, it's a twenty-dollar bottle. This afternoon in Nice, I paid three bucks."

"Taxes," I grumped. "About a thousand percent Canadian markup."

"Taste the wine," Annie said. "It'll do wonders for your mood."

She was right.

"Wowie," I said. "If this is a three-dollar bottle, I'd like to shake the hand of the man who crushes Beaujolais's grapes. Shake his foot, as a matter of fact."

Dinner was ravioli, salad, and the remarkable Beaujolais.

"So," Annie said, "what executive decisions came out of the office of C&G's president?"

"Chairman of the Board and CEO," I corrected. "Those are Swotty's titles. He's maybe going to get on to Jamie directly."

"Good luck to him if he expects to learn anything tangible. On the basis of this morning, I wouldn't call Jamie Haddon a motor-mouth. Coy, yes. A smartass, maybe. But forthcoming, no way."

"One of your strong points, Ms. Cooke, instant character analysis."

"Haddon's got a brain ticking over behind that bland face. A devious one."

"Ninety-nine out of one hundred women wouldn't agree with you on Jamie's looks. You think they're bland?"

"Or blah. Blond guys affect me that way."

"Fortunate me. Nondescript brunette."

"All the stuff about the name of his boat and the name on the disk, I find that cutesy and really, you know, cold-eyed." Annie put down her knife and fork, and folded her arms on the edge of the table. "Phoning Pamela and her father," she said, "now that's one thing."

"Two, if you want to be pedantic."

"But dealing with Mike Rolland is something altogether different."

"No argument from me. He has the disk in his desk drawer at Villa Pomme."

"What do you intend to do about it?"

"I think a reconnoitre might be in order."

"Whenever you invoke that word, I know you've got something silly in mind."

"Not to worry, my love." I reached over and squeezed Annie's hand. "It'll be under cover of darkness."

We finished the pasta and salad. "There's dessert," Annie said. She took the empty plates into the kitchen.

I went to the bedroom and made wardrobe adjustments. The jeans I had on could stay, but I changed my light blue sports shirt for a dark blue in the same model. I got my black windbreaker from the hall closet and pulled the new black beret over my forehead. The Rockport Walkers, in two shades of tan, didn't blend into the colour scheme, but they were the only shoes I'd packed that were remotely athletic.

I presented myself to Annie. "Who do I call to mind?"

"Not Cary Grant going over the rooftop in *To Catch a Thief.*"

"Aw, rats."

"He had on a turtleneck sweater. His pants were perfectly pressed. And I think his shoes were the kind that take a shine."

"Well, different eras, different costumes."

I took off the beret and windbreaker. Dessert was persimmons and goat cheese. I tasted some of both.

"Terrific combination," I said.

Annie pushed her plate to the centre of the table. She rested her elbows where the plate had been.

"Know what I think, big guy?" she said. "The reason you're being so tenacious about the Haddon business?"

"Well, finishing what I started, getting even for having been burgled, following through on promises, sticking it out to the end. Homilies of such nature."

"It's Pamela Cartwright."

I looked across at Annie.

She said, "You want to show her she made a mistake when she ended the marriage and rejected you."

There was a heel of Beaujolais left in the bottle. I tipped it into my glass.

"I'm not being critical," Annie said.

"Are you being accurate?"

"I think so. And, really, Pamela should be flattered, you pulling her chestnuts out of the fire for her. None of this means I think you want her back or anything."

"I hope I'm spoken for, thanks very much."

"In a way, it doesn't matter that Pamela's a woman. She just represents somebody, a person, who once judged you a schnook, incorrectly, and you're getting a kick out of having that person appeal to you, of all choices, in an emergency."

"Schnook?"

"Just a term to underline my thesis."

"You succeeded."

Annie picked up a stack of tourist literature from a chair. She had accumulated piles of maps, guides, and travel books. From the stack, she selected a small, brightly coloured map.

"If you're hell-bent on tonight's expedition," she said, "better study up on this."

It was a detailed drawing of Saint-Jean-Cap-Ferrat. There were two capes on the drawing. The smaller, Cap Saint Hospice, stuck into the Mediterranean past the little town of Saint-Jean to the east. The bigger cape, on the west, was shaped like a huge light bulb. It was Cap Ferrat, home to, among others, Mike Rolland.

"Right around the outside of the big cape," Annie said, tracing her finger on the map, "there's a sea walk. See, on here, it runs in a narrow public area between the backs of the private properties and the sea. Gorgeous in the day time."

"But the entrances to the houses are off the roads?"

"Yes. Avenue Jean Cocteau, all those. But keep in mind, it isn't all level on the cape."

Annie went over to the window. "Even from here, you can see the hills and trees." She was pointing south to Cap Ferrat. "And the rocks. The sea walk isn't a flat path. It goes up and down along the contours of the cliff. Not good for people with vertigo."

I tried to memorize parts of the map while I put on my windbreaker and beret. Annie and I hugged. "Don't do anything utterly absurd," she said.

"Who, me?"

CHAPTER SIXTEEN

I went a half-mile south on Avenue Denis Semeria and up a steep road that swept to the right. The silence was deep and total. I was in Cap Ferrat's residential district.

There was a three-quarters moon in the sky. And there were dim street lights spaced about one hundred feet apart. That was as much illumination as I cared for. I stuck close to the shadows thrown by long stretches of walls that were mostly stone and mostly fortress-like. The road I was on carried along the west side of the cape. I knew from Annie's map that it ended at a lighthouse. The lighthouse was old and historic, and marked one of Cap Ferrat's outer points. I stalked along, not making a sound. Somewhere on the road, Mike Rolland had his villa.

At each gate, at each gap in the long distances of walls, I examined the houses for indications of life. More than half had parked cars and lights and the flicker of people moving past windows. I kept on the move.

Damn.

It wasn't cars or lights or flickers I should be looking for. It was trees.

I switched my gaze upwards. Three estates further down the road, I got a reward. Against the early night sky, I was staring at the shape of an enormous apple. It swelled above the wall like a float at the Rose Bowl Parade, a cedar meticulously clipped into an apple shape complete with a stem at the top.

A name was embedded in the stone of the wall close to the gate. "Villa Pomme." On the house side of the gate, there were smaller trees and bushes trimmed in the rounded contours of Spys and Macintoshes and Deliciouses.

From the road, between the gate's metal bars, I could see all the signs of folks at home. Three cars were parked in an open space at the end of a short driveway. A large Mercedes, a Jag runabout, and some kind of outsized Japanese Jeep. And lights shone from both floors of the house. I applied a gentle shove to the gate. It had no give.

I slunk past Mike's place to the neighbouring mansion. No lights, no cars, no movement. Its gate was wood and had pointy spikes on top, but it was only chest-high. I boosted myself up and over gate and spikes. The house on the property could have been transported from Mecca. It had windows in crescent shapes and roofs like minarets. I trotted around the building and across the grounds to the wooden fence at the far end. The fence was taller, just above my head. I grabbed the top, swung my legs upward, and rolled over. Piece of cake.

I landed hard. And felt my heart do cartwheels in my chest. I'd come down, none too steadily, on a path that separated me from a long dive into the Mediterranean by no more than a yard and a half. Not such a piece of cake.

I was on the sea walk Annie had talked about. But she hadn't talked enough about crucial details like peril and danger and risk to one's life. By day, it was probably a frisky jaunt. By night, it was for fools and knaves.

I held my position, feet planted on the path, hands flat on the fence behind me. I waited until my eyes got used to the dimmer lights, until my nerves adjusted to the height. The path, from what I could make out, was manmade in some parts; big chunks of stone were cemented level to the ground. In other parts, it was earth and uneven, easier for goats to stroll than anything two-legged. The path had no railing, nothing between it and a plunge over the side of the cliff to the rocks and sea.

I looked down. Pretty impressive. In fact, incredibly dramatic. Whitecaps flicked on the surface of the black water that reached way beyond my sight in the direction of Muammar Qaddafi's kingdom. And it was noisy down there when the waves crashed against the craggy shoreline.

I turned north. Keeping my right hand on the fence for reassurance, I followed the path's twists and turns and rises and falls. I crept ahead until the shape of a big apple came back on the skyline.

Mike Rolland's fence on the path side was brick and seven feet high. A hardy bush grew out of the path next to the wall. I got a foothold in the bush and jumped for a grip on the wall's top. Pulling with my hands, pushing with my feet on the bush, I raised my head for a survey of Mike's domain.

He had two or three acres. The house was set a couple of hundred yards back from the wall. Between house and wall, there was an expanse of lawn, a swimming pool, and many more bushes and trees a la pomme. The house was white, cube-shaped, and had a lot of sliding glass doors. An architectural cross between Mies van der Rohe and Miami Moderne.

I dropped over the wall on Mike's side. Nobody saw me. At least nobody raised an alarm. I ran half the length of the lawn to a Granny Smith replica. I ducked behind it. Still no movement up ahead. The grass was cut as fine as the greens at Pebble Beach.

I slipped from cover, darted all the way to the swimming pool, picked up a lightweight aluminum chair from the pool side, and raced with it back to the wall. If I had to beat a hasty retreat from Mike's place, the chair would assist a quick scaling of the wall.

I made a return dash to the house. Most of the ground floor was visible behind the sliding glass doors. Inside, in a sprawling living room, there were tables, chairs, sofas, lamps, artistic knick-knacks, cabinets, rifles mounted on walls, and an air of furnished busyness. The lamps were switched on, but nobody was occupying the chairs and sofas.

I tried one of the sliding glass doors. Locked. There were doors inside the living room leading to the right. And there was a semicircular staircase built into the wall on the left. It went up to the second floor.

I stepped back and looked upward. The second floor had two long but narrow balconies. The room behind the balcony on the right was in darkness. On the left, the window streamed out light. I chose the dark one on the right.

I climbed onto a very large white box, probably a cover for machines that kept the swimming pool heated to Babette's choice of temperature. Or did she actually go swimming in that string thing of hers? I stood on my toes on the box and locked my hands on the railings around the balcony. I vaulted softly to the floor of the balcony. A vintage Cary Grant vault.

Another sliding glass door led off the balcony. I tried to open it. No dice. It was locked. What would Cary Grant have done? Easy question. He would have swung over to the next balcony. A swing wasn't precisely necessary in my case. A mere foot separated the balconies. I stepped across to the lighted balcony.

Another sliding glass door. It gaped wide open. I peeped in. It was a master bedroom for a master with inflated notions of space. It had about the same dimensions as the parquet floor at Boston Garden. At first, I thought the huge room was empty. The sounds told me I was mistaken. Whimpers and soft moans. They were coming from the far end of the room. Two people were on the bed. Making love.

At the moment I caught sight of them, they had assumed the female-superior position. The superior female's buttocks were aimed at me. I pulled my head out of the bedroom. Where did I stand on the topic of voyeurism? Against, for the most part. But this was a special instance. I was engaged in a necessary and dangerous mission.

I peeped back in. Tan lines ran very close to the crack dividing the two buttocks. They undoubtedly belonged to Babette. I was pleased to record that I had been correct that morning about the absence of cellulite.

If that was Babette on top, it must be Mike on the bottom. I was probably safe in assuming they would be occupied for the next several minutes. Good manners dictated I should leave them to their sighs and whimpers. I dropped to my hands and knees, and started across the floor to the open bedroom door.

Broadloom covered the floor, rust-coloured and thick. My progress was silent and as swift as my hands and knees could make it. I encountered obstacles along the way, clothes discarded in haste. Mike's silver-white pants. Babette's white dress. Mike's silver-white shirt. My hand got caught in a garment that was small, white, and silky. I shook it, but it insisted on sticking to my hand. Static-cling maybe. The garment had to be either Mike's breast-pocket handkerchief or Babette's knickers. There was no time to dwell on further identification. I crawled ahead with the object, whatever it was, fastened to my hand.

I got within two crawls of the door when there was much rustling from the bed. I flashed a look. The couple was shifting to the male-superior position. The male was Mike right enough. He didn't notice me. Neither did Babette. Too absorbed in the task at hand. I crawled into the corridor.

The small, white, silk garment had stuck with me. I stood up and peeled it off my hand. It was a Babette underthing. The label said it came from a Parisian house of couture, but the designer's name was universal. Mr. Sexy. And Mr. Sexy wasn't just kidding. I stuffed the underwear in the pocket of my black windbreaker.

The stairs were to the left. I tiptoed down them. I heard voices speaking French. Their source was a room beyond the living room. I stayed on tiptoes across the living room's length. It was fatiguing work, tiptoeing.

In the middle of the living room, I had an angle view into a section of the kitchen. A squat woman stood at the stove in an apron that trailed to the floor. The lanky Clutch brother with the greying beard sat at a table to the right. He was talking to someone out of my viewing angle. It didn't take a Sam Spade to conclude that the squat woman was the cook and that Lanky Clutch was talking across the table to his brother, Stove Clutch.

The kitchen was off the living room on the street side of the house. I opened the door that led into a room on the swimming pool side. It was Mike's den. It was dominated by a noble oak desk. Among other objects it dominated were the heads of many stuffed and mounted endangered species. All had their eyes fixed on me. I felt like the fall guy in a Gary Larsen cartoon.

The centre drawer in the desk was locked. So were the side drawers. No key sat in plain sight. Probably upstairs among the clothing strewn on the rust broadloom.

There was a letter opener on the desk, silver and slender and as pointy as a needle. I slipped the letter opener into the crack in the centre drawer and flicked at the lock. Two or three slow minutes went by, and I was still flicking. The burglar's touch eluded me until a pair of events occurred simultaneously. The letter opener broke in two, and the lock on the desk drawer clicked over. I checked the stuffed guys on the walls. They didn't seem to be interested in my triumph.

I eased the drawer toward me. Jamie Haddon's disk, Operation Freeload, waited in one corner like an old friend. I started to jam the disk into my windbreaker pocket, but encountered a problem. Babette's underwear was taking up most of the pocket space. What to do with the underwear? A calling card maybe? Zorro left a Z wherever he went. The Lone Ranger had silver bullets. With me, it'd be silk panties. I folded the underwear into Mike's drawer, transferred the disk to my windbreaker pocket, and left the library.

It was a cinch to release the lock on the sliding glass door in the living room. The principle was the same as on the sliding glass door to the balcony at the apartment on Avenue Denis Semeria. Push a small button under the door's handle. Pull on the handle. I pushed and pulled. The door opened.

A loud, insistent bell jangled through the house.

The damn lock was rigged to an alarm.

I took off like a sprinter on steroids. My feet skimmed over the ground. Across the patio, around the swimming pool, onto the lawn. Behind me, the clanging bell cancelled out other sounds.

I risked a look over my shoulder. Upstairs, Babette stepped on to the balcony. Not a stitch on her. The woman had no modesty. Mike Rolland wasn't in sight. Maybe coitus interruptus didn't agree with him.

Downstairs, both Clutches were steaming across the patio. The lanky Clutch, Georges, was in the lead, Emile right on his heels. Neither had impressive velocity. But they had numbers on their side. And a gun. It was in Emile's hand.

I scampered across the grass. The aluminum chair waited for me against the wall. Ten yards to go.

I heard the crack of a gunshot. I heard the whine of a bullet. It seemed to be far over my head. Emile must have fired his pistol. As a marksman, he wasn't up to the standards of his boss, the Deadeye Dick who had slaughtered half the pheasant population of Scotland.

Two yards to the chair. I drove into it with my left foot. In the same motion, I brought my right leg up to the wall in a high-jumper's kick. The chair acted with a trampoline effect. I went up, brushed the top of the wall, and thumped down on the other side.

It wasn't a graceful landing. And it wasn't on my feet. I hit ass-first. But I was on the sea path. And I was in one piece.

I scrabbled along the path, heading back the way I'd come. I kept moving past the high fence around the mansion from Arabian Nights. It was too close to Mike Rolland's place to serve as a refuge. Better to put distance between me and the scene of my theft.

Surefootedness, not speed was the number-one requisite on the sea walk. And considering the darkness, the skitteriness of the path, the prospect of a tumble into the Mediterranean, the possibility of the Clutches on my tail, I wasn't doing badly at putting my feet in the right places.

I covered about four hundred yards of path. My bum had a mild kink from its contact with the ground. My breath was coming in wheezes. I stopped to catch some air and check for pursuers. I leaned against a chain link fence on the inner side of the path. I inhaled deeply. My view back was impeded by the path's route in and out of the face of the cliff.

I waited. I watched. And I made out the beams of a couple of flashlights bobbing on the path about fifty yards back. The Clutches. My cue to skedaddle.

I took one more deep breath and felt something clamp down hard and wet on the left shoulder of my windbreaker. I turned my head. I was looking into the crazed eyes of a big, black, fanged, drooling, foul-mouthed dog. Its snout jutted through a space in the chain link fence. It snarled and tugged at the back of my windbreaker.

"Down, boy," I whispered. "Nice doggie."

Nice doggie? Who did I think I was talking to? Lassie? This beast was from the killer school.

"Goddamn it," I snapped, "it's my good windbreaker."

The dog pulled its muzzle back in a ferocious wrench. It slammed my shoulder against the fence. I made my own counter yank. The dog took that as a challenge. It jerked on my windbreaker. I banged backwards into the chain fence again.

Terrific. I was playing tug-of-war at night on a path over the Mediterranean with a dog whose grandfather had probably worked for the Gestapo.

I looked down the path. The winking flashlights were twenty yards closer. The Clutches' progress wasn't rapid, but it was steady. The tortoises and the hare.

"Okay, Rover," I croaked at the dog, "get ready for your best shot."

I gathered my forces for one Arnold Schwarzenegger heave. So did the dog. Both of us went at it. I won. It was something of a Pyrrhic victory. I left a chunk of my windbreaker in the dog's mouth, and I came close to pitching off the cliff. But I had reclaimed my freedom.

I scooted south on the path. At the same time, the dog broke into piercing yowls. Damn mutt was a sore loser. I took another glance back. The dog's racket seemed to have spurred on Georges and Emile. The flashlights were dancing ahead at a faster rate.

I stepped up my pace as much as I dared. The dog switched from yowls to yaps. Maybe the stupid beast would develop laryngitis. I pressed on.

The path dipped away from the outer edges of the cliff. It turned inland to a stretch where thick bushes grew on either side of the path and where the light was marginally dimmer.

I stopped.

Maybe this was the place and moment to mount an ambush.

I whipped off my belt. The bushes had sturdy little trunks. I looped the belt around the base of one of the sturdiest on the west side of the path. The belt was just long enough to reach across the path's width. I crouched in the bushes on the east side. I held the belt slack on the ground. I waited.

Georges and Emile thumped along the path. The winking from the flashlights preceded them. So did the sound of their gasping. The two guys weren't in tiptop shape for nighttime forays.

Georges came into my field of vision first. About three feet back, Emile followed. Neither guy was shining his flashlight on the path directly in front. Both were pointing the beams at longer range, probably hoping to catch me in the light up ahead. I couldn't tell whether Emile had his pistol at the ready.

Georges was three yards from me, coming at a jerky half-run.

Two yards. Emile, not quite on Georges's rear but close enough, had a slightly smoother stride.

One yard. Georges was almost opposite my crouching spot.

I yanked on the belt. It jerked off the ground. The taut belt caught Georges above his right ankle. He fell forward. His face made a smacking noise on the path. The flashlight flipped from his hand. It bounced across the ground out of his reach.

Emile pulled up fast, on his feet, but surprised and off-balance. He had the flashlight in his left hand, the pistol in his right.

I rose out of the bushes and the darkness. Emile didn't see me. He was concentrating on his flattened brother. I threw a right at his unprotected left cheekbone. It landed on target. A jolt of pain shot up my arm. The punch hurt me, but it inflicted more short-term damage on Emile. He crumpled into the bushes on the west side of the path. His flashlight flew somewhere beyond him. His gun dropped on the path at my feet. I kicked it in the same direction the flashlight had taken.

Georges was pushing himself off the path. He had his back to me. I slammed a Rockport Walker between his shoulder blades. Georges went down again. I stepped over his prostrate form. His flashlight was still shining. It lay a couple of yards along the path. I picked it up. Georges was giving himself another push off the ground. I cracked the flashlight across his nose. He sank back to earth. I hurled the flashlight over the path, over the bushes, over the side of the cliff, into the Mediterranean.

Georges was groaning. Emile was thrashing in the bushes. Both guys were temporarily on the disabled list. I got my feet churning and headed south again. I was alone on the path.

Ten minutes further on, around a sharp bend, something tall and slim with a knob on top rose against the sky. My first thought was more topiary. Maybe an ice-cream-cone tree? It wasn't. It was the old and historic lighthouse. Alongside it, stone stairs branched upwards from the sea walk. I climbed them as far as they went. Where they went was back to the residential streets of Cap Ferrat.

I chose a short road that bore to the right. It steered me straight at the inevitable wall around the inevitable mansion. Except this wall had a figure carved into it that set a memory tinkling. I moved closer. Two words, "Le Mauresque," were printed in the wall above the figure. I remembered where I'd seen the figure before. On the jacket of Somerset Maugham's novels. The mansion behind the wall was the old Maugham place.

Standing there, I got my bearings. Annie's map had indicated a street called Avenue Somerset Maugham. It ran down the middle of the cape comfortably east of the street Mike Rolland lived on. I was standing in front of the Maugham house, ergo, I was on the Maugham avenue.

I split off on the long road behind the house. It took me away from Rolland territory. I walked quickly. The Clutch brothers hadn't got a good look at their attacker on the path. At worst, they could be holding my belt hostage. It wasn't much of a clue, a black leather belt, size thirty-two. To Georges and Emile, I was a mystery man who had nothing to hold up his pants and a sweetheart of a right cross.

Mike Rolland would wise up when he discovered the disk was missing from the centre drawer of his desk. First he'd probably fasten on Dan Renzi as the robber. But he was sure to change his mind after he received a report from the Clutches about the rough stuff on the sea walk. Dan was not the sort for fisticuffs. Mike would switch his suspicions to other parties. And I'd be at the top of the list. I shrugged to myself. What the heck. I reached Avenue Denis Semeria and walked to the apartment without spotting Mike or the Clutches.

Annie met me at the door. I held up the disk. "Nice work, big guy," she said. She looked relieved. "You weren't gone much more than an hour."

"Time flies when a guy knows his business."

"Oh, yes?" Annie stepped back. "Then why does your best windbreaker look like something from a rummage sale?"

I fingered the rip in the windbreaker's shoulder. "I think it might've been the Hound of the Baskervilles," I said.

"A *chien mechant*?" Annie looked alarmed. "You got attacked by a *chien mechant*?"

"Who?"

"Most big houses around here keep them on the grounds. Tremendously vicious watch dogs."

"Damn French curs," I said. "If they aren't shitting on the sidewalks, they're chewing on people's windbreakers."

Annie wrinkled her nose. "You notice it's suddenly gotten gamey in here?"

I lifted my shoe and examined the bottom.

"Oh, yuck."

CHAPTER SEVENTEEN

I took the Miles Davis autobiography and a cup of coffee out to the apartment's balcony. It was late morning, and I had the place to myself. Annie was up in the hills conducting her movie-reviewing seminar.

I swallowed some coffee from the outsized piece of crockery in my hand. What the French drink their morning coffee from, Canadians eat their morning cereal from. I sat in the sun and felt superior. Couldn't help myself. If Mike Rolland concluded it was I who had invaded his apple villa and filched the disk, and if he and the Clutches set out to track me down, they'd start, and end, at hotels in the neighbourhood where Canadian tourists put up. They wouldn't think of a rented apartment, or locate my particular rented apartment. I basked in the sun and in my own splendid conceit, and I read the part of the Davis book where he described taking a fist to Cicely Tyson. Lovely trumpet player, lousy gentleman. At some point, I wasn't sure when, Annie was touching my shoulder.

"Huphurr," I said. I had a sour taste in my mouth and a crick in my neck.

"Dozed off, did we?" Annie said. She looked smart in her lightweight black suit. The skirt stopped at the middle of her thighs. There was no blouse under the jacket. There was nothing under the jacket.

"How'd it go?" I struggled in my chair for a return to dignity.

"The kids didn't have many points of reference. Not in pre-1975 movies. But on sci-fi stuff, things like *Altered States*, *Aliens*, any Lucas or early Spielberg, they were really analytical. And fiendishly well-informed."

"Makes me feel deprived I missed it."

"Don't be a grouch or I won't tell you about the news flash I brought back."

"The university wants me to show the students what a smooth-talking criminal lawyer looks like?"

"Better."

"Hard to top that."

"Just wait." Annie went inside, and when she came back, she was carrying two glasses of white wine.

"Lovely," I said. I tried to get out of the slump I'd fallen back into. "Is it that time of day?"

"Almost twelve-thirty." Annie stood over my chair looking down at me. "Know what that noise you made when I woke you up reminded me of?"

"Just resting my eyes."

"Of the name of the character Steve Martin played in *The Man with Two Brains*."

"Yeah?" I got straight in my chair. "Really? Dr. Michael Hfuhruhurr. The first h isn't silent. That's where most people go wrong."

Annie settled in another of the balcony chairs. The black skirt rode further up her thighs.

I said, "That's a movie you should've talked about this morning. Opened the kids' eyes to great and durable comedy."

"Crang, not everybody has seen *The Man with Two Brains* four times."

"Six. How do you think I mastered Hfuhruhurr?"

"Okay," Annie said. "My reward for the boon I have for you from the university is that you don't sit there and do recapitulations of your favourite scenes from *The Man with Two Brains.*"

"What you've got can't be that sensational."

"A computer expert who'll study your disk."

"I stand corrected."

"Optical disk?" Annie said. "That's the term?"

I nodded.

Annie said, "The president at the university introduced me to some faculty members, including this one guy whom the president called their resident computer genius. So I piped up and said I had a friend with an optical disk and nowhere to look at it."

"And no skills to do so."

"I added that. And I got the impression the resident computer genius, a Professor Nestor, was thrilled at the challenge of it all. He doesn't have the right machine at the school, but he can scare something up in Nice. Take a few days, which I said was certainly agreeable and very generous of the good professor."

"That long?" I said. "A lot can happen in a few days. Pamela could come batting over here. Swotty could get into the act somehow."

"You're sounding ungrateful, Crang. Nestor is the expert. If he says a few days, that's the necessary period."

"What's he like, Professor Nestor?"

"Oh, in his early thirties probably, but he looks about fourteen."

"Ideal. The man's ideal."

Annie shook her head in exasperation. "You insist on thinking that only kids or people who are kidlike can be trusted around computers."

"No, I think they're the only ones who should be permitted around computers. Maybe a universal law could be enacted, people over thirty-five have to abandon computers and return to instruments more compatible with man. The pen and pencil."

"With that kind of retrogressive attitude, you're headed for big setbacks before the twenty-first century."

"If it becomes absolutely necessary, I'll hire a kid to guide me."

Annie dipped her hand into her shoulder bag. It was hitched over the back of the chair. She pulled out the notes from her seminar. There were handwritten scribbles on the last page. She read from them.

"David Nestor is the genius's full name. He's staying in an apartment in Beaulieu, an address I think is just up the walkway past the tennis courts. It'll be convenient for him if we drop off the disk on our way to lunch."

"We're on our way to lunch?"

"Got it all planned," Annie said. "And much, much more."

She went into the bedroom to change and emerged wearing a light green cotton blouse, blue denim skirt, and Reeboks with three dark green stripes. The skirt wasn't any shorter than the skirt to the black suit. Or any longer.

"Something occurred to me," Annie said. She was back in the chair, the wineglass held in her lap. "Do you intend to tell Dan Renzi you recovered the disk? If so, Professor Nestor may be superfluous."

"Recovered the disk?"

"How you got it last night is something I would rest easy not knowing."

"It won't hurt Dan to wait until the professor tells me what's on the disk."

"A whole few days?"

"What Dan is worried about," I said, "is Mike Rolland using the disk to put the screws to Jamie Haddon, and Jamie thereby discovering it was his trusted friend and devoted admirer Dan who lifted the disk in the first place."

"Yes, that would cast Dan in a very poor light."

"But if Mike hasn't got the disk, he can't put the screws to Jamie, and Jamie won't discover Dan's duplicity, and Dan has no cause to worry."

"But Dan doesn't know that."

"Well, he'll notice nothing terrible is happening. Besides it'll be beneficial to his character to stew a little."

"I'm not sure," Annie said. "This is being kind of rough on Dan."

"Two answers, sweetie," I said. "One, it was Renzi who began this round-robin of disk snatchings. He doesn't rate any special compassion on that ground. And, two, I think we're of one mind, you and I, that none of that lot is conducting himself on the square, not Dan, Mike, or Jamie. Or herself either, Pamela. And, I guess this makes three, we'll never know what's up until the contents of the damned disk are revealed."

"That's Professor Nestor's field," Annie said. "Right, okay, I buy it."

"Was it the force of my argument?" I said. "Or you just want to let your mind roam to other pastures?"

"Some of the former, all of the latter."

Annie placed her wineglass carefully on the floor of the balcony. She hooked the shoulder bag over her arm. The glass had a couple of swallows of wine left in it.

"Get your Rockabees on," she said to me. "We're hitting the road."

"You know they're called Rockports."

We delivered the disk to Professor David Nestor at his apartment. He was medium tall and chubby all over, what in an adolescent is called baby fat and is expected to vanish before age sixteen. His face looked as if it needed shaving about every other Christmas. He held the optical disk like he'd been handed the Dead Sea Scrolls. I thanked him effusively for his services.

Annie and I walked another two blocks to a restaurant near the train station called Le Catalan. It was gruff and noisy and the air was thick with the smoke of one thousand Gitanes. It won my heart, the Gallic-ness of it all. We got a table in the window. Annie ordered pizzas.

Her arm disappeared up to the elbow into her shoulder bag. It emerged with a sheaf of articles clipped from magazines, notes she'd made from Michelin and other guides. "This file," Annie said, "tells you everything you might ever want to be briefed on in advance before we go to Haut-de-Cagnes this afternoon. It's one of the more accessible of the *villes perchées*."

"First principles," I said. "What are *villes perchées*?" Annie expounded. The pizzas arrived. They were, as was the case with almost everything else I'd encountered on the Côte d'Azur, a different species from the product at home. *Villes perchées*, Annie said, were villages that medieval folks built of stone at the peak point of the highest mountains they could get at in their districts. Annie said the reason the medievals built on the heights was that it helped them spot their enemies coming from a long way off. A lesson worth adopting in my own life, if I could just think how.

CHAPTER EIGHTEEN

I was feeling touristed out.

"Something funny's happening in my head," I said to Annie. "I have to think very hard to remember what day it is."

"Monday, big guy."

"I'd already thought very hard," I said. "Odd though, I'd decided it was Sunday."

"Sunday, yesterday, was when we went to Grasse, Vence, and Biot."

"Ah, yes," I said. "Grasse was the perfume factory. Vence was the Matisse chapel. And Biot was where the man with the mighty lungs blew into the long tube and produced the pretty glass that I bought to take home and drink vodka and soda out of."

The phone rang. Annie and I were dawdling over lunch in the sunroom at the apartment.

"That's probably someone calling to offer you a job as a tour guide, Crang."

"Bad move if they are. I'd lose track of the days."

I picked up the phone. *"Oui?"* I said. It was my best French word.

"Crang?"

It was an emphatic male voice.

"C'est moi," I said, two more I had down pat.

"Archie Cartwright here."

"Holy mackerel."

"You sound surprised."

"More like thunderstruck," I said. "Poleaxed. Knock me over with a feather."

"We have never been introduced."

"This'll do."

Archie Cartwright spoke with an upper-class Toronto honk. His voice was coming through without the underwater sounds of long-distance telephone.

I said, "Please tell me you're in Toronto, and this happens to be a fantastically clear line."

"We've just checked into the Negresco."

"I don't suppose you're on a Rotary junket."

"Pamela is with me." Archie paused. "Or, under the circumstances, you could say I'm with Pamela."

"Which circumstances would those be?"

"That's the subject I wish to discuss with you." Archie had the tone of a man who was accustomed to parcelling out instructions. "Let's set up a meeting for this afternoon."

"Well, ah, yeah, that'd be dandy, you bet."

Why did I turn into Jimmy Stewart whenever a Cartwright caught me on the phone?

"I'm free at this moment," Archie said.

"Free of Pamela?"

"I intend to meet you alone, Crang." Archie was just brusque enough that I almost slipped back into Jimmy Stewart. I rallied and suggested the outdoor cafe in Villefranche under the Hotel Welcome.

"In an hour," Archie said.

I was there in forty-five minutes. I ordered a coffee. A tour bus unloaded a crowd of sightseers. They looked middle-aged, well-upholstered, and German. Did I need the complication of Archie Cartwright? With him, the topic could be Pamela, if Archie had somehow picked up on her affair with Jamie Haddon. His remarks on the phone made that seem likely. Or maybe it was Swotty who had despatched Archie to call on me. On the whole, I would prefer Archie as an emissary of Swotty. Marital trouble was on a par with the European Community as a subject that buffaloed me. The language from the sightseers had echoes of the bad guys in World War II movies. Ve haf vays of making you talk, Herr Englische.

"Crang?"

It was the voice from the telephone, piercing and nasal. Archie Cartwright was taller than six feet. Even at rest, standing beside the cafe table, he emanated vigour. He had a long, firm-looking face. There was a deep cleft in his chin. His nose was too large, but its size added to the overall impression of energy. His hair was brown and cut short. He was wearing a grey-blue tweed jacket, grey dress shirt, a red tie bearing the insignia of a club I couldn't place, navy blue trousers, and black loafers. He asked the waitress for coffee in English. No messing about with lesser tongues.

"Good of you to meet me on short notice," Archie said to me.

"I had a choice between this and one more vieille ville," I said. "You got the nod."

Archie crossed his legs and did some fine tuning on the creases in his pants.

"I think," he said, "we would both prefer if I didn't beat about the bush."

"Could you hold the bush-beating for a minute, Archie?" I said. "My phone number over here, did Swotty give it to you?"

"Swotty?" Archie's face showed a flash of bewilderment. The face didn't look like it was used to an expression like bewilderment.

"You know," I said, "the mainstay of C&G. Old Whetherhill. Your father-in-law."

"Oh, I see, you were being facetious," Archie said. "Yes, John gave me your number."

"John? You call him John?"

"I like to think the two of us are intimates."

"Intimate enough for you to call him John? Not enough for Swotty?"

"Only his oldest prep-school friends use that.... Look, Crang, could we get on to other matters?"

"The dynamics of names intrigue me," I said. "When I held down a seat at the Whetherhill Sunday table, just keeping it warm till you came along, Arch, I didn't get as far as the John stage."

Archie seemed to regard that as a conversation-stopper.

"If Swotty supplied my phone number," I said, "is he why you're here?"

"John is not the reason."

"That leaves the alternative I was hoping it wouldn't be."

The waitress brought Archie's coffee. He said "Thank you" in English. She said he was welcome, also in English. Maybe Archie's air of total self-assurance drove her to bilingualism.

"I should warn you, Crang," Archie said, "John is certain to be ringing you himself. I'm not privy to certain executive matters at C&G, that goes without saying. But John told me in so many words he has a worry connected with the commission you are carrying out for him over here."

"Swotty's not a happy camper?"

"John wanted me to put you on alert."

It crossed my mind to play dumb and let Archie ease into whatever subject he wanted to chat me up about. But, what the hell, I'd spent a lifetime plunging straight into matters that were usually better left alone. Why break old habits?

"In the broad spectrum, Arch," I said, rushing in where angels fear to tread, "the piece of inquiry I'm doing for Swotty has to do with the guy whose name I bet you're about to bring up."

"Jamie Haddon."

"And, sorry about this, his affair with your wife."

Archie stayed steady as a rock. "To be clear on one point, Crang," he said, "John is completely unaware of Pamela's involvement with Jamie."

"Sure, and it's essential he stays in the dark," I said. "I realize that. I also think I know what Swotty's dander is up about. If I've read the portents correctly, he's fretting over a possibly large piece of possibly missing money."

"Haddon is involved in that too?"

"Possibly."

"Well, I must say this is grim news."

"But it isn't first among your concerns, it's not why you and I are meeting for the first time in beautiful downtown Villefranche."

"Quite right."

Archie picked up the little paper napkin that came with the coffee. He wiped the lip of his cup. Then he took a sip.

"My purpose in seeing you," he said, "is to save my marriage."

"I know how it feels, Arch. But if you don't mind me breaking into the preamble again, background may be important. How did you cotton on to the affair?"

"An informant. I've been brought into the picture in some detail."

"By Jamie?"

"That's preposterous, Crang."

"But not unprecedented."

Archie ignored my remark. Or didn't grasp it.

"When you had tea with Pamela ten days ago," he said, "you would have met our housekeeper, Hilda."

"Observed her comings and goings was more like it."

"Hilda is my informant."

"Hilda is? The woman who moves on little cat feet?"

"She is very loyal."

"Try that on Pamela. She thinks she's the one who's got Hilda's ear. Her silence too."

"I know," Archie said. "And Pamela is mistaken. Hilda was in my parents' house from the time I was a teenager. She only came to us, to Pamela and myself, after Mother died. She sees her first duty as being to the Cartwrights."

"The woman has to be deep as the ocean, fooling a smart cookie like Pamela."

"Hilda came to me with her suspicions. More than suspicions, in actual fact. I couldn't believe they were true, but I requested that Hilda find out more."

"Hilda got on the inside with Pamela?"

"Pamela took Hilda into her confidence, yes. This was a few months ago."

"Fantastic."

"And I made it my business to learn what I could. About the Rowanwood apartment, my wife's meetings there with Haddon, and so on."

"That's tough, Archie. It must have been painful."

"And of course Hilda advised me when you entered the picture."

"That was by invitation only, and purely investigational."

"I appreciate your status, Crang."

The waitress came by. I asked for a glass of white wine. Archie's confidences were making me thirsty. He had another coffee. Across the way, the portly Teutonic tourists were flocking into St. Peter's Chapel.

"Forgive my curiosity, Arch," I said, "if you've known about the affair all this time, why haven't you confronted Pamela? Played the outraged husband? Told Haddon to buzz off?"

"Fair enough that you should ask," Archie said. He sounded like a first-year psychology lecturer acknowledging a student's perceptive question. I didn't think the question was perceptive. To me, cheating, in or out of marriage, called for an immediate response. Punch someone's lights out.

"I decided patience was the wiser course," Archie said. "I love my wife, Crang. I value my marriage. There is nothing I wouldn't do to keep both."

Archie was speaking in tones that added a dash of sanctimony to his normal pedantry. The combination made him a pain in the ass to listen to.

"I looked at the affair in the cold light of day," Archie went on. "Believe me, that wasn't easy. But after due consideration, it seemed to me ludicrous that the affair could last."

I said, "Play the waiting game, I get it, Arch. Stick around to pick up the pieces, Pamela being the pieces."

"I also considered the scandal that would come to our families if I brought the affair out into the open."

"Very commendable," I said. "But there's one drawback, Arch. Your strategy has been a tad slow paying dividends."

"That is true. And it explains why I am relying on you at this juncture, Crang. The sudden decision of Pamela's to come to France, to where Haddon is, must indicate a turning point of some sort in their relationship. Would you agree?"

"That's exactly right, Archie."

Archie gave me a look of trust and anticipation. He was clearly waiting for me to continue. I didn't. The silence between us lengthened. And the expectancy drained from Archie's face.

"Well?" he said. He was annoyed. "I've just taken you into my confidence, Crang. Told you facts about my marriage I've revealed to no one else. Surely it's only fair that you share what you've learned from your investigations over here. After all, it affects me in the most fundamental way."

"Tit for tat doesn't count in this instance, Arch."

Archie looked bewildered again. Twice in one afternoon — probably a normal year's complement.

"Perhaps I've used bad judgment confiding in you, Crang," he said. He gave his words the brusque force he'd used on the phone.

"Hold your horses," I said. "If I'm keeping back information, it isn't because I'm invoking a solicitor-client privilege —"

"I hardly see where one could exist."

"— but because I'm coining a new privilege. Call it first husband-first wife. When Pamela opened up to me, she didn't foresee that her second husband and I would be exploring the same events from another side of the triangle."

"See here, Crang, I spoke of patience. But I assure you mine is not unlimited."

"I'm not about to blow Pamela's secrets," I said. "God knows most of them are almost public property anyway. But I'll tell you this much, Archie, trust me on it, whatever happens in the next day or so should make a winner out of your team."

Archie uncrossed his legs. He spread both hands on the tops of his thighs. His beautifully manicured fingernails were digging deep into his thighs.

"This is unacceptable," he said. He had plenty of edge to the normal bray of his voice. Maybe the edge was supposed to bowl me over.

"Well, I'm not talking about a happy ending, like in the movies. Fade to man and woman walking toward the sunset, anything like that. When one partner in a marriage tumbles into an affair for whatever reason, what comes after can't be unalloyed rapture. The other partner is hurt and wary, you in this case, Archie. But at least the chance is there for restoring the marriage to some semblance of a mutually trusting relationship. That's what I'm trying to tell you. Assuming the pre-Haddon marriage was a good one."

"Much more." Archie's voice was choked. The choke didn't bowl me over either.

I said, "This may sound strange, given the last year's history, but Pamela may be hurting as hard as you right now, Archie. Different kind of hurt, the kind connected with guilt and remorse, but equally rough on her. If you approach her the right way, both of you might come out just fine."

Archie sat with his hands pressing on his thighs. I sipped my wine. I was feeling like a noodle. What I'd told Archie could have been lifted from a primer for inept marriage counselors. On the other hand, I knew more than Archie about the current state of his wife's affair, knew that Pamela seemed to be on the verge of giving Jamie the gate.

Archie shook his head slowly. "It isn't satisfactory, Crang," he said.

"You're welcome, Arch."

"I showed Haddon hospitality from the day I married into Pamela's family. More than hospitality. Friendship. I welcomed him to our house. And this is the way he repays me."

"Archie, you're branching into areas I can't help you with."

"I don't understand the man."

"Archie." I held up my hand in a halt signal. Archie barged on through.

"I blame Haddon completely," he said. He was speaking into my face, eyes locked on mine. I couldn't look away. "Who else can I blame except Haddon?" Archie said. "I can't blame Pamela. I want her back. I can't blame someone I want back."

"So far she hasn't gone anywhere."

"Don't be a fool." Archie came down hard on the fool part. "Pamela may not have left me physically. But you can't sit there and tell me our marriage will be the same after what Haddon has done to it with his insufferable selfishness."

"The marriage could be better in the long run," I said. "It's been known to happen."

"You can't begin to comprehend my frustration," Archie said. "If the man was anyone except Haddon, I could take steps. I and my friends could. Haddon's name wouldn't be worth mentioning in Toronto. But since it is Haddon, my hands are virtually tied."

"He's Swotty's pet," I said. "If you spoke up about the affair, many walls could come tumbling down. I understand your dilemma, Archie."

"It has cost me heavily to keep my silence ..." Archie's voice faded out.

He looked down at his hands. The backs of them had gone white from the pressure of gripping his thighs. He lifted the hands. There were rows of oblong prints in his navy blue trousers. Archie smoothed them away.

I couldn't think of anything else to say, and it seemed to me Archie had shot his bolt. Probably he regretted that he'd been so frank with me. Rich WASPs aren't accustomed to letting their feelings run rampant.

Archie took a clip of franc notes from his pants pocket. He picked out a twenty and placed it under his coffee cup.

"I've no more time," he said. The Toronto honk was reactivated in his voice.

"For what my advice is worth, Arch," I said, "don't give up on the silence yet."

Archie walked away.

On the other side of the square, the jolly band of German tourists was preparing to descend on the cafe. I counted out enough francs to cover the rest of the bill. The Germans advanced. It looked like another breach of the Maginot Line. I left.

CHAPTER NINETEEN

I walked back from Villefranche on the elevated sidewalk that circled the harbour. The sidewalk was separated from the water by fifteen yards of sand and pebble beach. Dozens of bodies lay on the sand and pebbles, toasting in the warm spring sun. The female bodies wore no tops.

I stayed on the move and marvelled at the diversity of breasts, the differences in size, shape, texture. Nationality too. The two slim teenagers touching their upper bodies had to be French. No self-consciousness about them. But the three young women lying side by side, almost rigid, I was betting they were Yanks, tourists from Cleveland or Dallas experiencing their first toplessness. I couldn't classify the small woman with breasts to match, small but exquisite. She was wearing a black bikini bottom and a big straw hat plunked over her face and shoulders. And just to the left of her, two portly matrons with monstrous, spreading ...

Hey, didn't I know those small but exquisite breasts?

I picked my way through the prone figures on the beach and approached the big straw hat. I approached tentatively. If I had the wrong breasts, I might be explaining my error to the authorities.

"*Pardon, m'dame*," I affected a sexy baritone.

"Look, *señor*." The voice from under the straw hat was angry. "I told you once to take a hike."

"You did?" I used my natural medium-sexy tenor.

A hand reached up and removed the straw hat.

"Oh hi, honey," Annie said. "I already had to shoo away a Spanish guy making a pass."

"Nobody's blaming the Spanish guy." I was crouching on the sand and pebbles. "But what are you doing like that?"

"Like what?" Annie started to sit up.

"You don't have to sit up!"

"Why not?" Annie sat up. Her breasts glistened under a light coating of oil. "Crang, really, are you embarrassed on my behalf?"

"It's on my own behalf I'm embarrassed."

"Well, heck, look around you."

"I was."

"The beach is practically shimmering in bare hooters."

"Hooters?"

"I wanted to see what it felt like," Annie said. She set the straw hat on her head and began gathering her equipment. Tan oil, sandals, copy of *Cahiers du Cinéma*, bikini top.

"What's the answer?" I asked. "How does it feel?"

"Lying in the sun is boring any way you do it, with or without a top."

Annie strapped herself into the bra.

"I was having trouble with my reaction," I said. "Seeing parts of a loved one's anatomy in public that one is used to observing in privacy is disorienting."

Annie grinned at me. "Well, big guy, it was just a try at a new thrill."

Back on the elevated sidewalk, Annie asked me how I sized up Archie Cartwright.

"He's shortlisted for the Mr. Ponderous title," I said. "That's his personality in general. In particular, at the moment, he's only holding on by the fingernails. And who can blame him, the hand he's been dealt … the cuckold."

"He knows about the affair?"

"The housekeeper was playing a deep-throat role."

"Wow," Annie said. "What is it Archie's holding on to by the fingernails?"

"His temper, which I'd rate as explosive. His sense of the tightness of things. His self-esteem. The usual."

"What did he expect from you?"

"*Café* and sympathy," I said. "And information. Mostly information."

"That's kind of thick. You can't go on telling Archie what Pamela said, and Pamela what Dan said, and Jamie Haddon what Mike Rolland said ad infinitum."

"I held my tongue. Practically bit it off."

A trio of young French bucks lounging by an ice-cream stand gave Annie an up and down check-over. She had put on a shirt, unbuttoned, over her bikini. It made her look sexier than she had looked topless on the beach.

"After you left the apartment," she said to me, "Snappy or Sneezy or whichever of the Seven Dwarfs has you on retainer called from Toronto."

"Grumpy would be about right."

"Poppy?"

"That's George Bush," I said. "What did Swotty want?"

"For you to phone him straight back."

We went up the long flights of cement stairs that climbed majestically above Villefranche's harbour on the east side. At the top of the stairs, we walked along the back road to our corner of Pont Saint-Jean.

"Love your *chapeau*," I said to Annie.

"Three bucks at the supermarket in Beaulieu," she said, "and I bought a present for you."

"Something matching in straw?"

"A quart of Polish vodka."

"You found a liquor store?"

Annie shook her head. "Also at the supermarket," she said.

"Damn. Now that's my definition of a civilized society, Wyborowa alongside the Heinz and the Kraft."

I was behind Annie on the narrow stairs to our apartment. If the three young French bucks had had that perspective on Annie's figure, they'd have gone mad with lust. I was mature enough to control such passions.

"Which is first?" Annie asked. "Phone the guy in Toronto or pour the vodka?"

"I was thinking of jumping your bones."

"Be serious."

"I am," I said, "but in answer to your question, neither."

"Swotty sounded like he might have smoke coming out his ears. He's very upset and anxious for your call."

"I don't doubt it," I said, "and for the record, on your other point, you'll have noticed I have gone without Wyborowa for almost a week, and there hasn't been a whine out of me."

"The fresh supplies have arrived. What's holding you back?"

"Discipline is my middle name. I wish to carry out a job of work before taking my pleasure."

"Gosh, it's uplifting to stand close to such greatness."

I asked Annie to make a phone call I needed. It lasted longer than I expected, ten minutes of French. Annie sounded coquettish, unless that was just the effect of the language. When she hung up, she placed a second call. It lasted twenty seconds.

"Jamie Haddon's at the Beau Rivage in Nice," Annie said when she got off the phone.

"He's moved?"

"Sort of. That's what all the wheedling was about."

"I thought it sounded coquettish."

"The man on the other end of the first call was that pleasant concierge I spoke to last week at L'Hôtel de Paris. Haddon's keeping his suite there, but he's moved to the Beau Rivage for a few days and doesn't want the fact known. Those were his instructions to the concierge."

"How did you loosen his tongue?"

"He remembered me favourably from the last time. Then I threw in an extra persuader."

"What?"

"Said I was Jamie's secret and married amour."

"The spot is taken. But nice going, cookie."

"Haddon's definitely registered at the Beau Rivage. That was the second call."

I got the train schedule from the table in the front hall and set about deciphering it.

"Why visit Haddon?" Annie asked. She'd taken off the bikini and wrapped herself in a towel.

"Give the pot one final stir," I said.

I used my finger and tried to match up the names of the towns in the vertical column with the times of the trains in the horizontal column.

"Your brow is furrowing," Annie said.

"I like it that French trains run on time," I said. "I don't like it that I can't figure out what the hell the times are."

"You'll find there's one leaving Beaulieu for Nice in about fifteen minutes."

My finger stopped.

"Show me," I said to Annie.

She showed me.

"Oh yeah," I said, "the ever-reliable 16:05."

I had on tan cords, a shirt with thin stripes in olive and dark blue, and the Walkers.

"Think I'll pass muster at the Beau Rivage?" I asked Annie.

"Wear the snazzy jacket you bought last fall at that store on Queen," Annie said, "the navy blue."

I went into the bedroom and put on the navy blue jacket. Annie followed me in her towel.

"Fool that I am," Annie said, "may I express the hope this visit to Haddon is your last go-round with these people?"

"Almost home," I said. "Could you nudge along David Nestor while I'm gone? Ask if he'll please finish his mumbo-jumbo on the disk today or tomorrow."

"Sure."

I looked at myself in the hall mirror.

"Presentable?" I asked.

"Hey." Annie was standing in the bedroom doorway.

"Yeah?"

"You can jump my bones when you get back."

She let the towel fall.

CHAPTER TWENTY

I rang Jamie Haddon on the house phone. He said to wait for him downstairs.

The Beau Rivage was to L'Hôtel de Paris as Nice was to Monaco. No plumage, no excess. Its opulence was understated. I did my waiting in a sitting room off the small lobby which featured ribbed columns and glass cages. The predominant colour in carpet and furnishings was lilac grey. I sat in a Queen Anne chair. The room was empty except for me and a bellhop in a lilac grey uniform who subjected my person to stern glances. Maybe the jacket from the store on Queen Street wasn't doing its job.

Jamie was fifteen minutes getting from his room to me. He had on a black cotton turtleneck, black denim jeans with many pockets, and burgundy leather oxfords. Studiously casual. The bellhop greeted him with a slight bow of the head and went away. Jamie sat in a love seat that had vases of mimosa at each end. He wasn't wearing his nonchalant air.

"The stunned prick at the hotel won't do that again," he said.

"Which of your many hotels?"

"L'Hôtel de Paris. The concierge isn't supposed to tell anybody I'm down here."

"Ah, Jamie, don't blame the concierge. Poor chap was over-matched."

"Your girlfriend?"

I nodded.

Jamie said, "I just finished telling him on the phone his ass is in a sling if it happens one more time."

"Who are you hiding from?"

"Nobody." The grin was back on his face. "I just like to make things difficult."

"Pamela's in town," I said.

"Terrific." The grin stuck.

"With Archie."

"Even better."

"Close by," I said. "They're five minutes from here."

The Beau Rivage fronted on a little street called rue Saint-François de Paule, which ran past Nice's opera house in the direction of the old town. The back of the hotel was split into apartments and had a prospect across a wide avenue to the Mediterranean. Two or three blocks to the west, the avenue merged into Promenade des Anglais and led to the Negresco Hotel's doorstep.

Jamie said, "Pamela always stays at the Negresco." He gave the words a hoity-toity twist.

"I'd have thought it was more your speed too, more than the Beau Rivage."

Jamie held his hand out and wobbled it. "Variety, you know," he said.

"Yeah, the spice of life."

Annie had said Jamie wasn't forthcoming. That didn't get close to it. As a communicator, he might as well have been mute.

I said, "You're in deep shit, Jamie." Shock tactics.

"It's the other way around," Jamie said. "You don't know what you're talking about, Crang. I'm the one who's got other people in deep shit."

"Not if you're missing the disk."

"Well now, the disk. Jesus, Crang, you're so predictable. I already guessed you came here about the disk."

"It isn't in your safety deposit box in Toronto."

"You think I hadn't figured that out?" Jamie said. "The comedy act you two clowns put on the day we had the champagne?"

"Saw through it, huh?"

"Dan's got the disk. He's the only person who could have taken it from the deposit box. Or Rolland's got it. He might have conned Dan out of the thing."

"What makes you so sure I'm not holding it?"

"Have you discussed the disk with old Whetherhill?" Jamie asked. He had his legs crossed and he was swinging one foot in the air as he talked.

"No," I said.

"Or Pamela?"

"Nor Archie."

"Then you don't know what's on the disk," Jamie said. "If you did, you're the kind of guy who'd go running to the family."

"What kind of guy is that?"

"The honest kind."

"Now we're getting somewhere."

"Not really."

Jamie's swinging foot wasn't a nervous tic. It was a manifestation of arrogance. The way I was beginning to read Jamie, he was a natural-born show-off, the kind of guy who'd mail a lippy postcard to Swotty. Jamie probably figured he was invulnerable.

"Why aren't you hitting on Dan to get the disk back?" I asked him. "Or on Mike?"

"There's no rush."

"It's stolen property when you think about it. Stolen from you."

"Know something, Crang? You're a nosy bastard."

"I like curious better. Makes me sound more detached and scientific."

Jamie laced his hands behind his head and stared at the ceiling. His foot was still swinging. At the peak of its arc, the burgundy oxford came perilously near to clipping my kneecap.

"Okay," Jamie said. He'd finished his examination of the ceiling. "Dan's a nice guy, kind of an old maid sometimes, but I like him. The thing about him, though, he's a follower, not a leader, and the position he happens to be in right now, he can't afford to aggravate me."

"What if I said I thought you and Dan might've been, um, pretty tight at one time?"

"Pretty tight?" Jamie put some derision in the phrase. "I love it, Crang. What you're trying to say, you think Dan and I were lovers."

"Were you?"

"I'm bisexual. That plain enough for you?"

"Dan still seems kind of stuck on you, Jamie."

Jamie waved aside my comment. "Let's leave it. I swing both ways from time to time. Okay? A liberal-minded guy like you doesn't want to make anything out of that, right Crang?"

"Not me," I said. "But how about we get back to the disk? What if Mike Rolland's got it?"

"If he does, I'll buy him off. Either guy, Mike or Dan, I don't see myself losing any sleep."

"What beats me is why the hell you've been holding on to it? I mean, keeping something as potentially dangerous as the disk on hand?"

"You haven't asked me what's on it."

"I think I know the answer to that one."

Jamie laughed. "I doubt it. But the answer to your question is, for future reference. The reason I'm saving the disk, it may be a blueprint for something I might try down the line." Jamie's laugh wasn't long on mirth.

"Want me to tell you what I've doped out?" I asked him.

"About the program on the disk?"

"Among other of your criminal, quasi-criminal, and immoral deeds."

Jamie pulled back the sleeve of his turtleneck to look at his watch.

"This gonna take long?" he said.

Was it going to take long? Jeez, I was on the verge of explaining how and why I was convinced the man was a thief and homewrecker, and he wondered if he'd be running late for his next appointment.

"I'll condense as I go," I said.

"Okay. Why don't we have a drink? I've got fifteen minutes."

Jamie stood up from the love seat abruptly and walked out of the sitting room. I fell in two paces back. We went down the corridor to the right. Jamie's heels sounded like detonations on the marble floor. A man of authority. He wheeled left into a bar on the other side of the small lobby. The bar was subdued and tastefully furnished with dark wood. It made me want to check that my hair was combed, teeth flossed, deodorant functioning. We were the bar's only patrons.

"You'd be amazed at the house wine here," Jamie said as he sat down.

"I'll have it anyway."

The bartender brought the wine in crystal glasses. "Pouilly -Fuissé" Jamie said. "From a good year." Steal some money and turn into a wine connoisseur.

"Okay, shoot," Jamie said.

"You're a thief," I said. "About a three-million-dollar thief, I'd calculate. If you paid more than half a million for the Hatteras, you're probably holding at least five times that much for the blissful future you're savouring. The three mill came from Cayuga & Granark, and the information on the optical disk is the program, whatever the hell the term is, the record of how you engineered the theft."

"What did you say I'm doing about my future?"

"Savouring it."

"You got it," Jamie said. He turned in his chair and asked the bartender for a dish of nuts.

"No, no, Jamie." I shook my finger at him. "The true sophisticate doesn't sully his palate."

Jamie shrugged. "I like nuts." The bartender put down a silver bowl of almonds, macadamias, and cashews. Jamie picked out an almond. "Yeah," he said, "what else?"

"The theft isn't the best part of the story."

"Jesus, it sounded pretty great to me."

"No, the best part, the most interesting as far as drama goes, is the reason for the theft and the affair with Pamela."

"That's getting around?" Jamie looked pleased. "You heard talk about me and Pamela?"

"Come off it, Jamie. You started spreading the word yourself a month ago. That was the idea. Leak the news, make Pamela look bad, humiliate her. You initiated the affair. Now you're closing it down in the crudest way possible."

"Why would I do a thing like that?"

"Same reason you stole the money. To get even with the Whetherhill family."

Jamie popped a cashew in his mouth. "That's stupid," he said.

"It didn't make a hell of a lot of sense to me at first. As a motive, revenge seems like a classic case of cutting off your nose to spite your face. You get even with Swotty by stealing his money, messing up his daughter. But you're bound to be caught for the theft, maybe do time in prison. The trouble is, ridiculous as the explanation sounds, it's the only one that adds up."

"You haven't told me what it is I'm supposed to be getting even for."

"For what the Whetherhills did to your father, for the way —"

Jamie laughed. It was loud and sustained. A sneer I might have expected. A chuckle of scorn. But Jamie's laugh was the stuff of withering contempt. What had I said that set him off?

"You kill me, Crang," Jamie said. His laughing fit wound down. He took a drink of wine. "You really kill me."

I waited for Jamie to tell me why I killed him.

"You met my old man?" he asked me.

"I talked to him once or twice in the old days."

RIVIERA BLUES | 161

"When you were married to Pamela, right," Jamie said. "So you might remember he isn't exactly a rocket scientist."

"Indelicate as it may seem to say so, I think that's at the basis of my analysis."

"Like shit it is. The reason is, you're leaving something out."

"What've I left out?"

"Or maybe a hotshot criminal lawyer like you didn't happen to notice," Jamie said. "Sure, my father's in a dumb-ass job. The Whetherhills stuck him in it. I know that. You know it. Everybody knows it. But here's a fact you don't know, Crang. My father likes the job. He doesn't even recognize it's a shit job. He thinks he's doing important work for the company. The fucking trust company. And you want to hear something else? My dumb father, the guy who gets royally dumped on by the goddamned Whetherhills, he's actually happy."

"Your father isn't bitter?"

"The way he looks at it, it's a fucking honour to work for C&G."

"So, ah, you aren't nursing a grudge on your dad's behalf?"

"Don't be a jerk, Crang."

My revenge theory seemed to be out the window. Also in tatters and blown to the four winds. I busied myself with my glass of wine. Anything to gain a little thinking time. Across the table, Jamie wore a grin that set new records for disdain. I was wrong. Jamie hadn't been compelled by the desire to settle scores. But I was convinced that the rest of my analysis held up, that Jamie had stolen from C&G and had pulled a foul trick on Pamela.

"Who sent you to talk to me?" Jamie asked.

"Don't I get credit for personal initiative?"

"Pamela," Jamie said. "Yeah, you're sticking up for her."

He laughed again, short and sardonic. "Sure as hell it wouldn't be Whetherhill. You should've heard the stuff he said about you after the marriage broke up. Made what he called my old man sound like a compliment."

Control of the conversation had passed to Jamie.

"Swotty's a hard man," I said.

Maybe it was preferable to leave control with Jamie. Maybe he'd drop something that would get me back on the beam.

"Lucky for you you're out of the marriage, Crang. That's the truth." Jamie was looking at me over the top of his wineglass. His leg had gone into its bounce. "Pamela's a slut —"

"Hey, listen —"

"No. You listen. She's a slut. And I'll tell you what her father is. Whetherhill's bent out of shape. He's crooked. Pillar of the fucking financial community, my ass. The guy's about as upright as Ivan Boesky."

"Swotty? I can't —"

"I'm not finished." The formerly unforthcoming Jamie was on a communication jag. "These people, Pamela, the old man especially, you know what they did to me all those years? You really know, Crang?"

"Gave you an education?"

"That was shit."

"Well, I don't know, Ridley College is supposed to work wonders for a lad."

"They fucking patronized me."

In the small, empty bar, the sentence was as concussive as a shot.

"Patted me on the head," Jamie said. "Said they knew what was best. Told me one day I'd be on the thirty-second floor. Jesus, Crang, they thought I'd sit still for that?"

"The system seems to have worked for them."

"Them! That's what I'm talking about, man. Who are them? One of them is a bitch with round heels. And the other is the biggest goddamned hypocrite in the history of Canadian business."

"Well, allowing for a dash of hyperbole, Jamie, maybe you'd like to give me the particulars of Swotty's hypocrisy."

Jamie rolled back his sleeve again. His watch was a Patek Philippe.

I said, "Of his crookedness too."

"I gotta go." Jamie put his wineglass on the table. "Date with a beautiful mademoiselle," he said. He had pasted his grin back on.

"Not just when the story's reaching the juicy part," I said.

Jamie stood up.

I said, "Why don't I buy us another round of the Pouilly-Fuissé?"

Jamie brushed a stray fragment of cashew from his black turtleneck.

I said, "I'll even spring for one for the beautiful *mademoiselle*."

"I stole three million?" Jamie said. "Don't be a dickhead, Crang."

Jamie strode out of the bar. I could hear his heels on the marble floor of the main corridor, hitting with the force of little gunshots.

CHAPTER TWENTY-ONE

Annie said not to pour myself a Wyborowa.

"David Nestor's waiting for you this minute," she said. "The disk doctor."

"He's finished work on it?"

"Sounds like the work's finished him."

I hadn't even sat down. Annie was lying on the fat stuffed sofa in the living room. She had a paperback book closed on her finger to mark the page. The book's title was *Two Weeks in the Midday Sun*.

"The professor's excited about what he got off the disk?" I asked.

"He's cross. Mad as a wet hen. And the unmistakable message he conveyed on the phone is that the man he's cross at is you, with some residual animosity for me on account of I introduced you to him."

"Just what I need, another meeting where I'm on the end of a chewing out."

"Jamie Haddon was rude to you?"

"He was outspoken, believe it or not," I said. "What's the book?"

Annie held it higher. "It's sort of a diary Roger Ebert kept in Cannes when he was covering the 1987 festival."

"Ah, boning up."

"And starting to go about crazy in anticipation." Annie pulled herself to a sitting position on the sofa. "You'd better step on it, fella. Nestor's at the Café des Nations. It was fifteen minutes ago he had his temper tantrum on the phone. I told him you'd just about certainly come home on the 17:40 train."

"On the money, babe.... But why does it have to be the Café des Nations, wherever it is?"

"In Beaulieu, across from the supermarket. Because he refuses to be seen entering this apartment or to have you be seen at his."

"Seen by whom?"

"I just look after the quotes around here, and that one's verbatim."

"Well, keep the vodka chilled," I said.

The sign across the front of the Café des Nations claimed that it had opened its doors in 1897. On the sidewalk under the sign there were four or five arrangements of chipped metal tables and chairs. They could have been circa 1897. I didn't see anyone at the tables who looked like David Nestor, pudgy and under the legal drinking age. The legal drinking age in France was probably twelve and a half anyway.

I went into the cafe. The bar started immediately inside the door on the right and ran most of the length of the smallish room. The bar was zinc and unostentatious, a surface for resting glasses between drinks. More chipped metal tables lined the wall on the left. Overhead a big fan revolved in slow motion, leaving the thick cigarette smoke undisturbed. The customers were mostly men who had the blue work uniforms and browned faces of manual labourers. The house wine at the Café des Nations wouldn't be Pouilly-Fuissé.

David Nestor was the only drinker with a table all to himself. It was the end table in the row on the left. Nestor also seemed to be the only drinker drinking coffee.

I sat at the table. "Is it the down-to-earth quality you like here, Professor, compared to the groves of academe?"

"This is the first time I have been in the place, Mr. Crang, and the last," Nestor said. He was trying to sound angry. It came out prissy. "That was the point of meeting you where no one knows me. As I tried to make plain to Miss Cooke, I want the least possible connection with you and the disreputable contents of your disk."

"How disreputable?"

"Don't play dumb with me, Mr. Crang. Criminally disreputable."

Even in petulance, Nestor's chubby face didn't show a line or wrinkle. His eyes were small, as if tiny buttons had been pressed into the flesh. His hair was straw-coloured, thinning, and combed flat on his scalp. It was like sitting at a table with the Pillsbury Doughboy.

"Obviously," Nestor said, "what has occurred is that someone has diverted funds from a second party to his own use."

"You can tell that from what's on the disk?"

From the expression on Nestor's face, I might have asked about the Pope being Catholic.

"All right, Professor," I said, "I'm presuming on your good nature. There were strong indications to me that the disk's owner had been up to a piece of flimflam. I'll confess to that. But I have nothing on how or how much the man stole."

"I prefer 'divert.'"

"And I'll respect your preference," I said. "How much did he divert?"

"Twenty-three million dollars."

"Hey, I nailed the figure exac — how much?"

"Twenty-three million."

"Not three?"

"Twenty-three million."

"Oh my goodness."

I didn't register that the bartender had come out from behind the bar and was standing at our table.

"M'sieur?" he said to me.

My eyes took in the bartender's presence, but my mind was stalled back at the twenty-three million dollars.

"M'sieur?" the bartender repeated. He was a muscular Latin type and had a chunky gold chain showing through the unbuttoned top of his shirt.

"What do you want, Mr. Crang?" Nestor asked impatiently. "Beer? A glass of wine?"

"Something stronger."

"Le monsieur désire une boisson forte," Nestor said to the bartender. *"Ah, oui. Un pastis?"*

"If it's got a jolt, I'll try it," I said. *"Oui, un pastis."*

The bartender left to pour my drink. Nestor drew a newspaper from below the table. It was folded around a plain brown envelope. The newspaper was *Nice Matin*.

"I want these off my hands, Mr. Crang." Nestor shoved the *Nice Matin* across the table. "The optical disk is in the envelope with a printout of what is on it. And I assure you, this is the only print-out I made."

Nestor started to rise from his chair.

"Not yet, Professor," I said, "I need some interpretation. How do I account for the twenty-three million? Come on, let's kiss and make up."

"The printout is perfectly clear on how the diversion was managed."

"But I don't know a modem from first base," I said. "You're the expert."

Nestor hung in the air, half in and half out of his chair.

"Word has it," I said, "where computers are concerned, you're in the genius division."

Nestor was wavering.

I said, "Who else has the erudition plus the pedagogical talent to explain the workings of the disk to a bumpkin like me?"

Nestor's rump dropped back on the chair. "It was actually a rather ingenious piece of interception," he said.

The bartender put a small, thin glass and a pitcher of water in front of me. The glass held one ice cube and a pale green liquid. I poured water into the glass. Its contents swirled in little clouds, like something inside a beaker from the laboratory of Count Dracula. I took a swallow.

"Anything happening to me on the outside?" I asked Nestor. "Fangs sprouting? Other weird growths?"

"What are you talking about?"

"Never mind," I said. I had another sip. "This stuff tastes like licorice."

"That's what everybody says," Nestor said.

"Then we should move to more original topics," I said. "The diversion."

"Yes," Nestor said. He sounded instantly professorial. "It took only three minutes and thirty-seven seconds —"

"How do you know?"

"There is a timing device on the disk," Nestor said. "Well, then, the diversion began at exactly eleven o'clock on the morning of March fourteenth —"

"Amazing."

"What is?"

"That you have all this exact data."

"Mr. Crang, I haven't got near to describing anything remotely amazing as yet." Nestor laid his plump forearms on the table. He gave me a schoolmarmish look. "Furthermore, if you expect me to continue, you will have to stop interrupting."

"Promise," I said. "I'm all ears and no mouth."

"Very well." Nestor unpursed his lips. "The money came from the account of a company called ErnMax, the twenty-three million dollars. At the time I'm speaking of, March fourteenth at eleven a.m., a transfer was taking place. You will have heard of Cayuga & Granark, I suppose, the trust company. Well, they had the twenty-three million in an account at their Toronto office. They were moving it by computer to another account in a Swiss bank. In Zurich, as a matter of fact, but that isn't entirely relevant because the money didn't get there. The person who made the diversion tapped into the Cayuga & Granark computer precisely at the moment of the transfer of ErnMax's twenty-three million."

"You can call him Jamie," I said. "Less troublesome than repeating 'the person who made the diversion' each time."

"Yes, all right." Nestor didn't appear to mind the interruption. "Well, this is the stage where it becomes quite clever on the part of, ah, Mr. Jamie. You see, no one could simply break into the ErnMax account. There were safeguards in the form of entry codes. I'm keeping this very simple, Mr. Crang, but basically ErnMax had four entry codes. They were changed at regular intervals. Two codes were new each day, the other two each week. You follow me?"

I nodded.

Nestor went on. "And before anyone could access the account, he would have to know the entry codes for that particular day and that particular week."

"Which the man we're calling Jamie, mostly because that's his name, knew."

Nestor smiled. "No, he did not." The smile was owlish. It added ten years to Nestor's face. "Mr. Jamie knew the first three entry codes. That's clear from the material on the disk. He didn't know the fourth code. And this is where I give him high marks as a programmer. He used his knowledge of the first three codes to run through all possibilities until he arrived at the correct fourth code. And he managed it in three minutes and thirty-seven seconds. Very impressive piece of work."

"But morally reprehensible."

"Oh, of course. I was only speaking of technique."

"Understood," I said. "What was Jamie's move after he cracked the code?"

"He diverted the twenty-three million dollars to a numbered account at the Banco di Napoli in Monaco."

I took a long swallow of pastis.

"Whew," I said.

"Quite," Nestor said.

A man standing at the bar was staring at me. He had bushy black hair and a heavy drinker's flush. He was wearing a sweater that had Pittsburgh Boomers spelled across the front. The sweater rode over a bulging gut. Pittsburgh Boomers? Pittsburgh had the Pirates, the Penguins, and the Steelers. No Boomers. The French love sweaters and T-shirts with American sports logos, but they keep getting the names wrong. French jeans don't fit right either. The guy was still staring.

"But," I said to David Nestor, "wouldn't someone on Cayuga & Granark's computer take notice that funny things were happening to the ErnMax account?"

"Well, right now, of course, I'm sure the trust company and the ErnMax people are aware that the Zurich account doesn't record a twenty-three-million-dollar deposit."

"That wasn't my question," I said. "I'm talking about the three minutes and thirty-seven seconds of diversion on March fourteenth. During that period, could there have been a tipoff to Cayuga & Granark? Some sign that the Zurich transfer wasn't proceeding according to plan?"

"Oh, definitely. When the Mr. Jamie person made his interception, there would be a very perceptible voltage drop in the Cayuga & Granark computer. That would be enough to warn the operators of the unauthorized entry."

"Then what are we missing?"

"Missing?"

"Jamie got his hands and his computer on the twenty-three million. But I'm certain C&G doesn't yet know as much about the diversion, or where the money's gone, as you and I sitting here on the Côte d'Azur know."

"Hmm, yes. Well, there might have been a way of concealing the interception. But I can't think how."

"Maybe I can."

The guy in the Pittsburgh Boomers sweater had his hand on the bartender's shoulder. His other hand was pointing in my direction. The bartender shook his head, as if to say that, as far as he was concerned, I was a stranger in these parts. That didn't stop the Boomer from continuing his vigil on me.

"Suppose," I said to Nestor, "a breakdown happened at C&G's computer at eleven o'clock on March fourteenth."

Nestor started to answer. I stopped him. I hadn't got the memory straight in my head. What had Trum Fraser said when we had lunch at Coaster's? The company's computer had gone on the fritz. The crisis had lasted a few minutes before order was restored. The date of the breakdown seemed to me about right, two or three weeks before Trum and I had had lunch, which would place the computer trouble close to March fourteenth.

"Yeah," I said to Nestor. "Theorize with this, Professor. C&G's computer malfunctioned, and Jamie made his entry simultaneously."

"The computer was down?"

"Whatever term you people use."

"Well, a large corporation such as Cayuga & Granark protects itself against all eventualities. If the main computer went down, a backup would take over."

"But there's a transition period from the main to the backup?"

Nestor's owlish smile spread across his face. "Yes, I see what you're getting at," he said. "That's very shrewd."

"Not of me. Of Jamie."

"When the backup computer was taking over, during that short period, it wouldn't be possible for the operators at Cayuga & Granark to record the drop in voltage."

"Or to record the fact of the diversion? "

"The diversion would in effect be masked," Nestor said. There was a note of admiration in his voice. "An arrangement like that would require impeccable timing."

"That's been a specialty of Jamie's," I said. "So far."

There was a telephone next to a video game at the end of the bar. No one was playing the video game, but someone was making a phone call. The Pittsburgh Boomer was talking rapidly into the mouthpiece.

I said to Nestor, "So we can assume that C&G's computer people were oblivious to the diversion during the three minutes Jamie tapped in."

"And thirty-seven seconds."

"Them too."

"As I say, the coordination ..."

"Would have to be perfect," I said. "Sure. Let's give Jamie perfection right down the line, just for the sake of our theory. My next question is this, would the C&G computer itself, either the main one or the backup, record the diversion even if the operators didn't notice it?"

Nestor needed time to think about the question. He made faint humming noises as he thought. His gaze floated somewhere over my right shoulder.

"No," he said. His eyes focussed back on me. "In all probability, given a transfer between computers at the same time as Mr. Jamie's interception, the diversion wouldn't show up on the trust company computers."

I patted the copy of *Nice Matin* that was folded around the brown envelope. "It seems to me we've got an exclusive in here," I said.

"If you mean Mr. Jamie's disk is the only record of the diversion," Nestor said, "that appears to be true."

"Jamie is his first name."

"Oh."

"And I won't burden you with his last name."

"Thank you." Nestor nudged the *Nice Matin* closer to my side of the table. "You know, Mr. Crang," he said, "your, um, theory is intriguing. But it leaves unanswered questions."

"Well, yeah, a loose end here and there probably needs tying up."

"Much more than a loose end. For instance, how was Jamie certain that the trust company's main computer would go down when it did, at exactly eleven o'clock on March fourteenth?"

"He couldn't induce the breakdown from his computer at home?"

"Hardly."

"Let's see," I said. How had Trum Fraser put it? Some kind of massive short circuit? "How does this strike you, Professor?" I said to Nestor. "A short circuit in the computer?"

Nestor got a pitying look on his face.

"On a really large scale?" I tried.

Nestor shook his head. "And don't tell me about an act of God either," he said.

"You got any ideas?" I asked.

"Oh, it's patently clear." Nestor sounded superior. "Your Jamie had assistance. Someone else downloaded the system just before Jamie made his entry."

"Downloaded? That means putting the main computer out of operation?"

"Roughly."

"Okay," I said. "Jamie and a confederate synchronized their watches. At a couple of minutes before eleven on the morning of the fourteenth, the confederate commenced sabotage on the main computer. Two minutes later, Jamie tapped in."

Nestor nodded in a way that conveyed wisdom. "That's the scenario I had in mind," he said.

"Could the computer be sabotaged in two minutes?"

"Downloaded?" Nestor raised his eyebrows. "Probably in less than two minutes. But you would have to find the confederate and ask him."

"I will."

"You know who the confederate is?"

"I've got a choice suspect."

"Really?" Nestor considered that for a moment. "Well," he said, "I think you've probably told me enough, Mr. Crang, especially about personalities."

I smiled charmingly at Nestor. He smiled back owlishly.

"How about a drink, Professor?" I asked. "Celebrate the evening's accomplishments."

"That might be nice. A Perrier for me, please."

I looked up for the bartender. The guy in the Pittsburgh Boomers sweater had his back to me. He was offering a glad hand to a man who had just come through the door. I recognized the newcomer. He was the junior of *les frères Clutch*, Emile the Stove.

CHAPTER TWENTY-TWO

If it was possible for a man with the contours of a kitchen appliance to look natty, Emile Clutch pulled off the feat. He had on a three-button single-breasted glen-plaid jacket, a white shirt with French cuffs, a wine-red tie in a Windsor knot, and grey herringbone trousers. Mike Rolland must have put Emile on a generous clothing allowance.

But money couldn't spruce up Emile's face. It was broad and flat and battered. The features were crammed towards the centre, leaving vast areas of forehead and jaw. His eyes had the warmth of two stones.

"Professor," I said to Nestor, "I don't want you to panic."

"Do I have reason to?" he asked quickly. He was panicking.

"Someone has come into the cafe who isn't altogether friendly to me and my good works."

"He wants the optical disk?" Nestor slapped both hands on the table. "This is exactly the sort of trouble I wanted to avoid."

"I think what happened is Mike Rolland —"

"Don't mention names."

"— Mr. X did the French equivalent of putting my description on the street, and Pittsburgh Boomer over there got lucky."

Nestor started to turn his head toward the bar.

"Don't turn around, Professor," I said. "Keep your eyes on me. That's right. Pretend we're a couple of guys having a time on the town."

Nestor pulled back his lips in a nervous rictus.

"I meant having a good time, Professor," I said.

The Stove stood at the bar with a beer at his elbow. The Pittsburgh Boomer hovered at his side. Boomer's eyes kept spinning my way. He looked tickled pink. The Stove contented himself with occasional glances along the row of tables.

"Why can't I just walk out of here?" Nestor asked. His voice was plaintive. "You deal on your own with the robbers or whoever they may be." The brief spell of kinship Nestor felt toward me had evaporated.

"Emile may —"

"No names."

"The man at the bar may have reinforcements outside," I said.

Nestor slumped in his chair.

"If you'll allow me a moment's reflection, Professor," I said, "I'll brainstorm us a scheme to get out of here."

Nestor seemed on the brink of collapse.

"With the disk of course," I said.

Another man came into the cafe. It was hard to miss his entrance. He had a smile of thousand-watt voltage, and he was dressed in clothes of many colours. All the colours were electric. He had on a brilliant blue warmup suit, white Nikes with purple stripes, and a yellow and black Hamilton Tigercat football jacket. Over his shoulder, he held a small duffle bag in shades of maroon and gold. The bag carried McMaster University's name and crest. If this flamboyant fellow was French, I was Albert Camus.

The man slapped backs and shook hands all the way down the bar. He had handsome features, curly brown hair, a wide build, and a carrying laugh. He gave Pittsburgh Boomer a fraternal pat on the shoulder. He leaned across the bar for a cheery word with the bartender. He accepted a glass of beer and he steered himself to the table where I sat with the gloomy professor. Nestor, head down, didn't see him coming.

"Hey, Dave," the man cheered at the back of Nestor's head. "Never seen you before in this den of iniquity."

Nestor jerked around.

"Oh, hello, Jake." Nestor's voice was flat.

Jake switched his beaming smile to me. "The last name's Finney," he said. He gave my hand a pump worthy of a long-lost frat brother. "I haven't seen you in here either," he said.

"My first time, same as the Professor here," I said. I told Jake my name. "I'm new on the Côte d'Azur."

Nestor stirred from his funk. "Jake is a colleague of mine," he said to me, "in the English department."

"Hell," Jake barked, "I am the English department."

"Nice place to teach," I said, "if you have to teach."

"Better believe it." Jake's wide body was blocking my view of the Stove at the bar. "Tell you how good it is, I haven't missed a day of tennis since November."

"Right there, Jake, you got me jealous," I said. Even if I couldn't see the Stove, I knew he wasn't budging.

"You're a player, Crang?" Jake said. "Listen, I always need guys for a couple of sets. I've got an extra racquet. You want to take me on, name any day."

"Sorry," I said, "my friend and I are moving along to Cannes tomorrow."

"For the film festival?" Jake looked impressed. "We had a gal up at the university the other day talking about it."

"My friend is the gal."

"No kidding." Jake was noisily delighted. "I sat in on her seminar. Tell her I'm a fan."

"Of hers? Or of movies?"

"I'll put it this way, Crang, you're a lucky man. But movies, if you and she got time, I always keep a stock of videos at my place."

"That's nice, Jake, but —"

"Right now, if you want to come over, I got, let's see, *War and Peace*. That's the Henry Fonda one, not the ten-hour Russian deal.

I got *Sweet Smell of Success*, best movie Tony Curtis ever made ..."

Jake waxed on. He stood by the table, bouncing enthusiastically on the balls of his feet, beer in hand, the other hand describing eager little circles in the air. He remained in a direct line between me and Emile Clutch. Jake's McMaster duffel bag, full and bulging, swung back and forth from his left shoulder. He talked and bounced, and the shoulder bag swung, and an idea crawled to the surface of my brain.

"The fifth movie I got right now," Jake was saying, "kind of a minor epic, very minor, you know what I mean, it's the 1955 *Ulysses*, the one Kirk Douglas is in, and Silvana Mangano."

"Jake," I said, "speaking of movies, this may sound forward of me, audacious even ... but perhaps you might do me a favour."

Nestor came to life in his chair. "Don't pay attention to this man, Jake," he said to Finney. "Don't even think about it. Crang is a very dangerous person."

"Dangerous?" Jake's perpetual smile stretched another inch. "Now you've really got me interested," he said to me. "Give me more of this audacious stuff."

"The movie I have in mind," I said, "is maybe more along the lines of *The Third Man*."

"Absolute work of genius," Jake said. "Carol Reed, I love his movies, honest to God. That one, *Third Man*, it had Orson Welles, Joseph Cotten, the lovely actress Valli.... Who else?"

"Trevor Howard and Wilfrid Hyde-White," I said. "Okay, Jake, don't look around, there's a guy at the bar who wants something I have in my possession."

Jake didn't look around. Nestor did.

"Professor," I said, "I wish you wouldn't do that."

"Jake," Nestor snapped at Finney, "it's only my duty to someone I'm associated with to say you're putting yourself in jeopardy if you agree with whatever Crang asks of you."

"You've probably never seen *The Third Man*, am I right, Dave?" Jake asked him.

"No, but that has nothing to do with real life," Nestor said.

"See the movie first, Dave," Jake said. "Then we'll discuss real life."

Jake turned to me.

"The guy I'm talking about," I said to him, "is the party behind you who has the very low centre of gravity."

"I noticed him," Jake said. "With my pal who wears clothes from teams that don't exist."

"What is it with the sweaters?"

"He's got one for Los Angeles Lakers University," Jake said. "He keeps telling me his son is gonna head over there and study surfing."

"Anyway," I said, "the other guy with the face like he just swallowed a quart of vinegar, he's my problem. I'm holding these two items inside the brown envelope that the *Nice Matin*'s hiding on the table here. I want to smuggle the two items out of the cafe without the guy at the bar seeing the act of smuggling."

"So I'm the smuggler," Jake said. His expression was almost radiant. "I love it." He put down his empty beer glass on the table. "Here's how we do it," he said. His voice was low and conspiratorial.

"Hold on a minute, Jake," I said. "This is my play."

"Let me," Jake said. "I've seen it done a hundred times."

"What? In the movies?"

"Where else does anybody learn this kind of stuff?"

"You're probably right, but —"

Jake had the manner of a man with no time for quibbling over small matters of detail.

"'Kay," he said. He was tilting closer to me. "Can your man see what I'm doing?"

"No," I said. "You're shielding the table from him. Besides, you aren't doing anything."

"Now I am."

Jake switched the McMaster University bag from his shoulder around to his chest. He pulled back the zipper that ran down the bag's centre. A copy of *Sports Illustrated* sat on top of a white tennis sweater. Jake spread the magazine in front of me, open to an article about Mario Lemieux.

"What you do, Crang," Jake said to me, "you look real interested in the magazine, like I'm showing you something you're dying to read." Jake spoke as if he were Alfred Hitchcock coaching an actor whose talent he doubted. "Try to feel involved in the words on the page there.... Okay, without taking your eyes off the page, reach into the *Nice Matin* ..."

I followed Jake's directions. My hand fumbled at the newspaper.

"Relax into it, Crang," Jake said. His voice was trying for a soothing effect. My hand got a grip on the brown envelope, my head stayed over the *Sports Illustrated*. "Very nice," Jake said. "You're really getting into the part, Crang.... Now, slide the stuff out of the envelope over to me.... Not that slowly. Let's get this thing done in one take, know what I mean?"

Under Jake's coaxing, I slipped the disk and the printout to the table's edge. In one continuous motion, Jake accepted delivery of both. He folded them into the duffel bag on top of the white tennis sweater. I continued to act engrossed in the Mario Lemieux article. It speculated on the possibility of Mario scoring one hundred and fifty goals in a single season.

"You're not done," Jake said to me.

"The disk and printout are in your bag."

"What about the brown envelope?"

"What about it?" My eyes were still fixed on the Lemieux piece. I didn't give a fat hooray whether he scored fifteen hundred goals in a single season.

Jake said to me, "You shouldn't walk out of here with the envelope empty. Suppose the guy at the bar already saw it had something in it?"

"The *Sports Illustrated*?"

"I haven't finished reading it."

"Ah, *Nice Matin*."

"Atta boy."

I was improving at the surreptitious moves. I stuffed the newspaper into the brown envelope. The envelope bunched up as if it still held the optical disk and computer printout.

"Very professional," Jake said. "That'll be a wrap."

He took back the *Sports Illustrated*. There wasn't much room left in the duffel bag. But Jake squeezed the magazine on top of the disk and paper. He zipped the bag shut.

"Let me ask your opinion, Crang," he said. "Who do you see playing me?"

"Pardon?"

"If what we're doing is made into a movie, what actor'd take my role?"

"The old casting game, I get it," I said. I gave the matter some thought. "Van Heflin."

"Really?" It was Jake's turn for deep thinking.

"You know the Heflin type," I said, "decent but courageous without calling attention to himself."

Jake looked down at his brilliant blue warmup suit and his Hamilton Tigercat windbreaker. "I'd have to speak to the wardrobe department about different clothes," he said.

"Something more self-effacing," I said.

"Right." Jake retrieved his beer glass from the table. "Okay, Crang, you want me to hold the stuff in the bag at my place?" he asked me.

"It may be a few days."

Jake told me his address. He lived in an apartment building a few blocks west of the Café des Nations.

"'Kay, luck to you fellas," Jake said. His delivery seemed a trifle stagey to me, but it probably came across as typical Finney heartiness to the regulars in the cafe. "*Au 'voir*, guys," Jake barked.

He returned his beer glass to the bartender. It took him another five minutes to work the room. It was *bonsoir* to one guy, *ça va*? to another, an *au 'voir* here, a kiss on the cheek there. The kiss was for a toothless crone who looked about Madame Defarge's age. Then Jake was out the door with the disk and printout.

"Is he always like that?" I asked Nestor.

"Jake is quite outgoing," Nestor said, "if that's what you're getting at."

"Roughly."

Emile Clutch was still holding down a piece of the bar, nursing a beer and eyeballing me.

"Now what do you intend?" Nestor asked me. His question mixed sarcasm and resignation.

"Well, Professor, let's face the music."

Nestor groaned …

"And dance."

CHAPTER TWENTY-THREE

There wasn't a back way out of the Café des Nations. That cut the options to a precious one. I told David Nestor we would walk out the cafe's front door, me carrying the brown envelope, then we'd run like hell.

The first phase of the plan proceeded flawlessly. We walked to the door. Nestor looked like he might swoon at any moment, but he succeeded in getting one foot in front of the other. We stepped onto the small patio outside the front door.

"To the left —" I said to Nestor. And got no further.

From behind, Emile Clutch latched on to my left bicep. His grip was so determined that I developed an instant case of pins and needles in my lower arm. Pittsburgh Boomer's hand rested on David Nestor's neck. It was nothing like a stranglehold. It didn't need to be. Nestor's head hung down in despair and surrender.

Emile and Boomer quick-marched us to an alley that ran along the west side of the cafe. Mike Rolland was leaning against a car parked a few yards down the alley. The car was the Japanese Jeep I'd seen in the driveway at Villa Pomme. Georges Clutch stood to Mike's left doing fierce things with his eyes and mouth. Georges's face was conspicuous for the shining white bandage that covered most of his nose.

"Hey, fellas," I said, "together again."

Georges Clutch eliminated the space between him and me in four purposeful strides. Georges strode, and Emile's hand dug deeper into my arm. I was locked in the Stove's grip. Georges hit me in the stomach.

It was a punch worthy of Sugar Ray Leonard. It travelled no more than fifteen inches, and it struck me precisely in the solar plexus. Air hissed out of me. I couldn't breathe.

Emile let go of my arm. I sank in slow motion to my knees in the dirt and grit of the alley. My hands clawed at my stomach. Behind my eyes, black and red dots whirled.

Georges leaned over me. He was close enough for the longer bristles of his beard to scratch against my cheek. Georges's lips formed a grin. His teeth were brown stumps. He broke into a cackle. The breath that his laugh released from between the brown stumps was almost worse punishment than the punch. Georges's halitosis put him in a class with the *chien mechant* I had had the tussle with on the sea walk. I wanted to gag, but I couldn't muster enough air to make my throat function.

Georges straightened up. He put his hands on his belt and gave his trousers a hitch. Georges wasn't the fashion plate his brother was. His pants needed a press, and his shoes needed a shine. I knelt in the dirt, my lungs screaming for oxygen. Georges balanced himself on one unpolished shoe and pulled back the other. The son of a bitch was winding up to plant the shoe's heel in my face.

"*Non, non.*" Mike Rolland spoke unhurriedly from somewhere above me. "*Peut-être plus tard, Georges.*"

Georges returned his kicking shoe to the ground.

"Like you say, Crang, together again." Mike squatted beside me, his face as near to mine as Georges' had been. Mike passed the breath test. His smelled of alcohol with a mouthwash overlay. "Except I think you are not happy to see us, for sure," Mike said.

I could feel life begin to stir in my chest.

"Thanks for calling off Georges," I said. My voice sounded like a female impersonator doing Marlene Dietrich.

"What you have caused to Georges's nose, Crang," Mike said, "I think he is not finished with you."

I paused before I answered. Partly the delay was a matter of collecting sufficient wind to speak again. Partly it was a piece of fakery while I considered a way out of this predicament.

"We still best friends, Mike?" I wheezed.

I pushed myself off the floor of the alley. The little circles continued to spin in my head. And my legs felt like they could use some glue. Otherwise I seemed to be regaining health.

"I got the questions for you, Crang." Mike sounded combative. "You answer, okay, for sure we be best friends."

There was something different about Mike, apart from the hostility. It was his clothes. They featured a colour other than silver white. He had on a leather ensemble, pants and a windbreaker in sea-green. Maybe they were his battle fatigues. Mike stood aggressively close, his forehead to my chin. Ranged behind him, the Clutch brothers, Pittsburgh Boomer, and David Nestor waited for Mike's questions and my answers. Nestor's jaw was slack.

"Fire away, Mike," I said. The words came out with the normal amount of air.

"Who is this guy?" Mike asked. His thumb jerked over his shoulder at Nestor.

"The Professor is no threat to you, Mike," I said. "No help to you either. He's just a teacher at the Canadian university."

"Another Canadian?" Mike turned and gave Nestor an inspection. Maybe Nestor's nationality struck Mike as one too many coincidences. "What you teach, you other Canadian?" he asked Nestor.

"Zoology," I answered before Nestor could blunder into a reply that might blow the ball game.

Mike turned back to me. "Zoology?"

"Cutting up frogs, Mike," I said. "The study of animal life. You'd be a natural for the Professor's course."

Mike said something to Emile in French. The Stove spun Nestor around, braced Nestor's legs against the far wall of the alley, and kicked them apart. Emile showed a lot of expertise in his search of Nestor's clothes and person. His hands patted and poked every fold and crease and pocket. He finished and shook his head at Mike.

"Told you so, Mike," I said. "The Professor has nothing to hide. And neither do I."

Mike nodded Emile over to me. The Stove did his patting down with a shade more force than was called for. He probably resented coming up empty again. The brown envelope lay at my feet where I'd dropped it during the one-punch TKO I lost to Georges. Emile picked it up. *Nice Matin* fell out.

"Convinced, Mike?" I said.

"Crang." Mike had his barrel chest thrust forward. "Two times you take the disk from me."

"Now, Mike, let's be accurate," I said. I was feeling frisky enough to bend over and brush at the dust on the knees of my jeans. "The first time, at Jamie's apartment, the disk was up for grabs."

"I am getting very angry with you, Crang," Mike said. He looked very angry. "Where is this fucking disk?"

"It's, ah, with my client."

"Who is your fucking client?"

"Jamie," I said. "Jamie Haddon."

"What the fuck —"

"That's right, Mike," I said. My delivery was smooth and confiding, bordering on unctuous. "Jamie retained me by telephone from Monaco ten days ago to recover the disk from his apartment in Toronto. You're aware that Dante Renzi had appropriated it?"

"I know that already."

"Or, rather, misappropriated it."

"Crang, you trying to tell me —"

"And, of course, Mike, you have been apprised of the disk's contents?"

The expression on Mike's face was of intense exasperation. "Why the hell you think I am looking every place for the goddamn disk?" he said. I was cheered by Mike's exasperation. It deflected him from the more immediate emotion of anger at me. "Because I want to know what is on it, you dumb bastard," Mike said.

"On the disk, Mike," I said, "is a foolproof scheme Jamie has devised for redirecting several millions in Canadian funds from a financial institution in Toronto to a bank in Monaco."

"Yes? For sure?" Mike said. My mixture of fact and fiction seemed to be hooking Mike.

"This is a transaction without the potential for failure, Mike," I went on.

"On the disk this is?"

"It contains the blueprint for the scheme," I said. "Down to the most exacting detail. You can understand why I was required to take certain, um, drastic measures."

"And you give the disk back to Jamie, my friend Crang?"

"Gratifying to be back on the footing of pals with you, Mike," I said. "Yes, my duty to my client required that I return the disk to its rightful owner."

"Okay, so where is Jamie now?"

"Well, Mike, as I say, my duty —"

Mike motioned Georges to step forward.

"But," I said, "I can see my way clear to making an exception in your case. Jamie has rooms at the Beau Rivage in Nice."

"He is there with the disk?"

"Please don't reveal the origin of your knowledge," I said. "A favour to me, Mike."

"Jamie will need a partner in this job," Mike said. "I think for sure."

"You know Jamie, Mike," I said, "always open to an interesting business proposition."

Mike wasn't quite smiling. But he wasn't scowling either. The only member of the troupe who looked twitchy was Georges. He was probably thinking that all the chatter meant his chances of another shot at me were diminishing.

"My friend Crang," Mike said, "the other two times I talk with you, you tell the tall stories."

"Strictly on the level today, Mike."

"You invent the whoppers."

"The one change in our present discussions, Mike," I said, "is fear. It tends to bring out my honest side."

I marshalled my features into an expression that was intended to convey humility and deference. I felt like Uriah Heep.

Mike spoke in French to the Stove. The words "Haddon" and "Beau Rivage" were prominent in the conversation, Emile started out of the alley.

"*Attendez un moment,*" Mike called after him. Emile waited. Mike asked me where Annie and I were staying. I gave him the address on Avenue Denis Semeria. Mike wanted the name of the landlord. I said it was a landlady and supplied the name of Annie's French friend who had rented us the apartment. Mike recognized the name. He sent Emile on his way with additional instructions. I assumed Emile's destination was a telephone.

Georges growled a few words at Mike. Whatever he said drew a smile. "You know, my friend Crang," Mike said to me, "Georges enjoyed the punching."

"A man content in his work is a truly happy man," I said.

Across the alley, David Nestor was experiencing difficulty with a shimmy in his legs. I tried a reassuring smile on him.

Nestor was probably terrified that the network of half-truths and white lies I'd told Mike would come undone.

Emile returned to the alley. Mike absorbed his report. Mike's expression softened.

"All right, my friend Crang," Rolland said, "Jamie is registered at the Beau Rivage, like you say. And you have the rental at 68 Avenue Denis Semeria for two more weeks."

"Over and out," I said. I didn't even consider advising Mike that his information on my address was out of date, that Annie and I were moving down the road to Cannes the next day.

"You are not thinking of leaving Pont Saint-Jean, Crang?" Mike asked.

"Pull out of the garden spot of the Riviera?" I said. "Perish the thought, Mike."

"For sure," Mike said. "One day, everything work out, maybe I buy you the vodka on the rocks, my friend."

He got behind the wheel of the Japanese Jeep. Emile went around to the front passenger seat. Pittsburgh Boomer climbed into the back seat on the right. Georges seemed reluctant to depart. He glowered at me. I beamed at him. Georges turned to get in the rear seat beside the Boomer.

"Hey, Georges," I said.

Georges turned all the way back to me. I let go a straight right at a point just below his rib cage. I expected to hit a part of him with a layer of muscle. But it was like punching a water bed. Georges stumbled against the Jeep. His hands grabbed his belly. The parts of his face above the beard went suddenly pale. Georges bent over from the waist. One hand switched to his throat. Georges threw up. It was noisy and violent and messy.

"Oh, jeez, I'm sorry, Georges." I held his shoulders to steady him. "I hit you in the wrong place," I said.

Mike and Emile opened their car doors.

"I meant to hit you in the solar plexus." I tried to massage Georges's neck.

Emile was in the alley on the far side. Georges vomited again, Emile looked furious. Further ministrations to Georges seemed out of the question. I whipped around and ran out of the alley. David Nestor was fifteen yards ahead. Behind me, Georges was making retching noises.

CHAPTER TWENTY-FOUR

At eight-thirty, I was standing in the entrance to the apartment's sunroom, the telephone receiver in one hand, a Wyborowa on the rocks in the other. I watched a cabin cruiser with all lights running slide into the darkening Villefranche harbour. I was waiting for Trum Fraser to come on the line. By this time, he should have just concluded his noon-hour quest for the sublime martini.

"What's it you want this time, Crang?" Trum sounded irascible.

"Something wrong, Trum? Coaster's is closed?"

"I haven't been out of the damned building since I got here this morning."

I held my glass away from the phone so Trum couldn't hear the tinkling of ice cubes.

"And I feel like I'm coming down with the bends," Trum said. "Why are you calling long-distance?"

"Tell me about ErnMax."

"Jesus, Crang." Trum made a wounded noise. "Be right back."

I tucked the receiver against my chest. "Trum seems to be taking precautions," I said to Annie. She was on the sofa with the Roger Ebert book and a glass of white wine.

"Crang?" Trum was speaking close to the mouthpiece. "I had to shut the door to my office."

"Touched a nerve, have I?"

"How come you heard about ErnMax in wherever the hell you are?"

"South of France," I said. "There has to be quid pro quo, Trum. I answer your question, and you fill me in on ErnMax."

"I don't know. If you're screwing around, it'll be my nuts in the wringer."

"Listen, you mind asking the operator to switch the call to Swotty Whetherhill's office?"

"Okay, okay." Trum's surly mood was close to the surface. "I'll take a chance."

"Thanks, pal."

"Ernest Luphkin," Trum said. "You know who he is?"

"No. I've been living in Patagonia the last twenty years."

"Don't get smart."

"The guy who's ruined the skylines of more North American cities than anybody since King Kong."

"Luphkin's supposed to do that," Trum said. "He's a developer. He makes billions at it. You ready for this? Millions of the billions go through good old C&G."

"Luphkin is ErnMax?"

"It's his personal holding company. Him and his wife's. Her name is Maxene or Maxelle."

The cabin cruiser had docked somewhere in the shadows of Villefranche's quay. "How do you define holding company?" I asked Trum. "A place where billionaires hide their billions?"

"Sort of." Trum was slowing down the pace. "ErnMax — you probably gathered this from the way I reacted when you brought up the name — ErnMax is very hush-hush around here."

"Not to question your status, Trum, but how inside are you with ErnMax?"

"If I have to put up with insulting shit like that," Trum said, "what you got to trade better be sweet."

"In your wildest dreams, Trum." I took a swallow from my vodka on the rocks.

"I'm the only lawyer on C&G's ErnMax team," Trum said. "Very tight group, very small group, handpicked by Whetherhill himself. ErnMax is Whetherhill's special baby. My instructions from the start were, don't discuss it with the other people in the legal department, and all paperwork goes through Whetherhill's office."

"And right now, this afternoon in Toronto, there's an ErnMax crisis on?"

"Luphkin's staff's been camped out on the thirty-second floor since yesterday," Trum said. "I heard from a guy in securities that two Luphkin people stayed the whole night in the computer centre."

"Doing what?"

"Playing computer baseball." Trum's voice rose sharply. "How the hell do I know? I'm just the dumb cluck who's been told to stick around the office, hasn't had a drink all day, and hears ice cubes clinking over the long-distance phone."

"That's impressive, Trum. You got a great pair of ears."

"What're you having?"

"Polish vodka over ice."

"Maybe if you describe it to me, I'll feel better."

"The glass is still a little frosted on the outside, cold to the touch, and inside, the liquid looks thick, colourless but thick —"

"Enough," Trum said. "You're making it worse."

"Maybe we should go back to ErnMax," I said. I sat down in the fat stuffed armchair that matched the sofa Annie was on. The knees of my jeans still had dust on them from their contact with the alley beside the Café des Nations. I hadn't mentioned the fracas to Annie.

"Yeah," Trum said. "What's ErnMax got to do with the south of France?"

"Quite a bit," I said. I brushed at my knees. "Which is remarkable when you consider it should have more to do with Zurich."

Trum didn't speak.

"That's in Switzerland," I added.

"Sure," Trum said. "Chocolate, cuckoo clocks, and I know what you want me to say, you bugger, bank accounts that are more or less secret."

"In ErnMax's case, I guess it would ordinarily be more rather than less."

"Goon. What else?"

"Twenty-three million of ErnMax's dollars didn't make it to the Zurich account."

"Lemme get a file open at the right place." Trum became businesslike. "Twenty-three million?"

"Yes."

"Twenty-three million was supposed to go from us to Zurich on March fourteenth."

"It didn't."

"Shit," Trum said. "You mean that's what the Luphkin guys are chasing after in the computer centre?"

"They won't find a trace of the diversion at C&G's end."

"Where'd you get hold of a term like 'diversion'?"

"Ah, Trum, I'm experiencing all manner of new sensations over here," I said. "Only two hours ago, I was sipping pastis."

"Murky stuff, tastes like candy, I'll stick to gin."

"When you have access to it."

"Quit talking about drinking," Trum said. "How did you pick up on the twenty-three million?"

"This is going to call for all your diplomatic skills, Trum," I said. I folded my left knee over the right. The dust was more deeply imbedded in the right. "We're in a dicey area," I said. "Family."

"Whose family?" Trum asked, then answered his own question. "Oh, Whetherhill's.... Hey, Jamie Haddon."

"Right on the first guess."

"You're phoning from where he's gone on this leave of absence of his." Trum's voice had speeded up.

"Not far away."

"He's in Monaco."

"So's the twenty-three million," I said. "In an account at the Banco di Napoli."

"Sweet Jesus."

"You see why I mentioned diplomacy," I said. "Swotty wouldn't want a guy like Luphkin finding out it was Swotty's own relative who —"

Trum broke in. "Lemme have the name of that bank again."

"Banco di Napoli," I said. "The money's in a numbered account, but I guess C&G can deal with a little obstacle like that."

"Yeah." Trum was abrupt. "Look, I got to attend to a few things here, Crang."

"Is Jamie a member of C&G's ErnMax team?"

"Whetherhill brought him in a year ago. Get Jamie's feet wet, that kind of idea. Listen, Crang, I'll catch you later."

"You and a host of other Torontonians."

Trum hung up. My vodka on the rocks was almost gone. The thought of another of the same appealed.

"Give me five minutes' notice before you want dinner," Annie said. She had a few pages to go in the Ebert book.

"That's all you need?"

"The salad is made. Water's on the stove at low boil. The only thing to do is turn it higher and throw in the pasta."

I held up my empty glass. "One of these," I said, "always tastes to me like one more."

"Of course," Annie said. It was her mother-hen voice. "Now, would you care to explain how your jeans got dirty?"

CHAPTER TWENTY-FIVE

Annie was standing beside the bed holding out a cup of coffee to me.

"It's after ten, fella," she said.

"I overslept," I said. My voice was muzzy.

"When you're on vacation, that's called rising late," Annie said. "In addition to which, rolling around in that alley might've taken some starch out of you."

I propped two pillows behind my head and shoulders. Steam rose out of the coffee cup. "Yeah," I said, "I seem to have needed the sleep." Annie made stronger coffee than I did. Drinking hers was like injecting caffeine directly into the nervous system.

"You have a visitor coming in half an hour," Annie said.

"Oh, damn." Coffee slopped into the saucer. "You shouldn't break that kind of news when my guard's down," I said. "Not Mike Rolland and company?"

Annie shook her head. "My predecessor," she said.

"You haven't got a predecessor," I said. "You are a one and only."

Annie leaned over and kissed me on the cheek. "Pamela," she said. "She phoned at nine. Wanted to come right over. I told her to hold off a couple of hours."

I shaved, had a shower, and put on my other pair of jeans.

Annie had made a fruit salad. I ate most of it with a buttered raisin bun. Pamela arrived at eleven o'clock. She came in a large black American car. A guy in a cream-coloured suit and matching cap was driving. Annie and I watched the car pull up from the sunroom window. Annie went down to let Pamela in. I lingered behind and wiped butter and raisin off my fingers.

"I'm Pamela Cartwright," Pamela said.

Her voice carried into the apartment from the doorway.

"Annie Cooke," Annie said. "Please come in."

Their encounter was a long way from Debbie Reynolds and Elizabeth Taylor scrapping over Eddie Fisher. It was civilized and ordinary. When I walked into the hall, Pamela and Annie were shaking hands and smiling at one another. Maybe if I were a crooner whose bestselling single was "Oh My Papa," Pamela and Annie would have scrapped over me.

"I keep calling on you with questions, Crang," Pamela said to me.

"It happens this is probably one of the few times I've got some answers," I said.

Pamela might have been overdressed. She had on a sky blue dress in a silky material and shoes that colour-coordinated with the dress. The dress showed some décolletage. The shoes were high-heeled. She had a black patent-leather purse under her right arm and a floppy-brimmed hat in her left hand. Her face had more makeup than she'd worn at our meetings in Toronto two weeks earlier.

Annie offered coffee. Pamela thought coffee was a smashing idea. I said I'd have a second cup. Living on the edge. The three of us sat with our coffee at the table in the sunroom. Nobody remarked on the view.

"I don't question you saw Jamie at L'Hôtel de Paris, Crang," Pamela said to me, "but he isn't there now, and nobody's saying where he's gone."

"You spoke to the concierge?"

"He wouldn't reveal a thing," Pamela said. "I fed him every line in my repertoire."

"Including the one about you being Jamie's secret married lover?"

"The man practically laughed in my face."

Annie spoke up. "Pamela ... may I call you Pamela?"

"I wish you would," Pamela said, "Annie."

"What Crang is taking his time about telling you, Pamela, is that Jamie Haddon has checked into the Beau Rivage in Nice."

Pamela turned her eyes on me.

"True," I said.

"What's he doing there?" Pamela asked.

"Same thing he's been doing for the last year," I said. "Generating trouble."

Pamela opened her patent-leather purse. She took out the gold cigarette case and the gold lighter.

"Okay?" she said to Annie. Annie said, "Sure." Pamela didn't ask my permission. There was no ashtray in the apartment. Annie got another saucer from the kitchen.

"What is it you think Jamie has been up to?" Pamela asked me. "And if the details are grisly, don't spare me them."

"Cutting out most of the crap," I said, "Jamie has snookered you. Not just personally. Your family."

Pamela blew some smoke in the air. In the bright light of the sunroom, the makeup failed to conceal the purple smudges of sleeplessness under her eyes.

I said, "You told me at your house you felt Jamie might have led you on."

"Inveigled," Pamela said. "That was the word I chose."

"Your intuition wasn't false."

"Jamie admitted all of this to you?"

"Some of it is drawing my own conclusions," I said. "But they're based on Jamie's conversation with me. He set out to draw you into an affair with the intention of ultimately pulling the rug out. Or maybe that's pulling the covers off."

Annie elbowed me in the side.

"Am I being too direct?" I asked Pamela.

Pamela addressed Annie. "It's all right," she said. "Let Crang express himself whatever way he wants. I asked for it."

Pamela turned back to me. "Jamie wanted to make a fool of me?"

"Prove you had round heels. That's a phrase from the man himself."

"The son of a bitch." Pamela mashed her cigarette in the saucer. "When I think —" Pamela stopped. "Oh, shit," she said.

"Pamela," I said, "I don't know how much more of this you want. Or need. But one point is clear to me. You shouldn't bother visiting Jamie at the Beau Rivage or any place else. You should go home. Call it a day. Fold your tents."

"That's your advice?" Pamela said.

"Cut your losses."

"No."

I shrugged. From the moment Pamela came into the apartment, I'd been aware of something new about her, some quality I couldn't quite put my finger on. The quality seemed to be antagonism. I knew it wasn't directed at me.

"You'll get a laugh out of this, Crang," she said. She gave a hard laugh of her own. "As if I didn't have enough hassle, Archie flew here with me."

I heard Annie breathe a little faster.

"You couldn't dissuade him?" I said.

"Archie and I once had a lovely spring holiday along the coast from Nice to Saint-Tropez. When I told him I was coming over for a few days, he insisted we should recapture that spring. If only he knew."

"He doesn't?"

"Jamie Haddon's name hasn't crossed his lips in days."

"Right there," I said, "you have another reason for forgetting Jamie. So you can concentrate on your husband."

"For God's sake, Crang, I have to do something about Jamie, even if it's only to ask him one question. Why? Why did he do this to me?"

The coffee cups were empty. "There's no scotch on the premises," I said to Pamela. "How about a glass of wine?"

"Any alcohol," she said. "I've been up and upset since five."

Annie opened a bottle of Sancerre in the kitchen. She brought it to the table with three glasses.

"On the subject of why," I said to Pamela, "Jamie has a chip on his shoulder about your family. Actually the chip is the size of a board."

Pamela's eyes widened. "What he's inflicted on me is all about resentment?"

"Greed comes into it too."

"Greed? The money? You found out how Jamie is paying for his three months in Europe?"

"Jamie's stash isn't in the three-month category. It's good for a lifetime. Not coincidentally, that's about the number of years he has in mind for his leave of absence."

"He's not planning to go back to the trust company?"

"For Jamie," I said, "going back to C&G would come under the heading of returning to the scene of the crime."

Pamela held my gaze. It was silent in the sunroom. From outside, I heard the toot-toot of one of the tubby old fishing boats that ply the waters around Villefranche.

"My God, Crang," Pamela said. She began to shake her head back and forth. "You're just a bundle of glad tidings, you are."

Annie put her hand on my thigh under the table.

"My God," Pamela said again. She drank some of her wine. "There's no end to this. Now it's Daddy. A fax from his secretary was in my box at the hotel this morning. Daddy's arriving late tonight."

"He'll need to speak to me," I said.

"Is there a way of keeping Jamie's theft from Daddy?" Pamela asked.

I shook my head.

"This will absolutely destroy him," Pamela drank the rest of the wine in one gulp. "Destroy Daddy, I mean. He adores Jamie. I told you that."

"About now," I said, "Swotty's feelings about Jamie will be undergoing a comprehensive and probably permanent revision."

I didn't have Pamela's undivided attention. "Perhaps," she said, "perhaps if I speak to Jamie, he'll return the money."

"Pamela —"

Pamela's voice crossed mine. "May I have more wine?" she asked Annie. Annie filled Pamela's glass. She added a couple of inches to mine.

I tried again, "Pamela —"

"I know your advice, Crang," Pamela said. She seemed neither angry nor impatient. She seemed unyielding. "I also happen to think, no matter what you tell me, I still have influence with Jamie."

I turned my palms up. "Have a shot," I said.

"He was my lover for a year."

"But you should understand the money involved isn't all in the family."

"Explain."

"He stole from the account at C&G of a company called ErnMax."

"Never heard of it."

"How about Luphkin?"

"Ernest and Maxie...? Oh, I see. ErnMax. Isn't that tacky. Like something you'd name a boat." Pamela made a disdainful face. "Typical of those dreadful Luphkins."

"It's their money Jamie put the grab on."

"I'm still going to talk to him."

"You'll be talking about a serious sum."

"How much?"

"Twenty-three million."

"Oh." Pamela sipped more wine. "Well," she said. She dropped the gold cigarette case and gold lighter into her purse. "It's a lot, but not an impossible amount of money," she said. She took a longer swallow of wine. It emptied the glass. "Yes, all right," she said. She was trying to sound brisk and organized. "About Daddy, I know he has your number here."

I looked at Annie.

"The big guy and I are moving this afternoon," she said to Pamela. "The Monarch Hotel in Cannes. We'll be staying at it until the end of the film festival."

"The big guy?" Pamela sized me up. "I never thought of you in those terms, Crang."

"Well, maybe not that big compared to Archie."

"I didn't know Archie in the days when I didn't think of you as big."

Pamela went downstairs to her car and driver. Annie and I watched her from the sunroom. The car turned the corner on Avenue Denis Semeria and disappeared on the road that led to Nice by way of Villefranche. I took the empty wineglasses into the kitchen. Annie went into the bedroom to pack. Pamela's glass had deep red lipstick outlines on the rim.

CHAPTER TWENTY-SIX

Late Wednesday morning, Annie and I were drinking cappuccino in a restaurant on La Croisette.

"Up and down here," Annie said, "the four or five blocks along La Croisette from where we are, it's where all the festival action goes on. The public-type action anyway."

"Yeah, I noticed the girls doing the poses on the beach."

"They're rehearsing for when the paparazzi start snapping." La Croisette was a broad boulevard that wound along Cannes's waterfront. The beaches and the Mediterranean were on the south side of the boulevard; on the north side, it was hotels, shops, and cafes. To the east, the Carlton stuck out as the major landmark, a hotel in the confectionary mode. In the other direction, west, was the Palais des Festivals where most of the films were screened. It was a monolithic cement building with a spectacular flight of stairs up from a large plaza and the aspect of a five-dollar-an-hour parking garage. The cafe we were sitting in had directors' chairs with illustrious movie persons' names printed across the backs. I could see a Jack Lemmon, a Luis Buñuel, a Vivien Leigh.

"It's swell having your company, sweetie," Annie said, "but shouldn't you be waiting on Mr. Whetherhill's phone call?"

"I'm delaying the inevitable."

"I know what you're doing. But get it over with and you can resume what this trip's supposed to be all about."

"A holiday."

"Right."

"But I seem to have these lingering doubts about what all the characters are really up to in this little waltz."

"Oh, balls."

"Balls?"

"Listen." Annie was using her sergeant-major delivery. "I've got a screening in ten minutes. You go and report in to Swotty and meet me for lunch. Over and out."

Annie stood up.

"Who's on the back of your chair?" I asked.

Annie looked.

"Catherine Deneuve," she said. "What about yours?"

I looked.

"Who the hell's M.F. Siegler?"

Annie didn't have the answer.

I walked north on one of the little streets that ran out of La Croisette behind another ornate hotel called the Majestic. Cannes's main shopping street, parallel to La Croisette, was Rue d'Antibes. I sauntered past windows displaying pieces of chocolate shaped like fish, eyeglasses with lime-green frames, a little mink doggie jacket. At a tabac store, I bought the *International Herald Tribune*, and turned north again.

I was on the street behind our hotel. The Monarch was new, utilitarian, and nine storeys high. I sat at a table on the sidewalk outside a shoebox-sized cafe on the corner. More delaying of the inevitable. I asked the proprietor for a *café au lait* and read William Safire's column in the *Trib*.

The Monarch's main concession to variety in exterior design was the crisscrossed rows of tiny balconies. I had stood on ours the night before looking at the eastern view toward Cap d'Antibes. While I stood on our seventh-floor balcony, Annie stayed in the room. The balcony didn't accommodate two. Later we switched places.

I finished with William Safire and looked up at the hotel. A guy was resting his bum against the railing around one of the Monarch's balconies. From the back, I could see blond hair and a mauve shirt. I counted down. One, two. The guy was on a seventh-floor balcony, close to the middle, but toward the south end. So was the balcony that went with the room Annie and I were in. The guy had a familiar tilt to his head. The sun was in my eyes. I used my left arm to shade it out. The guy was Jamie Haddon.

I crossed the street and went in the Monarch's service entrance. The keys to the rooms were kept in little numbered boxes in back of the check-in desk. Opposite the boxes, there was a swinging gate that led behind the counter. Box 716 was empty. One assistant manager was on duty. He was at the other end marking something on a map for two middle-aged Americans in Ralph Lauren get-ups. I waited until the assistant manager had finished.

"Did anyone come to the desk for the key to 716 in the last little while?" I asked.

The assistant manager looked over his shoulder at the boxes. "You are Mr...?"

"Crang."

"Of course, Mr. Crang." He had a finicky manner, and he was wearing a faultless dove-grey suit. "I believe the lady took her key when she went out. Ms. Cooke? And you have yours?"

"In my pocket."

"That accounts for both," the assistant manager said triumphantly. "Did you require a third key, Mr. Crang?"

"No thanks."

The assistant manager smiled me away from the desk. I refrained from telling him I had watched Annie hand in her key at the counter an hour earlier. Might shake his faith in the Monarch's security system.

The hall on the seventh floor was empty and silent except for the sporadic whir of the elevators. A room-service tray from

Annie's and my breakfast lay on the floor outside 716. I put my key in the lock and opened the door fast. The room had a desk with a lamp on it, a chair for the desk, a double bed, and enough manoeuvring space for two people who were very fond of one another. Jamie Haddon wasn't in the room. I looked in the closet and bathroom. He wasn't in them either. The second key to the room sat on the desk.

Outside, on the street, voices were raised in a faint babble that conveyed something urgent. The glass door to the balcony was pulled back. I walked over and leaned out.

A man on the neighbouring balcony was looking down. He was a big guy with sandy hair and a sandy mustache. He had on white shorts and was bare from the waist up.

"G'day then," he said to me with an Australian accent. "You talk English?" he asked.

"It's my best language."

The big guy had his muscular forearms folded over the balcony railing. One forefinger was pointing down. "Poor bloke did a right job on himself," he said.

Jamie Haddon was sprawled face-down on the sidewalk. From above, I saw blond hair, mauve shirt, and splotches of dark blood. A couple of dozen excited people were keeping their distance from the body. My stomach gave a lurch.

"He came from up there," the Australian said. He turned his glance upwards. "Off the bleeding roof."

"You saw him, uh, fall?" I asked. My voice had a squeak in it.

"Nah," the Australian said. "But it's the only answer, isn't it then? The bugger didn't come out of my room. Or yours. Or any of those others."

I looked along the rows of balconies. On some, people were standing and staring down. A woman had a hand over her mouth. The glass doors on the balconies that didn't have people on them were shut tight.

"You must be right," I said.

An ambulance came from the bottom of the street. The sound of its siren bounced off the walls of the buildings. By now the crowd around Jamie had doubled in size. Two men got out of the ambulance and they stood over Jamie talking like two guys with minor problems in logistics. One had his hands on his hips. The other went back to the ambulance and dragged out a large black sheet. He draped it over Jamie.

"Waiting for the coppers," the Australian said. He sounded like he knew what he was talking about. Or maybe that was just a national characteristic; Australians always sound like they know what they're talking about.

On cue, two police vehicles careened around the corner at the top of the street. One was a sedan, the other was an oddly shaped van, tall and skinny, and both had their sirens on high. They stopped on either side of the ambulance. A total of eight police-men piled out of the vehicles. One wore a suit, the others were in uniform. Once they hit the pavement, none of the policemen seemed in a hurry.

"Fuck-all's likely to happen for the next half hour," the Australian said. His voice was blunt with certainty.

"It won't?"

"Ever met a French copper who didn't like to natter?"

"Never met any kind of French cop."

"Take my word, these blokes are champions at nattering. Bleeding time-wasters, that bunch."

The big Australian straightened up and stretched his arms. "Well, how 'bout it?" he said to me. "You and your mate want to go downstairs for a shout?"

"Pardon?"

"Few beers in the pub."

"Thanks," I said, "but I've got to see a lady about a change in plans."

CHAPTER TWENTY-SEVEN

Annie was on the steps of the Palais holding an armful of schedules and brochures. The two guys she was talking to with great animation carried the same loads of paper. I recognized one of them, Jay Scott, the *Globe and Mail*'s movie critic. Annie waved me a big greeting. I waited over by a bust of Georges Pompidou. Annie kissed Jay on both cheeks and shook hands with the other guy.

"Why the long face, sweetie?" Annie asked me.

"I'm about to rain on the parade."

"Oh, oh, now what?"

I took Annie's arm and steered her across the plaza toward the water. A line of metal chairs faced into the bay. Further out, inside the sea wall, a seventeenth-century wooden ship sat at anchor. It looked like the kind of boat that pirates sailed when they plundered the Seven Seas.

"Somebody pushed Jamie Haddon off our balcony at the hotel," I said.

"Our balcony? Pushed!"

"He's dead."

"Well, the seventh floor, I guess so."

I lifted the papers from Annie's arms. She sat down slowly in one of the metal chairs. I put the papers on the ground.

"He wasn't my favourite person, Jamie," Annie said. "Not if I judge him from the only time I've met him. But, holy cow, shoved off a building?"

I sat in the chair beside Annie, and told her about being at the cafe behind the Monarch, about seeing Jamie on the balcony, about the key missing from the box, about the Australian saying Jamie came off the roof.

"Are you sure he didn't?" Annie asked.

"Come off the roof?" I shook my head. "I've thought a little about this. Jamie must have got into our room to look for the optical disk."

"Oh God, that damn disk."

"By this morning, more likely as early as last night, he would've known that Mike Rolland didn't have the disk."

"Because Rolland probably went straight to the Beau Rivage after he had the chat with you in the alley."

"Right," I said. "Though he might have taken a detour to let Georges freshen up. Jamie's logical step after he convinced Mike he didn't have the disk ..."

"That might not have been a cinch."

"... would be to call in Dan Renzi for a showdown."

"Sure, I follow," Annie said. "If Rolland wasn't holding the disk, Jamie would hit on Dan as the next suspect."

"And when Jamie was satisfied Dan was in the clear, he'd finally conclude the only person who could possibly be in possession of the bouncing disk was me."

"He'd have been correct if it hadn't been for the smuggling services of that teacher in the Café des Nations."

"Jake Finney."

"So Jamie came over here and sniggled our room key," Annie said. "Then what do you figure happened?"

"Mike Rolland and the Clutches were keeping an eye on Jamie," I said. "They followed him. There was a contretemps in our room. Jamie lost."

"But why would the Rolland bunch kill Jamie? That leaves them without Jamie and without the disk."

"Hell, lots of explanations."

Annie was silent for a moment. "I suppose," she said. "Maybe a short fuse, for one. Those guys, the little I've seen and heard of them, Rolland and the Clutches, they seem to be the types to bash somebody and ask questions later. If the somebody is still alive and talking."

"That's a possibility," I said. "another is that Mike Rolland probably figures all he needs in order to get at the big bucks is the disk. Jamie's superfluous, and once Rolland was convinced Jamie couldn't produce the disk, he didn't care whether Georges and the Stove dispatched Jamie off the balcony."

"Oh, Lord, but what this process of elimination means," Annie said, "is that Rolland and his goons will be coming back after you for the disk."

"Doubt it," I said. "Not right away they won't. Mike's best move is to stay out of sight for a few days."

"Because of Jamie's death?"

"Yeah. And by the time Mike concludes it's all clear, I'll have passed on the disk to Swotty Whetherhill and the people who own the twenty-three million."

"Thank you for that small blessing."

"I'll unload the disk this afternoon," I said. "And take other steps to bail out of the case."

"It seems to me a third party is bound to join in any minute now."

"The police?"

"Of course," Annie said.

"They'll chalk Jamie's death up to an accidental fall."

"But you know differently."

"If I tell the police everything that's gone on," I said, "their heads will spin."

"This is murder we're discussing. Murderers are supposed to get locked up, and people in the position we're in, we're supposed to help lock them up."

"When I said police heads would spin," I said, "I meant they might spin in my direction."

"Ah, right, that's a worry."

"Maybe Swotty Whetherhill's the answer."

"At the start, for gosh sakes, he was one of the questions."

"Yeah, well, he's got clout and resources. If he agreed to put some of them on my side, maybe I could deal with the police from a position of strength."

"And respectability."

"That especially."

"You'll have to phone Swotty anyway," Annie said. "Somebody has to tell people about Jamie's death, tell Pamela and Dan and the others, and I think the somebody is you."

"In a few minutes."

Annie and I sat in silence on the metal chairs staring at the water and the wooden sailing ship.

"That's Roman Polanski's boat," Annie said after awhile.

"I thought it might be Captain Kidd's."

"Polanski had it made for a movie of his," Annie said. "*Pirates*."

"I remember that one," I said. "You reviewed it. Called it a bomb."

"Total," Annie said. "Polanski moored the ship out there to celebrate *Pirates*' premiere at the 1986 festival. The movie flopped, and I guess he couldn't afford to sail it away."

"Well, it looks good for the tourist trade."

"Unlike Jamie Haddon's plunge," Annie said.

CHAPTER TWENTY-EIGHT

I sat on the end of the bed and phoned. Annie was at the desk leafing through her literature from the press conference. She avoided the balcony. I tried the Negresco. Swotty Whetherhill had checked in, but no one picked up the phone in his room. Archie and Pamela weren't answering either. I asked the desk to have them paged. The desk reported failure. It was the same story at L'Hôtel de Paris. Dan Renzi didn't respond to rings or pages. I left my name and number at both hotels. Annie and I went out for a late lunch.

"If the police are looking into Jamie Haddon's death," Annie said, "they're doing it from deep undercover."

"I didn't identify any cops in the hotel lobby."

"Maybe we expect them to look like Philippe Noiret," Annie said. "Or like Peter Sellers."

We were in a restaurant near the train station. The other patrons were working guys with big appetites. They'd found the right place. The plat du jour offered three courses and large helpings. Annie and I ordered a lot of everything.

"I don't get it," Annie said. We were digging into a fish soup that came with pieces of toast, grated Parmesan, a thick garlic sauce, and other trappings.

"What?" I said. "That we're gorging ourselves a couple of hours after somebody we knew died a violent death?"

"I read somewhere it's a common reaction to eat this way in a time of tragedy."

"And drink," I said. I poured from a pitcher of red wine.

"The part I don't get," Annie said, "is not feeling the least bit guilty about gobbling the food, even if it is a common reaction."

"You didn't like Jamie, kiddo."

"There's that."

"For Pamela, at least," I said, "Jamie's death is one way of keeping her affair with him quiet."

"Now who's being insensitive?"

"As a matter of fact," I said, "almost everybody comes out better with Jamie dead."

We finished with crème caramel and walked back to the Monarch. In the lobby, the fastidious assistant manager in the dove-grey suit asked to speak to me. Annie went up to the room.

"The hotel apologizes for the inconvenience, Mr. Crang," the assistant manager said.

"Is it about the gentleman who fell from the building?" I asked. My tone was hushed and solicitous and about as genuine as a three-franc coin.

"I'm so glad you understand, Mr. Crang. An inspector from the bureau de police is having a short word with guests who occupy rooms on the rear south side."

"If there is any way I can contribute."

"It's just for the police records." The assistant manager leaned across the counter. "We asked the inspector to show discretion," he whispered.

"You can be assured of it from me," I whispered back. "Such a shame for the hotel, an accident like that."

"*Mais, oui,*" the assistant manager said.

He opened the gate in the counter and ushered me to an office behind the check-in area. There were two policemen standing against the right wall of the room. They had on the crisp blue trousers and the tailored sweaters that make French uniformed cops look like models for Yves St. Laurent. The man sitting behind the desk wore a wrinkled brown suit, a faded green shirt, and a splashy red and brown tie pulled tight at the neck in a small hard knot. He didn't look up from the paper he was writing on. I felt a slight tightening of trepidation across my chest.

"Mr. Crang of room 716," the assistant manager said. "Inspector Farinaud."

The assistant manager bowed himself out of the office. I sat in the chair on the customer side of the desk. The Inspector moved an official-looking blue form from a pile on his left to a position under his writing hand. The blue form had umpteen lines and boxes. It was thick with copies and carbons.

"Passport, please," Inspector Farinaud said without much inflection. He held his hand out and kept his head down. The trepidation in my chest tightened another notch.

I took the passport from my jacket pocket. Farinaud wrote slowly and laboriously. He used a fountain pen and filled in lines and boxes with information from my passport. I considered my defence if he checked on colour of eyes. The only sound in the room was the scratch of the fountain pen. I didn't think the squeezing inside my chest was audible to the others.

Farinaud handed back the passport.

"Where were you when the gentleman fell, Mr. Crang?" he asked.

Farinaud raised his head. He had round cheeks and thick eyebrows that strayed over his brow. His nose was bulbous, a wine-taster's nose, and his lips were thick and purply. The man looked about as threatening as Andy Rooney. The tightening and trepidation fled from my chest.

"That's hard to say, Inspector," I answered. "Where would I have been? In the lobby of the hotel maybe. Or on the elevator."

"You did not see the man fall?" Farinaud asked.

"I saw him on the sidewalk."

"That is known to me."

"Oh, really?"

Farinaud exhaled loudly through his nose. He leafed through another pile of blue forms neatly arranged on the right corner of the desk. The lines and boxes had writing in them. Farinaud selected one. "Monsieur Colin Terrill observed you," he said.

"Did I observe him?"

"That is for you to say, Mr. Crang." Farinaud studied the form in his hand. "Monsieur Colin Terrill," he read. "Address, Broadbeach Waters, Queensland, Australia."

"Ah. Big guy, mustache, brown hair, may or may not wear a shirt?" I said. "He was on the neighbouring balcony. The dead man was down below."

"*Bon.*" Farinaud resumed his writing. He filled in a box that took up a quarter of the blue form. "Monsieur Terrill observed Monsieur Crang," he said in a soft monotone. "Monsieur Crang observed Monsieur Terrill."

Farinaud wrote to the bottom of the box. He lifted the sheets of paper and scanned the bottom copy. The fountain pen was still in his hand. He looked across at me.

"Is there anything further you wish to state concerning the dead man, Mr. Crang?" he asked.

"I wish to state?" I put on my thoughtful mien. "Don't think so," I said.

"*Bon.*" Farinaud's fountain pen made a check mark in a small box on the blue form. He fitted the pen's cap over the nib.

"Do you have a name for the man who, ah, fell?" I asked.

"A countryman of yours," Farinaud said. He consulted another form. It was pale yellow. "Monsieur James Gerald Haddon," he read. "Born in Strathroy, Ontario, Canada."

"That's about two hundred miles southwest of Toronto," I said.

"*Oui?*" Farinaud appeared to warm up to the fresh fact.

"Always glad to be helpful."

Farinaud uncapped the pen. Behind me, one of the cops in the chic uniforms held the door open. I got up. The Inspector was writing in the margin of the pale yellow form. I left the room and took an elevator to the seventh floor.

Annie was lying on the bed in her blouse and skirt. She had her hands folded over her stomach.

"Swell timing, big guy," she said from the bed. She was giving me a crooked smile. "I've already fielded your return calls."

"What an idiot," I said. "Me, I mean." I sat on the bed beside Annie. "I should've thought of that."

"First, Archie Cartwright. Then Dan Renzi. Dan cried on the phone."

"Uh-oh. How much detail did you get into?"

"Hardly any." Annie raised herself on her elbows. "Just that Jamie was killed in a fall from a building. I didn't reveal what building or how far he fell or anything else sordid."

"And Dan wept?"

"Buckets," Annie said. "He was also full of questions. I referred him to the Cannes police."

"That was prudent."

"I don't know if this means anything," Annie said, "but Dan called from a pay phone. He was talking so long he had to drop in an extra franc."

"So he wasn't on a phone at L'Hôtel de Paris?"

Annie shrugged from her semi-horizontal position.

"Archie Cartwright," I said, "he wouldn't have shed tears."

"His voice got very resonant when I told him. Sounded like an announcer on one of those MOR radio stations. He said he'd 'advise the family.'"

"I bet."

Annie stood up. "I'm due for a meeting with Bruce Kirkland in fifteen minutes," she said. She walked into the bathroom. "At Le Petit Carlton Hotel. We have to organize schedules, allocate tasks, divvy up movies." Annie was studying herself in the mirror.

"Don't change a hair for me," I said. I was watching from the door.

Annie smiled. She continued her studies.

"What held you downstairs?" she asked.

"I was assisting the police with their inquiries."

Annie opened the cabinet over the sink. "What did you tell them?" she asked. She took a long white comb from a shelf.

"I answered questions with some compromising of the truth by way of omission."

"That got past the police?"

"The fellow who quizzed me wasn't Inspector Javert incarnate," I said. "Anyway, the official conclusion seems to be that Jamie took an unaided header off the building. Nobody is looking for facts that disturb the conclusion."

Annie used the white comb to sweep at the hair over each ear. I failed to spot what change the combing brought to the styling. Annie wore her hair cut short and as close to her scalp as a helmet.

"Jamie shouldn't have been killed," I said.

Annie turned away from the mirror. "Nobody should be killed," she said. She squeezed past me into the bedroom.

"What I'm getting at is that events had begun to assume an order," I said. I leaned my hip against the door frame. "All returns weren't in, but thanks to David Nestor, I'd nailed the how of Jamie's theft. And thanks to Jamie himself, I knew the Whetherhill family was his specific target. The case was close to a finale."

"Now the bad guy is dead," Annie said. "Horrible, yes, but could we call it a kind of retribution?"

"Maybe it's the timing that bugs me," I said. "If Jamie had been killed before I learned what was on the disk and where the twenty-three million went, I could understand. But afterwards? I don't understand."

"You lost me back there around the last bend, fella," Annie said. She was tossing equipment into her shoulder bag. Pens. Notebook. Film schedules. Publicity releases.

I said, "As of the other night when I told Trum Fraser about Jamie's handiwork, C&G knew its missing money had gone to the Banco di Napoli in Monaco. The trust company would've taken instant steps to grab back the cash. They'd have frozen the Monaco account within a half hour of me spilling the beans to Trum."

"Yes, I follow that part."

"And Jamie would have been bound to discover almost as fast that his personal net worth was back down around zero."

"I'm still with you."

"So the money would be out of reach of Jamie and of anyone trying to get at him for a share of the booty. With that incentive removed, why bump off Jamie?"

"Oh, sure, now I get it," Annie said. She stopped loading papers and pens in the shoulder bag. "But doesn't that raise another question?" she said. "Why would Jamie bother coming over here, to this room, to root around for the disk?"

"The disk is still evidence," I said. "It could put Jamie in the hoosegow. He wouldn't want it falling into unfriendly hands."

"Like possibly yours."

"Yeah."

Annie resumed the packing of the shoulder bag.

"That still leaves my main question up in the air," I said. "Why would anyone kill Jamie when the monetary reason no longer existed?"

"Hey, come on, I thought we had it all worked out earlier. It had to have been Mike Rolland and his thugs, them and their, you know, penchant for spontaneous violence."

"I'm having second thoughts."

"Listen, big guy," Annie said. She swung the bag to her shoulder. "Stop thinking like a Monday-morning halfback. Take the disk to Mr. Whetherhill. Give Pamela a peck on the cheek. Come back. We'll see some movies."

"It's Monday-morning quarterback."

Annie opened the door to the corridor. "Never mind the nit-picking," she said. She blew me a kiss and left for her appointment.

I phoned Jake Finney and said I'd be over in an hour to pick up the disk and the printout. Jake asked if I had time to watch a video. He had *3:10 to Yuma* starring Van Heflin as a decent but courageous farmer. I expressed my regrets. When I hung up, I changed from my jeans to the pair of pressed cords and put on a dress shirt and tie with my sports jacket. Swotty was at the Negresco. I didn't suppose it would be a jeans sort of place.

CHAPTER TWENTY-NINE

The guy wielding the blunt instrument missed his timing. He swung too soon. I caught a flash of something to my left, black and moving. I pulled my head to the right. The guy's swing caught me in the hollow between the skull and neck. It stunned me, but not as much as I let on. I let on it knocked me cold. I collapsed on the carpet. My head and shoulders were in the Monarch's corridor. My legs were in the room. I worried a little that the sports jacket and pressed cords were getting mussed.

I kept my eyes shut. If whichever Clutch had socked me knew I was conscious, he would strike again. Someone did a clumsy job of shifting the upper half of my body into the room and closed the door. I continued my shut-eye policy.

The guy started shuffling through drawers in the desk. I had no sense of anyone except the shuffler in the room. Why a single guy? Didn't the Clutches operate as a team? I opened my eyes a slit. My left cheek rested on the rug below the corner of the bed. I was looking at a pair of trim Italian boots with a lot of raised stitching in about a size seven. No Clutch would choose such fey footwear. No Clutch was a size seven. I lifted my gaze.

"For chrissake, Dan," I said. I started to get off the floor. "A simple knock on the door would've gained you admittance."

Dan Renzi looked stricken. I was on my feet. Dan had parked his weapon on the desk chair. The back of my neck was numb, but the rest of me felt vigorous. Dan's weapon looked like the handle to a hammer. He went for it.

"Dan," I said, "I'm probably more experienced at this sort of thing than you."

Dan chose an overhead chop with the hammer handle. That gave me time to throw a left jab before the hammer completed its trajectory. The jab popped Dan on the point of his chin. He staggered back. The hammer made contact with nothing except air.

"That was only a jab, Dan," I said. "Think of the damage a straight right would do."

Dan's second try was a sweeping clout from the side. I stepped inside it. The handle clipped me on the upper left arm. I hit Dan in the nose with a straight right. Blood spurted out of Dan's nostrils. He looked astonished.

"Hey," I said, "don't bleed on the rug."

I guided Dan into the bathroom. He held his head back. His mouth was making raspy swallowing sounds. I ran cold water in the sink. Dan plopped down on the toilet seat. I soaked a white face cloth under the tap and pressed the cloth over his nose. It turned instantly pink.

"Keep the cloth tight," I told Dan.

I went back into the bedroom. The hammer handle lay beside the balcony door. I put it in the closet. In the bathroom, the noise from Dan's mouth suggested a small and terrified animal. I soaked the cloth again. Dan calmed down.

"What was it, Dan?" I said. "Looking for the disk?"

Dan nodded. His face was all scared eyes and pink cloth.

"The bleeding ought to be stopped by now," I said.

Dan took the cloth a few cautious inches from his nose. There was no bleeding, but Dan's chin and upper lip were crusted in drying blood.

"Don't make any sudden movements, Dan," I said. "The nose could erupt again."

I filled the basin with cold water. Dan handed me the cloth. I wrung it out in the water.

"The disk wouldn't help you, Dan," I said.

It was cramped in the bathroom, me standing over the basin, Dan looking like a fallen warrior on the toilet seat, but I didn't want to risk a recurrence of bleeding in the bedroom. The management might bill the *Sun* for the damage. Dan said nothing.

"You think the disk will tell you how to get at the money," I said to him. "It won't. It shows where the money came from and how it got to Monaco. No more."

Dan took a minute to process what I'd said. "Jamie's dead," he said finally. He sounded beaten. He wasn't putting on a performance.

"That may be the least of your worries," I said.

"What do you mean?"

"You've got your own hide to look out for," I said. "The people from the trust company will discover how you helped Jamie loot their till."

"Me?" Dan said. The innocence was back in his voice. He was performing again.

"Wash your face," I said. "We'll talk in the bedroom."

I sat in the chair at the desk and waited for Dan. When he came into the room, he held himself in a gingerly way. He perched on the bed.

"You don't know what's on the disk," I said.

"I'm not very good with computers, Mr. Crang."

"That gets you points with me, Dan," I said, "but not with Cayuga & Granark."

"I just went along on Jamie's instructions," Dan said. His impersonation of a wide-eyed waif would have deceived anyone who hadn't seen it before.

"Jamie needed someone to knock C&G's main computer out of business at eleven o'clock last March fourteenth," I said. "How did he tell you to do it?"

Dan touched his hand carefully to his nose. The nose had begun to swell. Dan winced at the touch. "You seem to know a lot," he whimpered.

"Uh-huh," I said. "What's the answer to my question?"

"I set a fire."

"Jesus, Dan, they could get you on arson as well as theft."

"It was just a quick little flash." Dan spoke defensively. "Crossing some wires, that was all. Not a real fire"

"Where was this?" I asked. "In the trust company's computer centre?"

Dan shook his head. "In a place under the street. There's a system of wires down there connected to the computer. Jamie rehearsed me for weeks. Day after day, we went down there. He showed me how to cross some particular wires, wait four minutes, and put the wires back the way they were. I could have done it practically in my sleep."

"Jamie must have been pleased by the way you executed at your end."

"Well, the computer went down, and Jamie got the five million out," Dan said. "For all the good it's doing either of us now."

"Five million?"

"The money Jamie switched to that bank in Monaco."

"Ah, Dan, how can I begin to tell you."

"What's wrong?" Dan was indignant.

"The amount Jamie redirected to the Banco di Napoli was twenty-three million."

Dan reacted like I'd smacked him across the forehead with a two-by-four.

"Jamie lied to me?" he said.

I spread my hands, palms up. "No honour among thieves."

Dan thought for a moment. "But if I'd known it was that much ..."

"Yeah." I nodded my head. "You wouldn't have needed to consider blackmailing Jamie into calling off the heavy spending. You wouldn't have snitched the disk from the safety-deposit box. You wouldn't have set off the whole merry chase after that dratted disk."

"Oh, God." Dan was shaken, and it was no act. "I was afraid Jamie would go through the entire five million in a couple of years."

"Twenty-three million could have seen the two of you in clover for the best part of a century," I said. "But Jamie must have had other ideas."

"He never told me."

"There's more bad news, Dan."

"Do you think I'll go to jail?" he asked.

"That's probably the good news," I said. "If C&G starts criminal proceedings against you, the story of the theft will come out in the press. The second-last thing Cayuga & Granark wants is that kind of publicity."

"The second-last thing?"

"The last is to lose the twenty-three million."

"Well, they won't," Dan said. He sounded grumpy. "Not all of it anyway."

"You want the bad news, Dan?"

"Not really, but go ahead."

"Jamie's death wasn't an accident," I said. I shifted in my chair to face the balcony. "Someone pushed him out of this room," I said. I pointed at the balcony.

Dan got off the bed very slowly. He walked past me to the balcony doors. His legs moved like they were on automatic pilot. He opened the doors. Sounds of traffic came into the room. Dan looked at the balcony as if it might tell him how Jamie had gone over.

"Take my word for it, Dan," I said.

"Miss Cooke told me Jamie fell," Dan said. There was a tremble in his voice. It sounded genuine, but with Dan, there were no guarantees. "She didn't say it was from this hotel," he said. He shut the balcony doors.

"Not to mention from this very room," I said. "Annie was showing caution."

Dan hadn't gone back to his perch on the bed. "Why would someone kill Jamie?" he asked. He stood between the balcony and my chair.

"People were getting overwrought about the disk," I said. "About the way it wouldn't stay in one place."

"People?" Dan had a wary look. "What people?"

"Mike Rolland heads the list," I said. "He's my candidate for Jamie's murderer."

"Those men who work for him have killer written all over their faces."

"On the other hand, Dan," I said, "where were you this morning?"

"Oh, come on, Mr. Crang." Dan flapped his arms. "Jamie was my best friend. Despite everything."

"You weren't at L'Hôtel de Paris when I called an hour after Jamie hit the sidewalk."

"I just happened to be out. Big deal."

"And you rang back here from a pay phone. That might've been from some place close by this hotel after you called L'Hôtel de Paris and picked up the message I left for you."

"All right, I admit I was out looking for Jamie," Dan said. "Why shouldn't I be? I hadn't seen him for two entire days. And when we talked on the phone last night, we had a fight."

"About the disk?"

"What else would we fight about?"

"I can think of other topics."

"Like what?"

"Like Jamie planning to ditch you," I said. "He needed you for a job, taking out C&G's computer. Which you did. Very nicely too, Dan. But from then on in, never mind the fantasy about drifting around the world, I can see Jamie, the kind of guy he was, putting you on the dispensable list."

Dan sagged onto the bed. "Jamie could be cruel."

"Did he talk to you about calling it quits?"

"He said on the phone he'd give me five hundred thousand dollars."

"Just to go away and keep your mouth shut?"

"Well, I'd have to keep my mouth shut, wouldn't I?" Dan stirred, indignant. "Otherwise I'd be putting myself in trouble."

"Hey, now we're getting somewhere. This is progress."

"Closer to disaster, if you ask me."

"Let's go back to this morning," I said. "You went scouting for Jamie, correct?"

"Correct."

"Have any luck?"

"Stop doing this to me, Mr. Crang." Dan was working himself into a huff. "How would I even know Jamie was way over in Cannes?"

"By following him."

"Maybe I would have followed him, except I never discovered where he'd got to. He made a big issue last night of not telling me what hotel he was at. Or even what city."

I gave Dan my seeker of truth look. He held my eyes without turning away.

"You believe me, don't you?" he said.

"You don't have a terrific track record for staying on the level."

"I wouldn't lie when it involves murder."

"Okay, I think I believe you."

"Thanks for that."

"One thing I should advise you."

"What?"

"I can't think of a neater way of phrasing this, Dan, but don't leave the country."

"Fat chance."

"Why?" I asked.

"Because Jamie was the one whose name the bank account is in," Dan said. "I can't afford to pay the bill at L'Hôtel de Paris."

"You've got a problem, Dan."

CHAPTER THIRTY

I rode the train to Jake Finney's apartment in Beaulieu, picked up the disk, and caught a return train to Nice. The Negresco was a ten-minute walk through back streets from the station. I went at it by way of the Rue de Rivoli. The hotel floated above the side-walk, white and florid. Annie and the tourist brochures called the Negresco's architecture belle epoque. I called it intense glitz.

A clerk at the reception desk said Mr. Whetherhill and party were in the bar. Party? I hoped it didn't include strangers, particu-larly Luphkin strangers. That might queer the pitch I had in mind.

The bar opened a few paces to the right of the front entrance hall. It was two storeys high. The walls and pillars were of gleam-ing dark wood. There was lots of polished brass and decorative touches in maroon. It might have been a redoubt for the heads of the *Fortune 500*. I posed in the doorway trying to look like a guy between sessions with Donald Trump and T. Boone Pickens.

The Whetherhill party was seated at something that resembled a conference table near the centre of the room. It was a party of four with no strangers on hand, but one mild surprise: Trum Fraser. He, Swotty, Pamela, and Archie were clustered at one end of the table. Swotty was holding forth. He looked grim. Pamela had put on five years since Tuesday morning. Archie's manner said he was right on top of his game. Trum seemed to be making an effort to keep a shit-eating grin off his face. I crossed the room to their table.

"The reason I have summoned you all together," I said, "is the matter of the mysterious crime in our midst."

Swotty swivelled his head up. His expression would have looked good on a polar ice cap. "What in heavens is Crang talking about?" he asked Trum.

"It might be, sir, that he thinks he's Hercule Poirot," Trum answered.

Archie came briskly to his feet. "Do sit down," he said. He slid out a chair at the end of the table opposite Swotty. Trum was on his right, Pamela on his left. Pamela blew a plume of smoke in the air. She regarded me from infinitely sad eyes.

"Allow me to order you a drink, Crang," Archie said. He was playing the genial compeer for all he was worth. I smiled my thanks to Archie's offer. Archie made hand motions at a waiter.

I spoke to Trum, "Somebody unlock the chain to your desk back home?"

Swotty answered. "Trumball has demonstrated great initiative during these last trying days," he said. "The trust company is in his debt."

Trum winked at me. "I gave you credit for the phone tip, old buddy."

"It's what makes you unique, Trum," I said, "that little pinch of generosity."

Archie's signals brought a waiter in a white jacket to the table. Trum had a martini in front of him. The other drinks were amber-coloured. I asked for vodka on the rocks.

"You will be interested to hear this, Crang," Swotty said. "The trust company has recovered the best part of twenty-two million dollars."

Trum had a sheaf of much-thumbed papers at his elbow. He read from the paper on top. "Twenty-one million, nine hundred and eighty-six thousand, three hundred and fifty-four dollars, fourteen cents, in the bank account."

"How much for a Hatteras that's only been once around the harbour?" I asked.

"Our guys are grabbing it this afternoon," Trum answered.

The waiter served my vodka with a small flourish. I went into my jacket pocket for the disk and printout, and flipped them onto the tabletop. The gesture was more Travis McGee than Hercule Poirot. "Everybody want to listen up?" I said. I tapped a finger on the disk. "This is the inside poop on how ErnMax's money got from downtown Toronto to uptown Monte Carlo."

"I think not," Swotty said. "The trust company's computer department is preparing all the explanation I care to hear."

"Let Crang have his moment, Daddy," Pamela said. Her voice was strained. "He's earned it."

"Is that so, my dear?" Swotty's tone was gelid. "I hardly think you're the one to make the choice of topics in this gathering."

Pamela looked at me. "I told Daddy about Jamie and me last night," she said. Her eyes were rimmed in pink. "The whole godawful story."

"Yes," Archie said, "and Pamela and I had our own fruitful talk."

"Good for you, Arch," I said.

"Go ahead, Crang," Pamela said, almost a whisper.

I didn't wait for Swotty to butt in. "Give Jamie this," I started, "it was a cute scheme." Swotty stiffened in his chair, but said nothing. I described the way Jamie had plugged his NeXT into Cayuga & Granark's computer, the way he had used his insider's knowledge of the ErnMax account to pick up the first three entry codes, the way his computer expertise helped him dope out the fourth code, the way he had diverted the funds to the Banco di Napoli.

Swotty wore one of his chilly glares through the recital. Pamela allowed a small smile to come and go. Maybe, skunk that Jamie had been, Pamela couldn't help admiring the nervy nature of this theft. Archie appeared to be floundering on the procedural stuff about entry codes. Trum looked like he was waiting to pounce. I finished the explanation.

"One omission, Crang," Trum said. He poked a finger at me. "How'd Haddon put the main computer out of whack bang on at eleven o'clock that morning?"

"He had an ally."

"Oh, Jesus," Pamela said, "that weasel Renzi."

"He's the boy," I said.

"To whom are they referring?" Swotty asked Trum.

"A kid Jamie recruited," I said. "Name of Dante Renzi. Jamie drilled him in the art of crossing wires."

"That's how they took out the computer?" Trum asked.

"It was tidier than dynamite."

"This man Renzi," Swotty said, "he shares the guilt in Jamie Haddon's crime."

I said, "C&G would be out of its mind to start any legal action against Dan."

Trum nodded.

Swotty said, "That decision will be left to our lawyers, Crang."

Trum converted his nod into a dive at his martini.

I talked some more. I doubled back to Jamie and the optical disk and explained how he had saved it as a possible guide to future computer heists. When I couldn't think of anything left to say on the technical side of the robbery, I stopped. No one else spoke. I drank a little of my vodka.

Archie made a honking noise. "Well, Crang, you deserve congratulations," he said. It was a fight for Archie to keep condescension out of his voice, but he lost. "I know I speak for all of us at the table in expressing our, um, gratitude."

"Thanks, Arch."

Archie's eyes polled the others for reaction. It was minimal. He was on his own speaking for the table.

"Yes," he said, still sounding expansive, "quite remarkable. Absolutely."

I drank from my vodka. It wasn't Wyborowa, but it wasn't French domestic. French domestic was as wimpy as Canadian domestic. The Negresco's vodka tasted bracingly Norwegian.

"Okay, gang," I said, "if you'll keep Jamie's mechanical manipulations on hold, the next explanation is about motive and other skeletons in the closet."

"You have done enough, Crang," Swotty said. "Archie voiced our appreciation. If you will excuse us, we have family concerns to discuss."

"Swell," I said, "family fits right into the subject I'm coming to."

"My secretary will set up something for when you and I are back in Toronto," Swotty said. His words had a ring that was meant to dispatch me on my way. "A lunch at the Concord perhaps."

"The last time we ate there," I said, "you gave me a mission under false pretenses."

Swotty made a movement that was probably called bristling. "I'll ask you to retract that statement, Crang."

"Half a false pretense," I said. "You were worried that the postcard might indicate Jamie was somehow off the rails. You levelled with me that far. But you neglected to bring me up to speed on your deeper fear."

"Which was what?" Pamela asked.

"ErnMax," I said. "The squad your father enrolled at C&G to run the ErnMax account was small, elite, secret, and included Jamie. It wouldn't have been great for business if one of the squad, Jamie, was out of the country for three months doing an imitation of a loose cannon."

"That's another thing, the three months," Pamela said. "Why did Jamie make a point of saying he'd go back to Toronto in three months?"

"Pure smokescreen," I said. "Jamie used it as a cover for easing his way out of the city without raising any special questions. Just a young guy on a well-deserved sabbatical."

"He never intended to go back?" Trum asked.

"Not him, nor the twenty-three million."

"Jamie and Dan Renzi, the two of them on their own," Pamela said in a small flattened voice.

The other three gave Pamela uncomprehending looks. She paid them no attention. Her eyes were stuck on me.

"Jamie ditched Dan too," I said, speaking to her. "If that's any consolation."

"Not much."

"Okay, Crang." Trum's voice came riding in. "We follow what you're saying about Haddon's theft. But, Jesus, we could've hauled him back to Canada. There are laws, pal, and even if there aren't, there could be other ways."

I shook my head at Trum. "Jamie knew he had two lines of protection against you guys. One, the only evidence of his theft was on the disk. And he had it squirrelled away. Or so he thought. And, the second protection, Jamie knew that C&G didn't come to the table with clean hands."

"You have stepped beyond the pale, Crang." Swotty's voice cracked over the table at me.

"The way Jamie looked at it," I said, "the way the RCMP fraud squad might look at it, the team at C&G has been facilitating a crime of its own. Hiding assets. They run the machinery that's stockpiling the Luphkin millions in a Swiss bank account. In other words, out of reach of legitimate Canadian taxes."

"At this very moment, Crang," Swotty said, "our counsel are preparing a memo of law regarding the legality of each step the trust company has taken offshore on behalf of our clients."

Trum grinned at me. "That'd be the distinguished Fraser duo."

"I don't know, John," I said to Swotty. "About five years down the line, I can see your lawyers arguing in front of the Supreme Court of Canada. And losing."

"Did you call me John?"

"I'm not ready for the leap all the way to Swotty."

"If you speak of ErnMax outside this circle, Crang," Swotty said, "I'll see to it you are dealt with."

"Does this mean lunch at the Concord is definitely off?"

"You have had a warning."

"Maybe the damage is already done. Maybe Jamie Haddon's theft has made a blip in international banking that the justice people in Canada are charting."

"Impossible and irrelevant," Swotty said. He could have been right. What did I know about international banking? Hardly anything, but I liked the idea of throwing a small scare into Swotty.

"One point I am determined on," Swotty said, crisp and level, "I do not wish further mention of Jamie Haddon in my presence."

Pamela's eyes were on mine. "I told Daddy your theory about Jamie and his attitude to the family."

"More than theory," I said.

"Did no one heed the request I just finished making?" Swotty said. He looked more baffled than angry.

"Sit still for this much, John," I said. "Your cousin Jamie was a lot of things. Impatient. Clever. Sneaky. And, get this, resentful. He'd built up a snootful of anger over the Whetherhills and their superior ways. So he nursed the idea of taking the family down a peg and getting rich into the bargain. Package deal."

"That's all I was to him?" Pamela said. "Part of a package?"

"How about the icing on the cake?" I said.

"Far-fetched, Crang." Swotty smacked the palm of his right hand on the tabletop. "The boy was nothing more than a Haddon through and through. I should have recognized he was second-rate long ago and treated him accordingly. In any event, he's dead now and best forgotten."

"Not just dead," I said. "Murdered."

"Oh, now, Crang." Archie leaned forward. "I talked on the phone not an hour ago to the inspector in charge of the investigation. The death was accidental. A fall from a building."

"The inspector was a guy named Farinaud?"

"He struck me as extremely thorough."

"Bet he even knew where Strathroy is."

"As a matter of fact, that impressed me."

"Where Jamie's concerned," I said, "the inspector has a gap in his knowledge big enough to drive a Renault through. What Farinaud doesn't know is that Jamie made an assisted tumble from my room at the Monarch Hotel."

Something close to a sob came from Pamela's throat. The others stayed quiet and waiting.

I said, "We all know Jamie was too smart to fall off a seventh-floor balcony all by himself. And he was too stuck on his own all-round charm to jump. Somebody pushed him. That's murder."

The silence lasted almost a minute. Swotty broke it.

"Summon that waiter," he snapped at Archie. Swotty's glass was empty.

Archie caught the waiter's eye on his first try. The man had a knack. Silence took over again. I tried a reassuring smile on Pamela. She stared right through it. The waiter distributed drinks all round. Trum nipped at his martini and glanced toward Swotty. Swotty blinked. It may have been a signal.

"Okay, Crang," Trum said, "if you're right about the murder, how come you haven't passed on what you think you know to this French cop?"

"I'm not sure who the person was in my hotel room with Jamie, the person who did the pushing. Minus that piece of the story, Inspector Farinaud might get it in his head I was the person. And who could blame him?"

"Yeah," Trum said, "that'd be sticky."

"Even for a slick criminal lawyer like me."

Trum checked with Swotty. Another blink and maybe a slight inclination of the snowy head.

"But probably," Trum said to me, "you've developed something nifty about this mysterious guy in the room."

"Person in the room, Trum. I said person."

"Whatever."

"Could have been somebody sitting at this table."

"Hey now, old buddy." Trum put a touch of indignation in the words.

"Leaving you aside, Trum," I said, "everybody here had a good reason to see Jamie out of the way permanently." I looked at Pamela. "Sorry, but that includes you."

"I didn't kill Jamie," Pamela said in her very small voice.

"I don't think you did," I said. "On balance, it was more likely Mike Rolland."

Swotty put a hand on Trum's arm. "Is that a name familiar to us?" he asked.

Trum shook his head.

"He was another friend of Jamie's, apparently," Pamela said.

"The two of them had plenty in common," I said. "Mike Rolland is another guy who enjoys money and isn't choosy about how he acquires it. That character defect may have led to Jamie's death. He and Mike quarrelled over the disk and the twenty-three million it represented."

Trum said, "Let's suppose this Rolland's the guy —"

"The killer," I said. "He or the professionals he employs."

"— all right, the killer. Are you going to let the thing slide or what?"

"It depends on you people."

"What people?"

"The might and power behind Cayuga & Granark."

Swotty moved his hands impatiently. "You do not seriously contemplate that the trust company will associate itself with a murder?"

"Not a murder," I said. "A solution."

Swotty made a sound somewhere back in his throat. It conveyed derision. He was good at it.

Trum's finger beat a rhythm on the tabletop. "May I suggest, sir," he said to Swotty, "that we hear Crang out. I mean, he isn't going to shut up anyway, and we might learn something from him that'll benefit C&G in the long run."

"Here's my proposal," I said. "I go to Farinaud with what I know about Jamie, about the disk, about Mike Rolland insinuating himself into Jamie's recent life. But I don't go alone."

"Sure," Trum said, "you want somebody from Cayuga & Granark along to vouch for the stuff about Jamie's theft."

"You'd do fine, Trum."

"Jesus, that's not asking much."

"It's a hard case to make against Mike Rolland," I said, "and I don't know how good the French police are when it gets past the stage of filling out forms. But the only way to bring the killing home to Rolland is by investigation, pulling people in for questioning, putting together times and places. That's police work."

"And you're thinking it'll take C&G to get the cops off the dime," Trum said.

"More than they'll listen to little old me."

Trum went back to his martini. He had no more questions to ask, and the making of decisions wasn't in his domain.

"The ball has landed on your side of the court, John," I said to Swotty.

Swotty knitted his fingers together and rested his hands on the table. His head was cocked at an angle.

"You and I regard the world from vastly different perspectives, Crang," he said. "Yours is from the practice of criminal law, mine from a lifetime in business and banking."

"If this is a preamble to no," I said, "you can skip right along to the denouement."

"I may surprise you," Swotty said. He shifted himself further over the table. "Naturally," he said, "I wish to be cautious."

"A lifetime in business and banking does that to a guy."

"Fair but cautious," he went on. "Therefore I have a counter-proposal. I submit we bring in Canadian counsel. I'll grant that you may have strong reasons for suspecting this Rolland person in Jamie Haddon's death. But I don't think I am mistaken in saying we need legal guidance of a specialized and friendly sort. And I promise you, Crang, if our counsel see a way clear to pursuing your approach, I will put the full co-operation of the trust company at your disposal."

Trum spoke quickly on Swotty's heels. "You can't ask fairer than that," he said to me. "Get an opinion from home before the bunch of us mix it up with the *gendarmes*."

"Trumball will brief his father and brother by phone this afternoon," Swotty said.

"Give them a couple of days to get a junior looking up the law on murder and other stuff over here," Trum chimed in. He and Swotty were working as smoothly as Torvill and Dean.

The ice cubes had melted in my glass. It held about an inch of diluted Norwegian vodka. That would still make it punchier than most undiluted vodkas. I looked at the inch and considered the barrel Swotty had me over. He knew I was unlikely to approach Farinaud without backup from C&G. Too risky for my own legal position. But maybe I had him over a barrel too. He couldn't be absolutely certain I wouldn't try anything wild on my own. Drop hints to Farinaud, involve the trust company, drag the good name of Ernest Luphkin into the disgrace of public print. I drank the diluted vodka and decided I had nothing to lose in going along with Swotty's deal.

"Okay," I said.

"This means you buy it?" Trum asked.

"Jamie Haddon was killed," I said. "He wasn't exactly Albert Schweitzer, but somebody ought to pay for the killing."

There was a murmur of approval. It came from Pamela. The men waited close-mouthed for me to finish.

"If it takes assistance from the other Frasers," I said, "I'll put myself on hold until they report in."

"Very sensible, Crang," Swotty said.

"But no stalling," I said. "Right, guys?"

"We'll touch base in the next couple of days," Trum said.

I picked up my empty glass and gave it a little shake.

"Don't bother yourself about paying, Crang," Archie said in a lofty tone. "I'll see your drinks go on our bill."

"Thanks, Arch."

I got up and left. Nobody has to tell me when I've overstayed my welcome.

CHAPTER THIRTY-ONE

Annie and I ate an early dinner Thursday at a place near Cannes's old town called La Pizza. The old town had a name, Le Suquet. It slanted up the side of a hill that overlooked the rest of Cannes from the west. La Pizza was as homey as an old shoe.

Annie hurried at her food. She was booked for an advance screening of a movie from Quebec. She thought it had prospects of being the festival's sleeper hit. When she left, I ate my meal and finished hers. One more piece of pizza and I might turn into an anchovy.

In the lobby of the Monarch, I bought postcards for Ian and Alex and the dog. I settled on one with a cooked lobster for Ian, a soccer player with impressive thighs for Alex, and a poodle for Genet. I took the cards up to the room.

I needed elaborate preparations before beginning the writing labours. I hung my jacket in the closet. Sat at the desk. Rolled up the sleeve of my writing arm. Poised the ballpoint pen over the poodle card.

"Dear Genet," I printed, "you would meet many wonderful companions in the south of France, though you might be chagrined at their personal hab ..."

I put the pen down and looked at what I had written.

Companion.

"Ho, boy," I said out loud.

Companion. Friend. Pal. Mate.

"Ho, boy."

I got up from the desk and stepped onto the room's balcony. The door leading off the balcony next to mine was open. I called through it. "Yo, Mr. Terrill, you at home?"

The noise of heavy shoes clopping on the carpet came from inside. Colin Terrill appeared at the door. He had on his white shorts and a singlet in red and white stripes. His right hand was wrapped around a bottle of beer. The hand covered the label.

"G'day, mate," he said. He had a big Down Under smile.

"The very term I wish to inquire about," I said.

"What then?"

"Mate."

Terrill hooked one shoe on his balcony railing and gave me a questioning look. The shoe was the leather equivalent of a Dutch wooden clog.

"The other morning," I said, "the morning when the guy went splat down there on the sidewalk, you invited me and my mate to go to the hotel bar for a drink —"

"A shout."

"My point is you didn't mean mate as a partner in marriage, wife, female companion."

"Nah," Terrill said. "'Course not."

"Who did you mean?"

"I had in mind the bloke you were in there talking to yesterday. But I made a mistake."

"Maybe not."

"It wasn't you who was talking to the other bloke."

"Who was it?" I asked. "And did we seem to be at cross-purposes in this conversation?"

"You're a Canuck, right then?"

"So far, so good."

"Orright then," Terrill said, "I heard two blokes in your room. The voices on them were Canadian like yours. What I thought, one of them was you, or whoever had the room with the sheila. But later on, after I talked to you out here, after I thought about it, it wasn't you."

"Sheila?"

"Woman. Lady. Girl. The pretty little one with the dark hair."

"She's an Annie."

Terrill gave an impatient wave. Part of his hand came away from the beer bottle. It was a Tuborg.

"What's the time frame we're working on here?" I asked. "When did you hear these two voices?"

"Cripes, you got the bleedin' questions, haven't you then?"

"Appreciate it if you bear with me, Mr. Terrill. It could help on a matter I care about. Other people care too."

"Well, I don't mind," Terrill said. "The time I heard the voices, that part's easy. It was ten minutes ... something under that maybe ... five minutes, ten minutes before you came out where you're standing right now, on the balcony."

"That's also before the guy must have fallen off the, uh, roof?"

"A touch before, right."

"And you thought one of the men you heard in my room sounded like me?"

Terrill nodded his head and swigged from his Tuborg.

"But wasn't," I said. "And the other voice belonged to a Canadian too, but didn't sound like me?"

Terrill did more nodding and swigging.

"Okay, the big question," I said, "can you describe the second voice?"

"Bloody guess I can." Terrill was aggressively indignant. "It's my job, isn't it then?"

"What, accents?"

"Voices, mate. I'm a sound man for ABC."

"You work for the American Broadcasting Company?"

Terrill unhooked his clog from the balcony railing. "The Australian Broadcasting Corporation," he said indignantly.

"Chalk up what I said to North American parochialism."

"We got a unit here shooting a documentary on Paul Cox," Terrill said. "But you probably never heard of the bloke."

"One of the really original film directors around," I said. "He did *Man of Flowers*. Loved that one. Um, let's see, *My First Wife* and, what else, the movie about Van Gogh."

"Orright then." Terrill seemed mollified by my praise for Australia's own Paul Cox.

"The second voice," I said, "can you tell me about it?"

Terrill hesitated. "These two blokes lift something out of your room?" he asked. "Is that what you're on about?"

"Let's say they were uninvited guests."

Terrill's eyes were an acute blue, made even sharper by the coppery tan of his face. His eyes spent a few seconds looking into mine. I kept my mouth shut and concentrated on not blinking.

"No harm I suppose," Terrill said. He folded his arms. The Tuborg was almost empty. "This other bloke," Terrill said, "he sounded like he talked through his nose. Lot of Poms do that, English."

"So does one variety of Canadian."

"Bloke had a loud voice. Bit cranky, he sounded too."

"Think you'd recognize the voice if you heard it again?"

"Why not?" A hint of belligerence crept back into Terrill's tone.

"There's a catch," I said.

"Wot then?"

"The voice will be speaking over the telephone."

"No matter."

I tilted my head in the direction of the room. "Want to strike while the iron's hot?" I said. "Come in now and get on with the phone call?"

"Let me fetch m'self another piggy."

"Excuse me?"

"Bottle of beer, mate. Want one?"

I shook my head. "No, thanks."

Terrill disappeared in search of his beer. The first voice he had heard coming from my room on the morning of Jamie's death must have belonged to Jamie himself. His vocal inflections, the run-of-the-mill Southern Ontario pitch and timbre, were enough like mine, superficially anyway, for Terrill to have briefly supposed it was me in the room. It was the second voice that counted. It had to belong to the guy who pushed Jamie into space. From Colin Terrill's description, Mike Rolland wasn't the voice's owner, not if the voice was Canadian. And it wasn't the voice of a Clutch, not Georges or Emile. Hell, they didn't even speak English.

Terrill returned with another Tuborg and without the weighty shoes. He climbed barefoot from his balcony to mine. The distance was only a yard, but from seven storeys up, I wouldn't have taken it. Terrill took it in stride. One stride.

In my room, I dialed the Negresco Hotel.

"How many words you think you'll need for identification purposes?" I asked Terrill. "Hello be enough?"

"Bit of a natter is more like it, mate."

I asked the operator at the Negresco for the Cartwright suite. She rang through, and I held the phone to accommodate Colin Terrill's left ear and my own right.

"Yes." It was Pamela's voice.

"Not that one, mate," Terrill said to me. He had a wide grin on his tanned face. I put a finger to my lips to shush him.

"Yes?" Pamela said again. "Who the hell is this?"

"It's me," I said. "Crang."

"Someone's with you."

"Listen, sorry to bother you at a time of family crisis, but is Archie handy?"

"What do you want with him?" Pamela sounded out of sorts. "And answer me about whoever else is on the line."

"Just a neighbour dropped by to borrow a cup of vodka."

"Don't kid me, Crang. That was an Australian accent. Australians don't drink vodka. Nothing but beer in that miserable outpost they call a country."

Terrill made motions like he was going to vent some spleen over the telephone line. I clapped a hand against his mouth.

"This Australian is a sophisticated member of the film community," I said. "You mind if I speak to Archie?"

"What does anybody expect from a country settled by convicts?" Pamela grumped on. "They're a race of beer drinkers and women haters."

Terrill sputtered into my hand.

"I'll give you Archie," Pamela said, "But don't keep him. We're due for a conference in Daddy's room."

There was a thonk from the other end as Pamela set down the phone.

"Let me run this next voice past you," I said to Terrill, "and no comments till we hang up. Okay?"

I took my hand away from his mouth.

"Bloody woman," Terrill said. He upended the Tuborg bottle into his mouth. I dried my hand on my jeans.

"What is it, Crang?" Archie honked into the phone.

"Nice to hear your voice, Arch," I said. I looked at Terrill. He motioned for more conversation. He'd been too intent on guzzling beer to pick up on Archie's opening remark.

"The reason I called you, Arch," I said, "I want to thank you for taking my side yesterday afternoon. Damned decent of you."

Archie did nothing except breathe into his receiver. I held the phone closer to Terrill's ear and waited.

"Yes," Archie said. He stopped at the one word. Surely he didn't read anything fishy into my phone call. The call was a flimsy device, but it couldn't be transparent enough to raise Archie's suspicions about anything. Or could it?

"Nobody else in the family appreciated the work I did," I said. I was trying shamelessly to prime Archie's pump. "But you stepped right in there with a vote of approbation."

"You're welcome, Crang," Archie said. "I thought you did fine. Now, if that's all, you can understand we have a great deal on our plates over here."

"That's the bloke," Terrill said, not moderating the volume of his own voice.

I whapped my hand back on his mouth.

"Bloke?" Archie shouted from his end. "Who is a bloke? What bloke? Crang, are you there?"

"Time to go, Arch," I was speaking rapidly. "Just called to tip my hat to you. Thanks tons."

"Damn you, Crang, who was that? What foolishness are you up to now?"

"No foolishness, Arch. Cross my heart."

I hung up.

"You're sure?" I asked Terrill.

"Bloody right. You think I wouldn't recognize a stuck-up bloke like that one there?"

I plunked down on the bed. My energy had deserted me in a rush. Archie? He'd bumped off Jamie? It was my own little game, using Terrill, that seemed to have unmasked Archie as the killer. Still, the notion took the wind out of my sails.

"The woman who cheeked off Australia bloody annoyed me," Terrill said. "Who was she?"

"My ex-wife."

"Good-oh for you she's not still your wife."

"Somebody else told me the same thing the other day."

Terrill drank some beer. "Get what you wanted on the phone then, mate?" he asked brightly.

"Yeah. Thanks."

"You sure? I've seen happier blokes than you look right now," Terrill said. He was standing over me. The hairs on his legs were bleached white by the sun.

I raised my head. "It's one of those situations where I feel half-glad, half-sad," I said. "Know what I mean?"

"I don't see halves, mate," Terrill said. "You look all of a piece to me. Like a bleeding grave digger."

"Not a bad analogy."

I stood up.

"Better siddown a bit, mate," Terrill said.

I sat.

"I dunno what lark you're on," Terrill said, "but I'll leave you to it."

"Thanks."

"You look like shit, mate."

"Thanks again." I sank back onto the bed.

CHAPTER THIRTY-TWO

After I got over feeling shaken up, I felt angry. After that, I felt like a drink. The whole process of shifting feelings, beginning to end, took five minutes.

The pint of vodka I'd bought for room purposes was in the cabinet over the sink in the bathroom. I poured three fingers into a toothbrush glass. It tasted warm but potent. I carried the glass back to the bedroom and sat in the chair with my feet propped on the desk.

Something was sticking in my craw, and it wasn't the room-temperature vodka. Swotty Whetherhill had played flim-flam with a multimillion-dollar client account. Pamela Cartwright had cheated on her husband. The husband, pompous Archie, had dusted off the guy Pamela was cheating with. And who was it who got left with a moral and legal dilemma? Me. That's what stuck in my craw.

In order to bring Archie to account, I couldn't move through normal channels. Inspector Farinaud was the only normal chan- nel I knew, and I'd already deceived him. It would save both of us many complications if I continued to deceive the good Inspector.

Sure, I'd told the crew at the Negresco I was willing to speak openly and freely to Farinaud if I had the supportive presence of

Cayuga & Granark with me. But that was when I had thought open and frank speaking would rope in Mike Rolland. Now I knew it would rope in Archie. That put a different spin on the offer.

Actually the difference in spin wouldn't be so much in my offer as in its reception by Swotty. He'd be a heck of a lot less inclined to aid in the unmasking of Jamie Haddon's murderer if the murderer happened to be married to his daughter. He wouldn't be inclined at all. He'd go the other way. It'd be Watergate all over again. Cover-up. Stonewall. Erase the tapes.

I was working myself into a lather. I got up and paced. There wasn't much room for pacing. Not enough room to swing a cat in, either. I resumed my seat at the desk and thought over the events of the last couple of days.

When I'd seen Jamie resting his backside against the balcony railing on Wednesday morning, Archie Cartwright must have been deeper in the room. He was out of my range of vision, but Colin Terrill had picked up Archie's voice. Jamie was probably giving Archie some lip. Jamie was talented at that. He must have been rubbing it in about his affair with Pamela. Then what? Then Archie shut Jamie's mouth. Shut it for good.

As far as the murder went, my reasoning accounted for the two classic ingredients, motivation and opportunity. Motivation: Archie hated Jamie for what he'd done to Archie's marriage and self-esteem. Opportunity: Archie was the only other guy in the room with Jamie. Move over Sherlock Holmes, it was a tidy piece of deduction.

I stepped out on the balcony. There must have been a brilliant sunset going on. I couldn't see it, not from our side of the hotel, but I watched its reflection bouncing off the water and the buildings over toward Cap d'Antibes. Down below, the street was picking up with evening traffic. Jamie's dried blood was still visible on the sidewalk. The sight drove me indoors and back to my ratiocinations.

I had Archie nailed as the killer, but that left me with the problem of where to park my knowledge. Take it to Swotty? Rub his nose in it? Ridiculous. Forget that choice. Farinaud? That would raise awkward implications. Work through Pamela? No, again. She'd already lost a lover. Losing her husband wouldn't make for clear thinking on her part.

Well, who?

Trum.

I sat a little straighter at the desk. Trum, his father, and his brother. They weren't precisely neutral parties. C&G paid Trum's salary and paid whatever hefty amounts the other Frasers billed the trust company for services rendered. But the three of them were lawyers and officers of the court. They couldn't ignore a murder. Even if the murder had happened in a foreign jurisdiction? Well, hell, the dead guy and the guy who caused the death were Canadian nationals. That ought to bring the Frasers in for a share of my moral and legal dilemma.

I'd catch a cab to Nice and the Negresco, collar Trum, brief him on what I'd learned, and together we might brainstorm our way to a solution. Maybe it wasn't much of a plan, but it'd get me out of the hotel room.

I took a long shower and shaved for the second time that day. In the closet, there was a long-sleeved sweatshirt in black and a linen jacket in wheat. I put them on. I felt chic and well-groomed and calm and organized and decisive. I straightened the jacket on my shoulders, went into the corridor, shut the door and took the elevator to the lobby.

CHAPTER THIRTY-THREE

There were no taxis at the stand in front of the hotel. I walked south. There would be cabs cruising on Rue d'Antibes. I whistled the beginning of "If I Were a Bell." When I got to the part about "ding, dong, ding, dong, ding," I saw Archie. He was thirty yards down the sidewalk and coming toward me. He wasn't whistling.

Archie was dressed like Robert Redford in *Out of Africa*. Crisp khaki slacks and jacket, belt in loops around the jacket, open-necked white shirt. He looked bold and dauntless. A man on a mission. He didn't resemble a person who might run amok. But appearances could be deceiving.

I stood in the middle of the sidewalk. My mind shuffled through alternatives to waiting and watching Archie Cartwright bear down on me. I could take to my heels. I could request asylum from a friendly passerby. I could fall down on the sidewalk and kick my feet in the air. Each choice seemed beneath my dignity. The side pockets on Archie's safari jacket were wide and deep. He had his right hand shoved into the pocket on the right side. His left hand was free and clenched. I kept on standing still until Archie pulled up in front of me. At close range, his face seemed tighter and more constricted than it had from a distance.

"Listen, Arch," I said, "there are ways that lawyers can work this thing out."

"I have a knife in my right hand, Crang," Archie said. He was standing very close to me.

"A knife? That's ridiculous, Arch."

"Listen to what I say."

"But a knife. Arch. WASPs don't carry knives. Guys in ghettos, yeah, drug dealers. You should have something more traditional, a fowling piece maybe."

"Your mouth will do you no good," Archie said. His head was four or five inches from mine and slightly higher.

"Could you back off a bit, Arch?" I said. "Where you're standing is called crowding the other person's space."

Archie's left hand clasped my arm above the elbow. It was casually done, but the strength of the grip matched Emile Clutch's. Archie's purpose wasn't to hold me in place. It was to get me on the move. He swung himself to my left flank, his left arm reaching across his body to keep me against him, his right hand buried in the khaki pocket. I felt the tip of the knife through the fabric of his jacket and mine. We walked south, the odd couple.

"Where did you pick up stuff like this, Arch?" I asked. "A Mafia encounter group?"

"I am a major in the Queen's Own Reserves."

"They teach knives in the Queen's Own?"

"All weapons," Archie said. "Keep walking, Crang."

It was well past twilight. The street lamps had come on. People sauntered up and down the sidewalk, going to dinner, heading for home, glasses of wine, conversation, loved ones, a few laughs. I was linked to a nut with a shiv.

"This is crazy, Arch," I said.

Archie pricked the end of the knife into the flesh around my hip bone.

We crossed Rue d'Antibes. The back of the Majestic Hotel blocked out much of the southern sky. Archie steered us right, going west, on a narrow, quiet street. Most of one side of the street was taken up by a not particularly striking cathedral.

"With me, Arch, the signs are you intend to harm me. But I don't think you intended to shove Jamie off the balcony. That alters your defence in law for the damage you do to me. Canadian law anyway."

"You should have kept yourself out of this business, Crang." Archie talked like a guy who had the bit in his mouth. Raring to go. "You should have kept out from the very beginning."

"But you see what I mean about intent. If you stick the Queen's Own bayonet in me, there'll be no reasonable doubt that you had malice aforethought. Pardon the legalese, Arch."

"Shut up, Crang."

"Your goose will be cooked."

Archie concentrated on getting me past a small group of parishioners on the cathedral steps.

"But in Jamie's case," I said, "I'm betting there was no intent. That means no murder. Manslaughter at worst. It could be a light sentence for you, Arch. Suspended sentence even."

"Crang, you bastard, I intended to kill Haddon." Archie hissed his words. A mist of spittle sprayed my face. "When I followed him to your hotel room, I didn't know if I had any aim except to dress him down for the pain he caused me. But after the things the swine said to me, I pushed him over the railing, and goddam it, I had made up my mind in that instant to push him."

"That's what I'm talking about, Arch, a crime of passion. No insult to you, but under the circumstances, Jamie provoking you, driving you nuts and all, a good lawyer could make a plea of temporary insanity stick."

"I felt relieved when I killed the bastard."

"By good lawyer, I didn't mean myself necessarily."

"You are quite correct in one assumption, Crang."

"Don't bother telling me, Arch."

"I intend to kill you."

We came out of the shadows of the cathedral street to lights and people at Rue Maréchal-Joffre. The crossing signal was against us. We stopped. Archie didn't slack off his grip on me. There was a guy on my right side waiting for the light. He was large and black. He had on a short-sleeved djellabah, a knitted wool cap, and thonged sandals. His right arm was draped in strings of beads. He had pieces of purple and green fabric slung over both shoulders. They were either very small rugs or very heavy scarves. He had rings dangling loose on his fingers above the knuckles, five or six rings per digit. Wristwatches marched up his left forearm from wrist to elbow. The watches had silver stretch bands and glinted green in the overhead street lamps.

"These things actually keep time?" I asked the black guy. I flexed the watch band at the top of his forearm.

"Don't speak to him." Archie's sibilance gave my face another sprinkling.

"Want a good watch, boss?" the black guy said to me. His voice was of James Earl Jones resonance. "Best prices on the Riviera, boss."

I was still fingering the top watch. The crossing indicator flashed the signal for walk. Archie forced me forward. My fingers squeezed on the watch. I tugged hard and down. The tug stripped half a dozen watches off the black guy's arm. They tinkled and clattered into the gutter.

James Earl Jones erupted. "What you fucking do to my watches, man?" He hovered between going for me and going for the watches. I ducked after the watches. Archie's left hand went with me, still clutching my arm but loosening the intensity of the hold. I swept up four watches and flung them in Archie's face. He let go of my arm.

"You fucking ruin my business, man," the black guy roared at me.

Archie's right hand stayed in the pocket and on the knife. His left hand was fending off the flying watches.

"Make it up to you later," I said in a rush to the black guy.

I belted across Rue Maréchal-Joffre. My Rockports thwacked on the pavement, my unbuttoned jacket flapped open, my body strained ahead, my eyes felt as if they were bulging out of their sockets. A pretty young woman walking toward me regarded my running form and giggled behind her hand. No laughing matter, lady. I heard clumping behind me. I didn't glance around. It would not be friendly pursuit back there.

I ran as fast as I could. On the right, there was a string of food places, a cafeteria, an oyster bar, a restaurant called Le Brasserie au Boeuf. On the left, a dirt square broken by rows of stubby plane trees. Customers in the windows of the eating places turned their heads and charted my progress. My lungs hurt.

Beyond the restaurants, I ran past a boule pitch. Beyond the boule pitch, a bandshell in another dirt square. Beyond the bandshell, a street thick with cars and people. I dodged and darted and flitted through the brief gaps between pedestrians. Me and O.J. Simpson.

I looked over my shoulder. Archie was ten yards behind. He ran like John Cleese. High knee action, upper body rolling, loony face. People heard him coming. They cleared the track. Archie's right hand remained jammed inside his jacket pocket. The posture slowed his progress. His speed wasn't world-class anyway. Hell, I was building a lead on Archie.

The street was Rue Félix Faure. It led straight at the hills of Le Suquet, less than half a block ahead. I aimed for its tiny, twisty alleys. Good prospects in there for shaking Archie and his stiletto.

I cut sharp right at Rue de la Boucherie. It wasn't so much a street as a flight of stone stairs with a pair of ruts on either side. I went up. The muscles in my calves screamed at the climb. I was alone on the stairs. The sudden quiet struck me as eerie. The dismal light wasn't reassuring either. It was the sort of area I'd ordinarily avoid, prime hunting ground for muggers. Maybe it would be helpful if I ran into a mugger. I could point him at Archie.

Rue de la Boucherie turned abruptly to the left and into a covered passageway. The light got gloomier. Other, small alleys branched to the right and left. Some of them led down to the busy street I had just left. I slowed my pace. What if Archie had continued further along Rue Félix Faure and looped up one of the side alleys to intercept me? What if this was the neighbourhood where he intended to use his blade on me anyway? Maybe it had been a lousy idea to slip into the old town. Maybe I had outfoxed myself.

The street got steeper. I proceeded with all caution flags flying. Up ahead, at the very top of the hill, there seemed to be a castle outlined against the sky. A couple of turns and more climbing lay between me and the castle. The light in the alley wasn't growing any brighter. I tried for stealth as I crept forward. My hands reached out like a sleepwalker's, feeling my way.

I heard Archie before I saw him. I heard huffing and puffing in the shadows of a recessed doorway. I slowed up. Archie lunged out of the doorway. He held the knife in front of him in the manner of a duellist with a sword. The stance made Archie look foolish. On the other hand, he gave the impression he knew what he was doing.

"Chrissake, Arch." I kept my hands up and out. I was backing off slowly. "This can't be what the Queen's Own trained you for."

Archie came forward in a kind of stutter step. He carried the knife low, in position for an upward thrust. I eased back. There wasn't much room in the cramped alley for manoeuvring, nothing to duck behind. Archie sprang at me. He let out a grunt, his right foot slapped the ground, he swung the knife in an arc that was on course for my belly. I juked left, feet off the ground, arms over my head, stomach pulled tight. My linen jacket flew wide open. The knife swept past my gut, nicked my black sweatshirt, and cut into the open jacket. Archie tugged at the knife. It seemed to be caught in the fabric. The knife ripped the jacket, but didn't come loose. I pulled back. The jacket ripped some more. I turned away, pointing in the direction up the hill. More ripping. I yanked at the jacket. The knife came loose, and Archie lost his hold on it. The knife fell to the pavement. Archie stooped for it. I took off up the street toward the castle.

The steep climb slowed me almost to a walk. There were still no people around, though the lights got brighter as I went higher.

I passed a pair of signs, Résidence de la Citadelle and Musée de la Castre. Sounded worthwhile if I was on a sightseeing spree. I tramped up a steep driveway. I looked back. Cannes was spread out far below me. I could pick out La Croisette and the Palais des Festivals. I could also pick out Archie. He was coming up the steep driveway. He had the knife in his hand.

I hurried across a courtyard. The route took me down a slight slope, through a small passageway, and up a short set of stone steps no more than a couple of feet wide. The steps put me on the parapet of what looked like the remains of an ancient wall around the castle. Very ancient. Eight or nine centuries old. Standing on the parapet, the top of the wall came up to the middle of my thighs. On the far side of the wall, in the direction of downtown Cannes, there was a drop of maybe eighteen or twenty feet. The fall on the other side, the open side, was five or six feet. A parapet of an old wall didn't offer me a really strategic place to make a stand. I stopped anyway. I needed a pause to catch my second wind. I wasn't sure I had a second wind.

Archie clumped up the stone steps. He was exhaling like a runner in the last hundred yards of the Boston marathon. The knife was in his right hand. He held his left hand to his heaving chest.

"Arch, we're both frazzled," I said. "Let's call off the war games and talk the situation over."

"You bastard." Archie's voice was hoarse.

"Aw, be fair, Arch. I'm the guy with the torn jacket, and you call me a bastard?"

Archie panted. "I'm going to kill you."

"Come off it. You hardly got enough breath to talk. Never mind the strength to skewer me with that stupid piece of cutlery."

It was the wrong line to take with Archie. My words didn't persuade him to pack it in. They stung him back to action. He launched another sweep at me with the knife. I danced out of range. The move called for no fancy footwork. Archie had lost much of his quickness. But he still had the damn knife.

"Time out, Arch," I gasped.

"Kill you."

Archie sounded fanatical. He drove at me, flicking the knife in my face. I ducked left, weaved right, moving back and back. The knife flicks were getting more threatening. I kept up my dancing retreat. Archie persisted. My right foot caught a loose stone in the parapet. I kept my balance, but the stumble broke the rhythm of my escapes from the knife's thrusts. Archie's eyes went wide at my stumble. He switched tactics. He raised the knife over his shoulder. I tried to get myself straight and out of danger before the knife descended. Archie grunted. The knife didn't descend. Archie was frozen in his pose, body reared back, hand over his shoulder.

"Who's gonna pay for my watches?"

It was the James Earl Jones voice. The face of the large black street vendor rose over Archie's right side. The vendor had grabbed the hand that wielded the knife.

"Hey," I said, "the cavalry has arrived."

Archie groaned. He pulled at the black vendor's grip. The vendor wasn't giving way.

"That a knife?" he said. "What you people at?"

"Don't let go," I said. "I'm the good guy in this. He's the bad guy."

The black vendor had ditched his merchandise. He stood tall and unencumbered behind Archie, his right hand around Archie's wrist. The black guy's face showed incomprehension. I couldn't blame him.

"I can explain," I said.

"I don't want no explaining, man," the black guy said. "Want my money."

Archie let out a roar. The noise shocked the black guy into relaxing his hold. Archie's knife hand came loose. He drove at me. I made a little shift to my right. At the same time, I threw a right cross at Archie's face. His thrust was wild and out of control. The knife missed its target. My right cross didn't. It clipped Archie on his prominent jaw. He staggered against the low wall and pitched over. I grabbed for his left arm. The black guy reached fast for Archie's right arm. Both of us hung on. The force of Archie's fall jerked my shoulder. I almost lost my grasp, but didn't. The black guy had no trouble with Archie's right side. Archie dangled against the face of the wall, his shoes a dozen feet above the dark ground. The black guy and I, hanging on to him, leaned over from the parapet. The knife was still in Archie's hand.

"Drop that, Arch," I said, "and we'll haul you up."

"Fuck you, Crang."

"Oh, great."

"You going to pay for my watches?" the black guy said to me.

"Let's deal with this present emergency first, the one at the end of our hands."

"My watches are an emergency, man."

"All right, listen, how many watches?"

"Six, man. Top-grade timepieces."

"Forget six. I'll buy one."

"Five."

"Two, my outside offer. What am I going to do with more than two watches?"

"Three of my best, better than Rolex. Twenty-five dollars apiece."

"Make it twenty."

"Sixty dollars. You got a deal, boss."

Archie squirmed. He was weighing heavy on my hands.

"What we do with this fella, boss?" the black guy asked me.

I looked down at Archie. "You going to let the knife go, Arch?"

"Fuck you, Crang."

I turned to the black guy. "How do you feel about dropping him?" I asked.

The black guy shrugged.

We dropped Archie.

CHAPTER THIRTY-FOUR

Annie passed up a chance to interview the guy who had written the new John Travolta movie, and came with me on the train to Nice.

"What's the latest on Archie's ankles?" she asked.

"Still broken, the last I heard."

"Was that the phone call this morning?"

"From Trum, yeah," I said. "Maybe Archie's physical state'll wring the hearts of the judges at his trial."

"You think he'll actually be tried?"

"So far the cops haven't been brought in. Trum says it's only a matter of Swotty holding off until Trum's brother wings over from home. That's supposed to be a couple of hours from now."

I looked at my watch. It had a silver band and a greenish sheen. I shook the watch.

"Damn thing's stopped," I said.

"Oh, well, you've got two more of the same."

"That's the trouble."

The train was an express and got us to Nice without any stops between it and Cannes. Trum had said to meet him at a restaurant in the Old Town. It was called Nissa Socca.

"Wheee," Annie said.

"What?"

"Socca. It's the yummiest food in the world."

The restaurant was Trum's kind of place, snug and frayed around the edges. It had an open kitchen and tables placed in parallel rows. The customers sat cheek by jowl. Trum had empty plates and the remains of a litre of red wine in front of him. Annie and I sat across from Trum, and I made the introductions.

"I told you you were wasting your time, Crang," Trum said to me, "coming over here."

"Nice to see me, though, right, Trum?"

"Nice to meet Annie. But as for you, what you and C&G and the family got to settle can be done through the mails."

"That's the official Whetherhill line?"

"I would've thought you'd take the hint, Pamela and Swotty not returning your calls."

Annie smiled sweetly at Trum. "I think that's why Crang wants to talk to you. To get the answers no one else is willing to provide. Or perhaps that should be able to provide."

Trum didn't dissolve completely under Annie's charm, but he gave signs of loosening up.

"I'll fill you in on Archie's story," he said to me, "if that's gonna make you happy."

"He bumped off Jamie," I said. "What else?"

"A lot. Background stuff I'm talking about."

"Background's a start."

"From your standpoint, old buddy, it's also an end."

"I assume what you're about to reveal came from Archie's own lips."

"His version, yeah," Trum said. "Well, last week he followed Pamela to an apartment you guys were staying at."

"In Pont Saint-Jean," Annie said.

"Wherever."

"He followed Pamela for what reason?" I asked. "He thought she and Jamie were renewing old acquaintances?"

"Right," Trum said. "Archie didn't say it in so many words, but if you ask me, he was hoping to catch his wife and that asshole Jamie in flagrante delicto. That'd give him a dynamite bargaining chip."

"Followed Pamela to our place," I said. "Then what?"

"He kept on following her when she left."

"To the Beau Rivage?"

"I forget the name," Trum said. "The hotel where Jamie was staying. Except when she got there, Pamela, Jamie wasn't in, and she left right away."

"But now Archie knew where Jamie was."

"You got it," Trum said. "So he started following Jamie around."

"Why'd he switch from Pamela to Jamie?"

"My opinion, I figure the poor bastard was feeling guilty about tailing his own wife, never mind she'd been playing fast and loose on him for a year."

"Okay," I said, "that put Archie right behind Jamie last Wednesday in Cannes."

"The guy was so cuckoo he thought Pamela and Jamie were getting it on way over there, a hotel in Cannes."

"The rest of it," I said, "is as plain as the nose on your face."

"That a personal crack, Crang?" Trum was fingering his red, veiny proboscis.

"Just a figure of speech, Trum. The thing is, knuckling down to the legalities, though I'm not all that au courant on French law, Archie ought to be pretty solid on a defence of provocation."

"I suppose." Trum didn't sound intensely involved.

"He goes busting into our hotel room, Annie's and mine, and he's expecting the ultimate confrontation. Instead, major disappointment, it's his adversary all by himself, Jamie the rotter, who gives Archie some heavy stuff about Pamela and her recent love life. Archie goes hairy. Boom, Jamie's off the balcony."

"Sure, sure." Trum's interest hadn't picked up.

"Well, there you go. I imagine French courts are very receptive to arguments based on a man standing up for his honour. You know, European machismo and all that."

"I imagine."

"Not to mention the sanctity of marriage. It works in Archie's favour. Your brother ought to make plenty of yards with that one."

"Crang." Trum's expression was deadpan. "You don't get it yet, do you? The reason why my brother's flying red-eye to Nice."

"Because your father's tied up?"

"I'm not kidding."

"Well, to represent Archie's interests in particular, and in general to oil the wheels of justice."

Along with the deadpan expression, Trum seemed to have added two very cold eyes. He said, "My brother's coming over mainly ... no, make that exclusively ... to be sure the lid stays on."

The waiter was a short, dark guy in a long smudged apron. He had a voice that made him sound like he was broadcasting from the bottom of a rain barrel. Annie engaged him in the usual French palaver.

"I ordered us a large socca," Annie said to me after the waiter left.

"I ate here twice before, three counting today," Trum said. "Had the cannelloni every time."

"Socca's the house specialty," Annie said.

"Really?" Trum said.

"From the name. The place is called Nissa Socca."

"I figured that was just the owner," Trum said. "You know, like Pierre Socca."

Annie shook her head.

"Not that I know what the hell socca is."

"Trum," I said, "how do you mean your brother's making sure the lid stays on."

"It isn't complicated. I mean Archie's heading home soon's the doctors okay him for a pair of crutches."

"Your brother isn't going to negotiate with the French cops?"

"That's what he's being paid to avoid."

"Goddamn it, Trum." I could feel two red spots beginning to burn on my cheeks. "Archie killed a guy."

"No doubt about it."

"And you're going to let him walk without even a trial? Without a peep out of any of you? Out of you or your brother or Swotty?"

"Look, fella, don't go getting yourself all hot and bothered," Trum said. "Just think the thing through. Sure, Jamie's dead. But the guy was a useless tit anyway. Stole from C&G. Left messes wherever he stepped. So he's dead, but the French cops got it down as an accident. That's the status quo, and there's no reason to disturb it. No sensible reason. What the hell, if Archie went to trial, he'd get off for the reasons you just said, provocation and whatnot."

"You're leaving something out, Trum."

"No, I'm not."

"You're leaving a lot out, but one item in particular."

"Not even that one particular item. Swotty and me got there ahead of you."

"Archie took a run at killing somebody else. Me, for Pete's sake, me. And when he did it, it was not in defence of the family or marriage. The son of a bitch was looking to stick me with a knife about the size of Excalibur because he knew I knew he'd done in Jamie."

Trum pushed his chair back. It bumped the man sitting behind Trum. The man spilled some of the wine he was drinking on his suit jacket. He gave Trum a dirty look. Trum noticed none of the small drama behind him.

"You go home, Crang," Trum said, "you go down to your office, you look through the mail, you open an envelope that's got no marking on it, no return address, you open it, and in your hand, you got your fingers on a bank draft."

"I'm trying to pretend I'm not hearing this."

"Twenty-five thousand dollars' worth of bank draft."

"Ah, jeez, Trum."

"Twenty-five thousand." Trum repeated the amount very slowly.

"This is for keeping my mouth shut?"

"The way Swotty phrased it last night," Trum said, "he said, 'Crang deserves compensation for the time he expended on this unfortunate episode.' His exact words."

Trum got up and left the restaurant.

"Holy mackerel," Annie said.

"*Très chaude, m'dame,*" the deep-voiced waiter said from behind Annie. He was holding a large platter with both hands on a wooden handle. The food on the hot platter was light brown and looked like an enormous pancake. Annie used her fork to break off a piece and lift it to her mouth.

"Ambrosia," she said.

The waiter came back with a litre of white wine.

"What would you think of this?" I asked Annie. "What would you think of stretching the holiday? Staying here longer? Two more weeks maybe? Whatever it takes?"

Annie hesitated for a bit. Her mouth was full of the stuff from the platter.

"It'll need some arranging with the radio station back home," she said. "But you don't have to twist my arm."

"Swell."

"What's up?" Annie said. "And, listen, you've still got those red spots on your cheeks. Not that I don't understand. That was disgusting, what your friend Trum just laid on you."

"Could you ask the waiter with the impressive lungs if he's got a phone book I could borrow?"

"Sure," Annie said. "But eat some of this socca."

It didn't taste like a pancake. It had a texture and consistency and flavour that reminded me of a weird combination of pasta, cake, and bread. Except it was more refined than those three. I might not have been giving the socca my full attention, but my taste buds seemed to be enjoying themselves.

"You want me to look up something for you?" Annie asked. She had the phone book on her lap.

"It's simple enough. I can handle the job."

I leafed through the listings for Cannes.

"When it comes to the actual phoning," I said to Annie, "I'll need you to lead off."

"A phone's over there on the wall. I think the drill is, a customer makes the call and pays the waiter afterwards."

I got on the right page of the phone book and ran my finger down to the listing I needed. There were six digits in the number.

"Okay," I said to Annie, "dial this number and get through all the operators and minions, and I'll take over when you have my party on the line."

"This party speaks English?"

"Enough."

"What's the name? Who do I ask for?"

"The guy I mentioned to you the other day."

"Yes?"

"Inspector Farinaud."

VISIT US AT

Dundurn.com
@dundurnpress
Facebook.com/dundurnpress
Pinterest.com/dundurnpress